MAX'S DANCE

GINA M. IACIOFANO

DEDICATION

THIS IS DEDICATED TO THE READER: LIFE CAN THROW YOU A LOOP, BUT ITS ALL ABOUT WHAT YOU DO WITH IT. LET THE SPARK ALWAYS CARRY YOU IN THE DANCE THAT WE CALL - LIFE.

CHAPTER ONE

The fire started off small and slow. As it gained more heat and oxygen, it started to grow. Yellow turned into an orange hue. There were tints of blue as that could be seen too. The smoke started off in puffs and now climbed higher and higher in the air. The crackling was intense and grew louder and louder. The light grew bigger and bigger. The fire jumped and danced like a dancer on center stage. Tonight, it was contained. As the wind starts to blow, the flames danced along with the flowing air.

Maxine "Max" Brandon sat close to the warmth of the fire. She watched it dance and flicker in the air. She closed her eyes and saw herself on stage. Dancing among nine other dancers. All of them just as good as the one standing next to them. They were a crew. They were a team. Most of them had known each other since they were young kids. They had once all played together in a sand box on the playground. They had all run and chased each other.

Max thought about their performances as dancers. It was Max and two other girls and seven guys on the team. They auditioned together.

The fire grew intensely. The smoke billowed up way above. Max heard the sirens but didn't give it any more thought. Then she was being jarred out of her thoughts as someone pushed her out of the way.

"What? What is going on?"

"Someone called 9-1-1 saying that there was a fire and there was smoke."

"It's a fire pit," Max said forcefully.

Her neighbor came rushing outside. "That's her. That's the fire starter. I want to press charges. I want her to suffer. I want her to pay."

"Shut up, Mrs. Stanley."

"You're a horrible neighbor. Why don't you just move the fuck out? It will make all of us happy."

"Go in your house and mind your own business."

The police also responded to the call. Max didn't look at them as they came into her backyard. An older woman in a pants outfit came right in front of Max. "You know the rules," she said to her.

"I didn't leave my house. I didn't go anywhere. I'm allowed outside in my yard."

"Put the fire out or we will," the woman officer said.

"But I wasn't in the wrong. I wasn't harming anyone. I'm not burning anything that I shouldn't be burning."

"Gentleman, put the fire out now."

The fire hose came on with such force that it knocked the pit off its foundation. Max watched as the fire was violently distinguished.

"That monitor is around your ankle for a reason."

"Yes, I know that, but I didn't do anything wrong. I was minding my own business."

"Max, what don't you understand about no fires."

"But it's a beautifully cool evening, and I wasn't hurting anyone."

"Go inside, Max."

"But Mrs. Stanley is always trying to get me into trouble. It's just not fair."

"Max, go inside please."

Max gripped the wheels of her wheelchair. Her newest hellish prison. She lowered her head as she went towards the house. She was locked out. She gripped the doorknob hard and firmly turning it over and over and was jerking and pulling on it, but it wouldn't open.

"NO!" her mother said from inside the house. "You know the rules."

"Oh, come on. Don't do this. You know what will happen."

Joanna Norris turned from the others to see what the problem was at the door. She watched Max pulling and jerking on the knob and it not budging a bit. She walked over to see what was going on.

"Max, what's the problem?"

"My mom locked me out of the house."

"Why would she do that?"

"Max, I have told you over and over again that you have to be nice to the neighbors. I've told you that there are things that you aren't allowed to do, and yet you don't listen to a damn word I say. Actions have consequences and this is one of them," her mother shouted from the kitchen window.

"She won't let me in."

"Come on. We will take you…"

"I don't want to go to jail."

"That's not what I was going to say."

Max lowered her head. She put it up against the cold door. "I hate my life," she said.

"Come on. I know a place that you can stay tonight and until we work this out."

Max transferred herself from her wheelchair to Joanna's car. Joanna put the wheelchair in the back of the car. Then she got into the car.

"Where are we going?"

"To a safe place."

"Yeah. Whatever that is."

Joanna drove to her house. Her husband came to see why she was home early. He saw Max sitting in the front seat with her head tilted back against the head rest. "Stay in the car. I'll be right back. Did you hear me?" She tapped Max on the shoulder. Max looked at her. "Stay in the car. I'll be right back."

"As if it were an option."

"Max, please."

"Yes, ma'am."

"I'll be right back."

Joanna got out of the car. Her husband stood on the driveway looking at them. "Are you bringing work home with you?"

"She needs a place to stay for a few days."

"Well, then bring her in."

"I need for you to put out the ramp."

He looked at her questioningly before he went into the shed and pulled out the ramp. He attached it to the front porch. Joanna had gotten the wheelchair out of the car. Max slid herself into it.

"Grant, this is Maxine…"

"Max," she snapped angrily.

"As I was saying. Grant this is Max. Max, this is my husband Grant."

"Nice to meet you," he said.

"Yeah. We will see what you say in the morning."

"Max!" Joanna said. Max looked at her. "It's just for a couple days. Please come inside."

Max pushed herself up the ramp. She entered the house behind Grant. "Do you have anything with you?"

"No."

"We will give you something to change into."

"Like a different body," Max mumbled.

"What did you do?" Grant asked.

She looked at him. He gestured towards the chair.

Max knew that she was blowing her first impression.

"How did it happen?"

"You probably read about it in the papers. You most likely saw it on TV."

"Counseling starts tomorrow morning," Joanna said.

"Counseling? Counseling for what? For who? I'm not going."

"It's no longer an option. The consequences are either you go for counseling or you go…"

"Yeah, I got it. Do you have a bathroom? I have to pee."

Joanna showed Max the bathroom. Max went in, closed the door, and let out a scream like Joanna and Grant had never heard. Max used the bathroom and then came out.

"Are you ok?" Grant asked.

"Yeah, man, I'm fucking wonderful."

"Come. Let me show you where you're going to sleep." Max followed them down a hallway. They brought her into a room with a day bed set up. "This will be your room," Joanna said to her.

Grant had gone into a room and came back with clothes for Max. He now put them on the bed. "These should fit you."

"I guess you want me to say thank you."

"No, I don't. Breakfast is at seven, so make sure your ass is in the kitchen at that time."

"I don't have my phone, so I can't set an alarm clock."

"There's one on the nightstand already set. Good night.

"Whatever," Max spat out.

"Max, it's only for a few nights," Joanna said.

"Yeah, sure."

The sound of a siren screaming started to go off at five in the morning. The sound was muffled at first until Max rolled her head on the pillow and then heard the screaming alarm. Max jumped at the sound. She reached for the nightstand but didn't see the clock. "Where is it? Where is the fucking clock?"

Grant came into the room and the clock went off. "Get up and get dressed. Be in the kitchen in five minutes."

"But you said that breakfast wasn't until seven."

"You have to work for your breakfast."

"I have to do what?"

"Get dressed and come in the kitchen within the next… now you are down to four minutes."

Max got out of bed. She dressed and pulled her shoes on. Then she went into the kitchen. Grant was watching the clock. "That's not good enough," he said.

"Good enough for what?"

Grant bent down in front of Max. He had a special key. He removed the ankle monitor that had been around her ankle for awhile now.

"No. I can't."

"Here you can. Let's go."

"Go where?"

"Work for your breakfast."

"I don't understand."

"You will," Grant said. "Let's go."

She followed him outside. Grant led her to a track. "What the fuck do you want me to do?"

"A mile. That would be four times around this."

Max went into the gated area. She went out on the track. She looked to her right and then to her left. "It doesn't matter which way you go. Just start in either direction right now."

Grant joined her on the track. Max went to her left. She started pushing and pushing until she got the wheelchair moving. She had a pace going. Grant kept up with her the whole time. They did once around the track. Twice around. Three times around. And then they finished with the fourth. When they were done, Grant led them back to the house.

"Breakfast is at seven. After you eat, I'll take you to your appointment."

"What do you get out of it?"

"What's that?"

"What's in it for you?"

"Just be in the kitchen for breakfast."

"Yeah, whatever. Can I watch TV?"

"No."

"Why?"

"Because there are things that need to be done."

"Like what?"

"Go make your bed. Take a shower. Change your clothes. You can't wear that to your appointment, now can you?"

"I don't know."

"No, you can't, so go."

Max went into the room and made the bed. Then she went into the bathroom. To her surprise it was a fully handicap accessible roll-in shower with a built-in shower bench. She got into the shower. Once under the water, she cried the whole way through. Then she wrapped the towel around herself and got out. There was a toothbrush and tooth paste on the counter. She brushed her teeth. She ran a comb through her wet hair. Then she went back into the bedroom, where she dressed. Max went into the kitchen before seven.

Breakfast: scrambled eggs, pancakes, bacon, and a glass of water and another glass of juice sat on the table. Max gobbled down the food in just over a minute.

"You don't have to eat so fast. No one is going to take it from you."

"I'm starving. I haven't eaten since lunch yesterday."

"Are you ready to go. It's about an hour or so drive to the counselor's office."

"Yeah, I'm ready."

Max went outside with Grant. He lifted her into his truck. He put her wheelchair in the bed of the truck. Max was quiet. "So what happened to you?" Max didn't answer him. Grant found himself tapping Max. She looked at him. "How did you wind up on house arrest?"

"Because they lied," she said staring out the window.

"Who lied?"

"They did."

"Who are they?"

Max leaned her head against the window and closed her eyes. Grant saw the tears roll gently down her cheeks. Max slept the rest of the way. When they got there, Grant woke her. "We are here. Come on. Let's go get you signed in."

"Signed in? Am I going to stay in the place? I don't want to stay here. I don't want to go in there."

"Settle down. It's not that kind of place."

Grant put her in her wheelchair. He then took her by the hand. They went into the building together. Grant gave Max the clip board to fill out the paperwork. Max signed her name and nothing more.

"You have to fill that out," Grant whispered to her.

"Naw. I'm good."

"Fine. Suit yourself."

"Yep."

"I'll be back for you in an hour and a half."

"What? You're not staying? Why aren't you staying?"

"Because this is for you to do. I'll be back."

CHAPTER TWO

Grant had left her sitting in the waiting room. Ten minutes later, a tall woman came into the room. "I'm Dr. Michelle James. Are you Max?"

"Do you see anyone else here?"

She smirked. "Come with me please. Can I push you?"

"NO! Fuck off. I can do it."

Michelle wrote in a notebook. **BELLIGERENT!** "Here. We are going right through here."

"Whatever." **RUDE!**

"Here we are. Make yourself comfortable."

"And how the fuck do you want me to do that?"

"Whatever way you'd like. Let's start. What caused you to be in a wheelchair?"

Nothing. No response.

"How long have you been in the wheelchair?"

Nothing. No response.

"How did your accident happen?"

Nothing. No response.

"Why were you arrested?"

Max blew out a deep breath. No words were spoken.

"How long are you on house arrest for?"

Max shrugged. **GOT MOVEMENT. A SHRUG. NOT MUCH, BUT IT'S SOMETHING.**

"Who do you live with?"

Nothing. No response.

"Do you still see your friends?

Max, who had been looking down, now turned her head to the right, but spoke no words.

"Do you miss your friends?"

Nothing. No response.

A series of questions were asked, and nothing was verbally answered. When Grant came back, Max went with him. He asked her how it went, and she didn't answer him. There was radio silence in the truck on the way back.

"MAX!"

Max looked at Grant.

"Jesus Christ, kid, I've been talking to you for the past five minutes. Haven't you heard anything I've said?"

Max looked away from him. They were about twenty minutes from the house. He pulled over, came around the passenger side of the truck. He opened the truck door and reached in to take her out.

"No! I don't want to get out of the truck."

"You are going to find your way back to the house."

"What? Why?"

"Because I don't tolerate rudeness from anyone. If I don't put up with it from the kids that I coach, then I am sure in the hell not going to put up with it with you." He put her in her wheelchair. "The house is down this road. Maybe we can talk when you get there."

Maybe he was expecting her to tell him off. She didn't. Max started to push her wheelchair in the direction of the house. He drove slowly towards the house. He drove around her when they were just about a block from the house. When she got there, he was waiting for her. He was sitting on the front porch.

"I spoke with the counselor. She said that you didn't speak to her at all today. Why?"

"I had nothing to say."

"You know that you are going to have open up before you can go home."

"But last night I didn't do anything wrong. I lit the fire pit in the back of the house. My neighbor called the police and the fire department."

"What were you burning?"

"My soul."

"What?"

"I was a fucking dancer. I have danced since I was five years old. It's the last thing that my dad saw me do before he left."

"How did the accident happen?"

"Jackasses didn't tighten the line on the baton rail. I was in the air when the fucking thing came crashing down. I was hit with such force that it knocked me out of Elliot's hands. They all took off running, but I couldn't get up and run away with them. I couldn't move. My legs no longer worked."

Joanna had returned from work. She stood listening.

"Then how did you wind up getting arrested and being put on house arrest?"

"Because they lied."

"Who lied?"

"They did. They said that I stole something and that it was in my bag."

"What was it?"

"I don't know. I never got my stuff after that show. I was in the hospital for over a month and rehab for much longer than that. I don't know where my stuff is. I don't know what happened to it. They fucking left me. The day I left rehab; the police were there waiting for me. I thought they were going to tell me that something happened to my mom. Then the one guy took the cuffs off his belt. He said things that didn't make sense to me. He asked me if I understood. My brain was like a tornado inside of my head. I couldn't make out what he was saying. I kept asking him to face me so I could see his lips, but he thought I was being a smart ass. I wasn't. Like in the truck with you earlier. I didn't hear you. I wasn't being rude. I didn't know that you were talking to me. From the accident, I lost complete hearing in my left ear.

"If the counselor was speaking to me the whole time today, I wouldn't know." Max dropped her head.

Joanna walked over. She touched Max's back. Max sat up, and she turned to look at her.

Grant sat on her right side. "So why were put on house arrest?"

"I couldn't answer the questions. They said that I admitted guilt by staying silent, but I didn't know what was being asked of me. I still don't know why I am under house arrest or for how long. I don't know."

Joanna tested it for herself and for them to see. She came on Max's left side and said things and Max never heard her. Max felt her breath on the side of her face, so she turned to look at her.

Joanna left her with Grant while she went to the house to talk to her mom. "Why isn't it reported that Maxine is deaf?"

"Because she isn't."

"She is. On the left side. She can't hear a thing."

"It's an act. An act for attention. Well, I'm fed up with it. I am done dealing with her bullshit."

"What are you saying?"

"The trouble making thief of a child that I have can't stay here any longer. If she does, I will be evicted. She can't live with me anymore. Did you take her to jail last night?"

"She's in a safe place."

"Good. Let her stay there. She cannot come back here to live with me ever."

"You're breaking your terms of the agreement."

"You think I give a shit. One day, I had a healthy abled bodied beautiful daughter, and now I have that thing. She is on house arrest, which means that my life is over too until she gets off it. So I am done. Let her be someone else's burden."

"Here. Sign this then."

"Whatever you like. I will sign whatever it is."

"Don't you want to know what it is?"

"Nope. I don't care. I really don't."

"Can I get some of her things?"

"You can have all of her things. Take it or I will put it out in the trash."

Joanna found Max's bedroom. Her mother gave her a box of garbage bags. Joanna packed up the clothes and other things as best she could in the bags. She took the trophies, medals, and ribbons. "Here. Take this too. Max would die without this stupid thing." Her mother handed Joanna a well-worn out stuffed elephant. When Joanna left, her car was full of all of Max's things.

Joanna called Grant. "She surrendered her."

"What?"

"Grant, she had me pack up all of her stuff. Grant, she… where is she?"

"She's sleeping on the couch."

"Has she said anything more?"

"No. The counselor called. She wants to see her again tomorrow."

"Can you take her again?"

"Yes."

Grant had cooked dinner. He woke Max when it was ready. He knew that she could transfer by herself, but he lifted her off the couch then placed her in her wheelchair. Joanna came in moments later.

"Max, is what you said true?" Joanna asked. She was standing on her left side. Max didn't respond. Joanna came in front of her. Max looked at her. "Is what you said true?"

"Yes. Why should I lie?"

"What was stolen?"

"I…don't know."

"When was it stolen?"

"The night of my last dance."

"Were there people there?"

"Yes. It was a packed house."

"Tell me what led up to it."

"What? I don't know what you mean?"

"You know. What happened before everything went wrong?"

"I don't know," Max said. She covered her face. "There were new people there. A new crew. They were creepy. They went through all our things. They kept pulling the rails down from the rigging. We kept having to tell them to tie them down tighter. There shouldn't be any slack. I kept thinking that someone was going to get hurt. Five minutes or so before we were going on, they played with the rails again. Scott or Dean yelled at them to stop it. We asked them if everything was tight. They had said yes. We took their word. I went in to change, but my bag was gone. I thought that maybe Lucy moved it in with her stuff. I didn't give it another thought. We took our places. The music was loud. The lights were flickering. Everything seemed normal. Elliot lifted me high over his head and we heard the boom and the pop and then the lights got brighter and brighter as the rail came crashing down upon all of us. The light hit me hard in the back. Elliot dropped me. I laid on the stage. They all went running. One of them kicked me in the left side of my head. The pain was excruciating. I didn't have pain in my back. I should have from being hit by the lights and the rail, but there wasn't anything. My legs no longer worked. I couldn't move. I lay on the stage face down. People thought it was part of the show until the lights came on and I was pinned down under a hot light. The next thing I knew there were fire fighters and paramedics. I was put in a neck brace. Because I was flat on my stomach, they put the backboard on top of me before they rolled me to strap me down. Someone said it was going to hurt, but I never felt anything. My head hurt. I know that people were yelling, and it must have been extremely loud, but it was muffled in my right ear and there were no sounds in my left ear. There was blood coming from my left ear.

"At the hospital, they kept yelling, but I couldn't answer them. They gave me something and everything dimmed out to blackness. They did emergency surgery on my back."

Grant tapped Max, so she looked at him. "Did they check your ear and your head?"

"Yeah, but I don't know. I was in an induced coma for a month. Then they brought me out of it, and I went to the rehab center."

"Did anyone ever come and talk to you about that night?" Joanna asked.

"No. When I was leaving the rehab place, the police were there. I was arrested. I was brought into a room where a woman officer yelled at me to tell her where the stuff was, but A) I couldn't make out what she was saying, and B) I didn't know what she was talking about."

"Did your friends come see you?"

Max looked away from them and shook her head.

"Have they seen you since that night?"

Max didn't respond at all. Joanna tapped her. Max looked at her. "Have they seen you since that night?"

"No. Not one single one of them. Well, they were in the court room. They testified that I took the stolen things, but I still don't even know what was stolen. I don't know the value of it. I haven't a fucking clue what it is. What is it?"

"A combination of jewels and drugs."

"What? I didn't take anything. I have never taken drugs and jewels. I don't wear jewelry. I was a fucking hip hop dancer. I wore baggy clothes and dressed like a thug, but I am not a thug. I have never stolen anything. There have been opportunities galore over the years, but I never touched anything that didn't belong to me. My bag was moved. My stuff was missing before the show ever started. We were all excited because rehearsals had gone exceptionally well that day. We were nailing everything."

"Why did you want to change?" Grant asked.

"Because we going to do something new with trampolines that night. It was why Elliot was holding me above his head. The lights were supposed to flash; I was supposed to dive from Elliot's arms to the stage floor… Am I allowed outside?"

"Yes, but you have to stay on the property," Joanna said.

"I will."

Max pushed herself out of the room and out of the house. She went to the track. She went out on it and this time she went to the right. She did lap after lap. She literally pushed herself until all her strength had left her body. As Grant was pouring himself a drink for the night, he looked out the window and saw Max slumped over. He put the glass down and went running out the back door. He ran to her.

"Max! Max!" She was unresponsive. He lifted her from her wheelchair and ran with her in the house. "JO!"

Joanna came in the kitchen. "What? What did she do?"

"I don't know."

"What did she take? Max, what the fuck did you do?"

"We need to call for the medics," Grant said.

"Dammit to hell!" Joanna got on her phone and called 9-1-1. "Yes, I need an ambulance at Twenty Twenty-one Palm Oaks Drive. Yes, this is Sergeant Joanna Norris."

In ten minutes, an ambulance had arrived and still Max was unresponsive. "Hey, I know this girl," the medic said. "She looks great since the last time I saw her. Honey," he said touching her cheek. "I think she just over heated. We will take her to the hospital though just to make sure."

"Can I ride with you?"

"Yes, Sergeant."

When they got to the hospital, Max was brought into to an examining room.

"Before you take off, can I ask you what you meant about what was said at my house?"

The medic looked at Joanna.

"How long ago was that?"

"Three years ago. I was new to the field. The fire department was called, us: the paramedics and the police. When we responded to the scene, we walked in thinking that it was going to be a recovery not a rescue. Her chest, face, and her torso were flat to the floor, yet her legs were twisted in a way that nobody's legs go. She should have been screaming in pain, yet she was silent. That is why we thought that it was a recovery. She was pinned down tight to the floor. Her spine was crushed at just above her belly button. There was a pool of blood on the floor coming from the side of her head. After a few minutes of getting everyone to calm down and clearing people out of there, she said that she couldn't move. We got the lighting system off her, we put her in a neck brace, and then we put the board on top of her. We rolled her gently as not to hurt her, but she never made a peep. She said that she had a headache. She showed signs of paralysis before we even got her in the ambulance to take her.

"If someone spoke to her on the left side, she couldn't hear them. We could tell that she had ear trauma, head, and back trauma right away.

"I would go and check up on her every once in awhile. She was in a coma for awhile and then she went to a rehab place. She was there for about six or eight months. I was there when she was released. They told her that her ride would be waiting for her outside. She wasn't thrilled to have to be going to her mother's house, but she was thrilled to be getting out of that place. Her mom didn't come for her. The police were there instead. She was arrested."

"Did they say for what?"

"Burglary. Drugs. Selling drugs. They went down a list of things."

"Did she say anything?"

"No. Other than that day of the accident hearing her say that she had a headache, I've never heard her speak."

"Thank you."

"Connor."

"What?"

"It's my name. Connor Redder."

"Thank you, Connor."

"Does she speak? I mean is she able to speak now?"

"Yes," Joanna said.

"Oh, good. Thank you."

"No. Thank you."

CHAPTER THREE

Joanna did some investigating work. Grant had come to the hospital with Max's wheelchair and a change of clothes for her. He now stayed in the hospital with her while Joanna took his truck and went to find out all that she could about this case. She wanted to know what exactly was said to be stolen.

The doctor's admitted Max. She was checked out and they found that she was exhausted. She had over pushed herself. She was given plenty of fluids. Max slept right through to the next day. When she woke up, Grant was in the room with her.

"What? Where am I? Why am I here? No. No. No. I don't want to be back here."

Grant upon hearing her voice had gotten up and was standing next to the bed. "You need to calm down."

"Why am I here?"

"Yesterday, you overexerted yourself and you were unresponsive."

A woman doctor came in. "What drugs do you do?"

"What? I don't."

"We did a tox screen when you were brought in. Your alcohol levels were above…"

"Your nuts," Max said. "I don't drink, and I don't do fucking drugs."

"Well, the tests don't lie," the doctor said.

"They have to," Max spatted at her.

"Aren't you, Daniella Granger?"

"No, you asshole. I'm Maxine Brandon and I don't do drugs. And I don't drink."

"I'm so sorry," the doctor said.

"Fucking asshole!"

"Max!" Grant said.

"Well, she is."

"She made a mistake."

"A mistake is what landed me in that goddamn chair and ended my dancing career."

Another doctor came in. "My name is Maxine Brandon. I go by Max."

"Well, then you are the person I came into see."

"Can I go?"

"Yes, you are going to be released today. Do you know why you are here?"

"Nope."

"You dehydrated yourself and you were overheated."

Max shook her head. "What?"

"Well, with the injury that you sustained, you probably don't feel when your body temperatures are changing do you?"

"I don't know. I guess I don't."

"When was the last time that you have done this type of activity?"

"Yesterday."

"Yes, I know that but before that."

"Yesterday," Max said again. "It's the first time that I've been outside and allowed to move around in three years."

"Well, you just over did it. Make sure you are drinking plenty of fluids."

"Can I go now?"

"We spoke to your mom and she said that you can't come back to her house."

"Yes, that's correct," Grant said. "She will be coming home with me."

"Have you been fitted for a hearing aid?"

"I was told that it won't work with the amount of hearing loss that I have."

"Well, would you want to try?"

"Yeah, I guess."

"You can get changed and into your wheelchair. The discharge papers are being drawn up right now."

"Thank you."

Grant looked at Max. "Do you need help dressing?"

"No."

"Do you need anything?"

"If you could just move the chair closer to the bed for me."

"Yes, of course."

"Thanks."

"I'll be right out in the hall if you need anything."

"Thank you."

Max got dressed. She transferred into her wheelchair and then came out of the room. Grant met her. They went to the nurses' station together. Max looked at the nurse behind the counter. "Lucy?"

"Oh, hi. Um. Let me get you my supervisor."

"Wait a minute."

"I can't. I can't talk to you right now."

"I deserve the right to know what the fuck happened that night."

"Listen, Xine, it was a long time ago. Things are different now. We are all different now."

"Yeah, no shit, Luc."

"That's not fair."

"No, this isn't fair. You said that you knew that crew. You said that they did great work."

"I trusted them."

"And I fucking trusted you and our team. Yet when the shit came down, you all ran for your lives. Well, you left one behind. You all let me take the fucking fall. I still don't know why I was arrested, why I was prosecuted, and why I have been on fucking house arrest for the past two and half years. What the fuck happened that night, Lucy?"

A security guard came over with a police officer. "Is there a problem?"

"No," Grant said. "We are simply waiting for the discharge papers."

"Lucy, is that true?"

"Yeah, it's nothing Tim."

The papers were signed; they left the hospital. "Where's your truck?"

"Joanna has it."

"Then how are we getting back to the house."

"Jason is going to drive us."

"Who is Jason?"

"He is one of my boys."

"You have children?"

"Yes, but Jason is one of the boys on my team."

"Where are your children?"

"They are grown. They live close by."

"What do you have?"

"Two of each. Do you have siblings?"

"Yeah. They are younger than me. When I went on house arrest, they had to go live with their dads."

"Dads? As in plural?"

"Yes."

"Do any of you have the same dad?"

"Yeah. Me and my brother. Then our two younger sisters share a father, and our little brother has his own father. I don't know them though. I mean my sisters or my little brother. I have only heard about them. My mom's good kids. The one's that she kept."

"So why didn't you get to do house arrest at your dad's house?"

"Because he's remarried and has other kids."

"You don't consider them your siblings?"

"I don't know. I never met them either."

"Why not?"

"Because when I was twelve, I ran away from home. I became a street kid. It's how I survived. I danced every day with my team. Not that we all were street kids. But I was."

"Did your parents ever report you missing?"

"I don't know." She laughed.

Grant's daughter pulled up. "Sorry, dad," she said. "Mom called me over an hour ago. Sorry."

"Ashley this is Max. Max, this is my daughter Ashley."

"Hi," they said together.

"How do you know my dad?"

"Your mom and I know each other."

"But mom is a cop."

"I know that." Max said.

"Oh, wait. I know who you are. Dad!"

"It's ok, Ashley."

"She's a thief."

"I never stole a damn thing in my life."

"That's not what the newspapers said."

"Yeah, like they knew."

"So how did you get that way?" Ashley asked.

"Listen! Are you going to give us a ride back to your parents' house or not?"

"Get in the fucking car," she said to Max.

"Both of you stop it." Grant reprimanded.

Once in the car, with Ashley on Max's left, Max couldn't keep up with the conversation. She sat staring out the window.

"Max! How old are you?" Ashley asked. Max never wavered. She continued to look out the window. "What's wrong with her?"

"She's deaf because of the accident that she had."

"Seriously?"

"Yes," Grant said.

"So she hasn't heard any of this conversation?"

"Probably not enough of it to follow along."

When they got to the house, Grant helped her out of the car. "I want you to go inside the house." He was on Max's left side. Max didn't hear him. Grant came around her. "I want you to go inside the house."

"I wanted to stay outside awhile."

"No. You heard the doctor."

Max shook her head. "I didn't. I heard her say that I was being discharged. Did she say more than that?"

"Yes. She said that you have to take it easy for a few days."

"Ok."

Max went into the house. She saw the trash bags full of her stuff. She lowered her head.

"I don't want her staying in my room," Ashley said.

"She isn't staying in your room."

"Dad, she is a thief."

Joanna came home. She saw Max looking through the bags. "It's not here."

"What are you looking for?"

"It's not here," Max said again. "Where is he?"

"He who?"

"My elephant. Where is he?"

"He's on the bed."

Max pushed herself into the room. She closed the door. She took the elephant off the bed, held it tight in her arms and cried. Joanna came in the room. She came and sat on the bed.

"She kicked me out," Max said. "I am going to go to jail." She looked up at Joanna. "Am I going to have to go to jail? I still have years left on being under house arrest."

"We are going to talk to a lawyer."

Tears streamed down Max's face. "I don't understand them when they talk. They talk too fast. I get lost."

"It's ok. Grant and I will be with you."

"But where I am going to live? I lost my place after the accident."

"You had your own place?"

"Yes."

"A house?"

"An apartment. I shared it with Lucy, Genevieve, Elliot, and Scott. But it was my apartment. I bought it. I paid for it with my own money. It is in my name."

"Where is it?"

"On Charles and Jameson Street. The apartment is on the fourth floor."

"Is there an elevator?"

"Yes."

Max's cell phone rang. Joanna found and looked at it. "No," she said. "Have you been using your phone?"

"No, ma'am."

"When was the last time you used your phone?"

"I don't know. It would be on there."

"I'm going to have your phone records ran."

"Ok," Max said.

"I'm taking this."

"I don't want it."

"Give me the elephant."

"Why?"

"I have to see something."

Max reluctantly handed it over. She watched as Joanna felt every surface of the elephant. She felt for any tears or openings. There weren't any. She handed it back to Max.

Grant opened the bedroom door. "Dinner is ready."

"Dinner is ready," Joanna said.

Max sat the elephant on the bed and then left the room. Upon entering the kitchen, there were more people there.

"MAX, THESE ARE MY BROTHERS HARRISON AND DALE AND OUR SISTER REBECCA."

"Why are you yelling it at her?" Dale asked.

"Because she's deaf," Ashley said.

"Can I make your plate?" Grant said to Max.

"Yes, sir, thank you."

"Is she troubled like your boys, dad?" Harrison asked.

Max ate quietly. When she was done, she was still hungry, but she wouldn't ask for more.

"MAX, DID YOU GO TO COLLEGE?" Ashley asked.

"Why are you yelling every time you speak to me?"

"WELL BECAUSE YOU CAN'T HEAR ME."

"I've heard you."

"SO IS YOUR DEAFNESS A GAME YOU PLAY?"

"A what?"

"I THOUGHT YOU SAID YOU HEARD ME?"

"Ashley, stop it," Dale said.

"May I please be excused?" Max asked.

"No," Grant said.

Max lowered her head.

"So how come you are in a wheelchair?" Harrison asked.

"I was a dancer," Max started. The words caught in her throat. She fought not to cry. "The lighting crew messed up and one of the rails came crashing down. I had been lifted into the air and the light hit me like a mac truck and knocked me to the ground before it continued to fall towards the stage. I was pinned under it. I couldn't move."

"That must have been painful," Rebecca said.

"No. I don't think it was."

"How did you lose your hearing?" Dale asked.

"Someone kicked me in the head as they went running away. From the pressure and the force of being knocked down the way I was and then getting kicked in the head, blood rushed out of my left ear. I felt the pain in my head."

"Does it hurt being in a wheelchair?" Harrison asked.

"No."

"It must be hard though." Rebecca said.

"What do you mean?"

"Alright. Enough of this," Grant said.

"But dad we have right to the know why she is here and what she is doing."

"No, Ashley you don't," Joanna said.

"I don't want her sleeping in my room."

"She's not sleeping in your room."

"How long is she staying here?"

"That's not your concern," Joanna said.

"Can I please have some more," Max asked.

"Yes. Help yourself."

"Mom. Dad. I have to get going. I have a test that I have to study for," Dale said. "Thank you for the distraction and for this great dinner."

"Yeah, we have to get going too," Rebecca said about her and Harrison.

"Do you have siblings?" Rebecca asked.

"Yes," Max said. "I have four brothers and two sisters."

"Your mom has seven kids?"

"No. My mom has five kids. My dad and my stepmom have the other two."

"Do you see them?" Dale asked.

"No. I haven't seen my dad since I was twelve," Max said.

"What?" Ashley asked. "Why?"

"Because when they divorced, I wanted to live with my dad. I ran away when he said that I couldn't. I didn't want to live with my mom."

"Where did you go?" Ashley asked.

"When?"

"When you ran away. Where did you go?"

"Just away."

"How long were you a runaway?" Dale asked.

"Till I was eighteen."

"So you were alone for six years?" Ashley started drilling.

"I was never alone. I had my friends from the dance crew. Some of us have been friends since we were little."

"Did you go to school?"

"Yes. I graduated high school." Max graduated at the top of her class. "They each put money in a trust fund account for me when I was a baby; they added to it over the years too, but I couldn't touch it till after my twenty second birthday. At twenty-two, I took some of the money out of the bank and I purchased my apartment."

"How old are you now?"

"I'm thirty. After the accident happened, I lost my scholarship for the doctorates program."

"What were you going for?" Rebecca sweetly asked.

"It doesn't matter," Max said.

Ashley started again. "So the accident happened three years ago?"

"Three and half. I was twenty-six."

"When did it happen?"

"May…May… I don't remember the date." Max lowered and grabbed the front of her head.

"When is your birthday?"

"November twelfth."

"Mom. Dad. We are going to go. It was nice meeting you," Ashley said.

"You as well."

Ashley leaned into hug Max goodbye and whispered in her left ear, "Don't you fucking steal anything from my parents." Max didn't hear a word of it.

CHAPTER FOUR

Within the next few days, Grant and Joanna took Max to meet with a new lawyer. The lawyer was an older man, who had been in the practice for twenty years. Max was given a packet to fill out. "Once you fill that out, we will go from there," he said.

"Thank you."

"What do you want to see done here?" the lawyer asked with his head down so Max didn't hear him.

"Max," Grant said. "He is speaking to you."

"I'm sorry. I didn't hear you. His head is down. I can't make out what he is saying."

The lawyer was testing her. He now went on her left side and asked the same question again. Max didn't even move a muscle.

"She can't hear you when you are on her left side."

"I know. You told me," he said. "I was testing it." The lawyer came back around Max. "What do you want to see done here?"

"I want my apartment back. I want off house arrest. I want my name and record cleared."

"One thing at a time."

"NO!" Max said. "I didn't do anything wrong. I was injured and they let me take the fall for someone else's bullshit."

"Ok, but how did it happen?"

"How did what happen?"

"Where were the things that were stolen?"

"I don't know. I don't even know what was stolen."

"It's here. A gold diamond tennis bracelet. Necklaces. Pearls. Emeralds. Rubies. And two hundred thousand dollars in cash and there was supposedly a bag of drugs."

"I never saw any of that stuff. I don't wear jewelry. I don't know what colors gems are. What are pearls?"

"They look like white beads strung together."

Max shook her head. "How could I have possibly taken the shit that was stolen? My back was crushed that night. Everyone else ran out of there. I was taken out on a fucking backboard."

"Was anything different that day?"

"There was a new crew working in the theater. They were creepy. Lucy knows them. Friends of hers or her brother's. I didn't know them. They kept messing with everything. They went through our stuff. They said that they could hang lights and I wound up like this because they didn't know shit about it. One second I'm having the dance of my life, and the next life as I knew it was over."

"Lucy? Who is Lucy?"

"She was one of my teammates."

"How many teammates do you have?"

"Nine. There were ten of us in total. It was me, Lucy, Genevie, Scott, Elliot, Dean, Mike, Jack, Shawn, and Brian."

"I need last names to go with those first names?"

"Lucy Smutbrook. Genevie…I never knew her last name. It's long and hard to say. Scott and Dean have the same last name, but they aren't related. Their last name is Sanders. Elliot's last name is Berk. Mike's last name is Faulk. Jack's last name is Preston. Shawn's last name is Collins. And Brian's last name is Aaronberg."

"Where are they now?"

"I don't know. Well, Lucy works in the hospital."

"When's the last time you saw all of them?"

"The night of the accident. This May will be four years ago."

"What were you prosecuted for?"

"I don't know."

"How long are you sentenced to be on house arrest?"

"Forever," Max said.

"Come on!" the lawyer said.

"I don't know. Five years total was it or six or… I don't know. I didn't understand what they were saying. I couldn't hear anything that was said on my left side. And my brain wouldn't process what they were saying. I don't know. I know that when court was over, my mother was pissed like I've never seen her pissed before. My siblings had to quickly pack up their things or have their things packed for them and go live with their fathers. I was just as mad to have to go back to live with my mother, who I haven't lived with since I was twelve years old."

"What does your mother say?"

"She kicked me out of the house the other night when the stupid shit neighbor next door called the fire department and the police because I was enjoying a fire burning safely in the fire pit in the backyard."

"Do you have anywhere else to go?"

"My apartment was taken away from me after the accident."

"Who has it?"

"Lucy, Dean and Scott lived with me."

"Did you share the expenses?"

"No. I had bought it when I was twenty-two. It is mine. I wasn't charging them rent or anything. Maintenance was the only thing I had to keep up with. Oh, and utilities. But those were all in my name. I paid the water, phone, and electric bills."

"So, they stayed scott free?"

"Yes. They sometimes chipped in for the laundry to be done, but never too often."

The lawyer's name is David Morgan. When Max left with Joanna and Grant, David got on the phone. He started making phone calls. He called an investigator. "I need for you to check on where nine people are living today and where they were living four years ago." David gave the investigator all of the names and as much details as he had, which wasn't much.

"What is this about?"

"It's a case where a young woman was charged with burglary and she's been on house arrest for quite some time now."

"So what is the issue?"

"There is no way that she could have done this."

"Ok, I will look into everything that you have asked me."

"Thanks."

"Do you want to drive?" Grant asked Max. "Have you ever driven?"

"Yes. But I have never had a driver's licenses or my own car. No. I can't drive."

"Well, what do you say you learn."

"I can't use my legs."

"You don't have to. You can use your hands."

"What? No. I've seen you and Joanna drive. You use your feet."

"I know that we do, but you can use your hands."

"Grant, how?"

"Well, let's go find out. It doesn't hurt to find out right?"

"No. No, it doesn't."

Grant took Max to see about getting her driving lessons. The lady behind the counter handed them a driver's manual. "First you learn all the rules of the road. Then you come back and take the test. From there, you get your license and then we go from there."

"Thank you," Max said. Grant paid for the driver's book.

When they left there, Max saw a sign for dance classes. "Grant, can we check that out."

"Check what out?"

"The dance class?"

"Yes, for a few minutes."

"Am I still on house arrest?"

"Yes and no," Grant said.

"I don't know what you mean."

"We will talk about it later."

They went in. The place was lined with mirrors, so everyone saw the wheelchair. The dance instructor turned from facing the mirror. "Can I help you?"

"I. I. Um. No. Sorry. Grant, let's go please?"

A girl did a move and didn't open up enough to finish the move, so she fell. Max moved forward. "That was good, but you fell because you didn't open up enough."

The girl got up, put her hands on her hips and spat out, "And how would you know?"

"I don't. Sorry. Sorry to interrupt your class." Max spun quickly. With the speed that she moved with it appeared that she was running. Grant ran after her. "Can I walk back to the house?"

"No. We aren't going there yet. Come on," Grant said. He lifted her out of her wheelchair and into the truck. "What was it like when you danced?" He tapped Max, so she looked at him. "What was it like when you danced?"

"What was it like?"

"Yeah, that's what I asked."

"It was an escape. I was free as a bird. I would cover the whole stage. My feet were hardly ever on the ground." Max closed her eyes as she envisioned herself dancing. Grant gave her the moment. She opened her eyes when they had stopped. "Where are we?"

"The grocery store. Do you cook?"

"I used to until I had to go live with the thing."

"Come. You are cooking for Jo and I tonight."

"Ok."

While they walked around the grocery store together gathering things for dinner someone was watching them. It was Dean. When they went to pay for the groceries, Dean started. "Did you break the ankle monitor?"

He was on Max's left side, so she didn't hear him, but others did.

"So what? You're not going to talk to me?" Dean said a bit louder. "Xine, why are you out?"

Grant stood there. "Leave her alone."

"Hey, man, stay out of it."

"No, man, leave her alone."

"She's not supposed to be out in public places. I've phoned the police. Max, did you hear me? The police are coming for you."

"She's completely deaf in her left ear," Grant said. "So therefore, you moron, she hasn't heard a word that you said."

The police came into the store. "That's her," Dean said. "She's on house arrest. She cut off her ankle monitor. She's on house arrest because she's a thief."

Max just noticed that there was a commotion going on around them. "What's going on?" She turned to the register for the first time. "DEAN!"

"No. I'm not allowed to talk to you. You are violating your house arrest and punishment."

"What? No, I'm not."

The police had cleared the registers of other customers. Grant was still right behind Max. "Sir, please step away."

"This girl is with me. She hasn't done anything wrong."

"Check her stuff," Dean said. "She's a thief."

"What? I'm not. I've never stolen anything in my life."

"Xine, you know that isn't true. The last time we were all together, you stole stuff. She…she…she has a gun."

That got the police moving faster. Grant was shoved out of the way. Max was grabbed by the police.

"What? What's going on? I didn't do anything wrong. Grant! Grant, please."

"Where is it?" an officer asked yelling.

"Where is what?"

"The gun?"

"What gun? I don't have a gun."

"Can you stand up?"

"No."

"We need to pat you down."

"You need to do what?"

"We need to pat you down and search you."

"I don't understand. I didn't do anything. I don't have anything. I don't even have any money. I am here with Grant Norris."

"Norris? As in related to Sergeant?"

"Yes," Grant said.

They had taken Max over to a wall. She was facing it. "Put your hands up on the wall," the officer on her left said.

"She can't hear you. She's permanently deaf in her left ear," Grant said.

The officer grabbed her wrist yanking it up. "What do you want me to do? I don't know what you want me to do."

The officer on the right side of her said, "Put your hands on the goddamn wall and leave them there."

Max did. She was frisked by the police. She didn't have anything on her person. Sergeant Joanna Norris came into the store. Max still had her hands up as high as she could on the wall. Joanna walked over to her. She touched Max on the shoulder and then stepped back as she crumbled.

"What the hell is going on here?"

"This man called 9-1-1 saying that a woman in a wheelchair had a gun."

"That's false allegations you know that?" Joanna said.

"I thought I saw that she had a gun," Dean said. "She's trouble. She steals. I thought that she might be stealing groceries. And she is supposed to be on house arrest for eight years. It definitely hasn't been that long. And what? She acts deaf now? I was talking to her and she never acknowledged."

"Were you on her left side?"

"Yes."

"Then she couldn't hear anything that you were saying."

"The man said that."

"Well, the man is correct. She is now stone deaf in her left ear."

When they got to the house, Max went into the bedroom. She closed the door and got on the bed. She took the elephant and tucked it under her arm. Then she laid there crying. She cried herself to sleep.

Grant and Joanna were in the kitchen. "So what happened?"

"We were in the store. I told her that I wanted her to cook for us tonight. Everything was going fine until the guy behind the register recognized who she was. He kept saying that she should be at home and on house arrest. I never saw him call the police, but all of sudden they were there. They cleared everyone away. Jo, I think maybe she is partially deaf in her right ear as well. It was loud in the store and people were running and rushing around, and she didn't seem to know what the hell was going on. We need to know the extent of her injuries."

"I agree with you there."

"Didn't her mom tell you anything."

"No. Just to take all of her stuff. We should see what she is doing?"

"I'll let you do that. I don't want to walk in the room if she's not decent."

"Ok," Joanna said with a smile. "Ok." Joanna went to check on Max. She found her sleeping on the bed. Joanna saw the tears on her face. Joanna covered her. Max never moved.

At four in the morning, Max was wide awake. She got dressed and went out to the track. She did three miles before going back in the house. She showered and got dressed for the day. Joanna came and found her. "You have to come with me today. Grant has to go be with his boys today. We can't leave you alone just yet."

"No. It's ok. I understand."

"Bring somethings to entertain yourself with."

"Ok."

"Grant and I are going to set up to take you to the doctor."

"For what?"

"Well, with you having a new lawyer on the case, we all need to know the extent of your injuries."

"What will I have to do?"

"Just get some tests done. Nothing too invasive."

"When?"

"Don't worry. Not for a few days or so."

Max went with Joanna to the police station. Joanna put Max in a room. "I'll come get you when I go to lunch. Do you need anything?"

"The bathroom."

"It's right through there. Here is money for the vending machine."

"Thank you."

Max sat at the table. She put the driver's manual on the table and started reading it. An officer walked over to her with a bottle of water, cookies, and pretzels. "It's not much, but it's something," he said. "What do you have there?"

"Thank you. Grant is going to take me for my driver's license."

"So what happened if you don't mind me asking."

"I don't mind. My dance team and I were having a performance when we heard something boom and pop, and the next thing we knew a lighting rail was coming down fast on top of us. It hit me in the back because I was up in the air at the time. I fell to the floor and I was pinned under the railing."

"Was it painful?"

"No. I only had pain in my head from someone on my team running past me and kicking me in the head."

"Someone kicked you in the head?"

"Yeah. Hard enough to make blood come from my ear. It was a lot of blood though. And then everything went quiet."

"Are you deaf in both ears now?"

"No, but if things are going on behind me, I don't hear it."

"Well, I'll leave you to your reading."

"Thank you."

An hour later someone else came over with another bottle of water. It was a woman detective. "Hey, can I talk to you for a minute?"

"Yes."

"Can I sit here?"

"Just not on my left side. I don't hear from that side anymore."

The woman detective took a seat the table. "So Jo tells us that you were a dancer."

"Yep."

"What happened the day or night of the accident?"

"Lucy, a girl on the team, brought this new stage crew in to do the lights." Max shivered. "They were creepy. They went through all of our stuff. They kept screwing with the rails and the rigging."

"What's that? What do you mean?"

"In a theater there are rails high above the stage. Things can be hung on them. Like lights and scrims, which are like backgrounds. Props can be hung from the rails too. And they are all on a pully system. Kind of like on a boat. They are all tied down really tight especially after a lighting system has been put on it. So all day while we were rehearsing, these guys were loosening the rail lines. We all kept telling them to stop. Scott, Dean, and I had gone over an hour before the show started, and we made sure that they were all tied down tight.

"But things just seemed off that night. I went to go change before the show and my bag was moved. I got distracted with other things, so I didn't give it a second thought. We all warmed up again and then we started on time. Elliot had me in a lift when we heard a boom and then a pop and then the lighting rail was coming down fast. It hit me in the back and knocked me out of Elliot's arms. It continued to drop until it couldn't anymore. The light was right on top of me. But I didn't feel it. I knew I couldn't move my legs. And then everyone in the crew went running off stage and someone kicked me hard in the head on the left side. I lost my hearing that night."

"So what happened to the jewels, the necklaces and drugs?"

"I don't know. I never saw anything. I had been distracted most of the day. My dad, who I haven't seen since I was twelve had called me out of the blue and asked if he could see the show with my stepmom, who I've never met and my half-brothers. It threw me off a bit. I mean I was focused on the dance, but my head was swimming. I hadn't seen either of my parents since I was twelve. I couldn't imagine how he had gotten my number."

"Tell me more about these guys. What do they look like?"

"One was a tall skinny black guy with long dread locks. He had an accent of some kind. Maybe French or something from the islands. He was really hard to understand. There was a total of six of them. One looked like a blond surfer. He had come into the space with no shirt on. He was ripped up with muscles on his abs and his legs were pretty built up too."

"Do you know or remember any of their names?"

"One was Diego Vert. Lucy would know them though. Or her brother for sure would know them.

"The others were all with dark black hair. They kind of looked like models. They didn't care anything about safety."

"Did you have a dance coach?"

"Yeah. Her name is Hannah Grace."

"When was the last time you saw her?"

"She was there during practice or rehearsal that day, but she didn't come back after we took our dinner break."

"Was she usually there when you had shows?"

"Yes. She was always there."

"But she wasn't there that night?"

"No."

"Did she come see you in the hospital?"

"No. None of them came. I went to the rehab center for like eight months. I was told that my ride was coming to get me, and I could wait outside. I was arrested that day. Then I was in court, but I didn't understand what was going on. In like four days they said that I was guilty and then the judge put me on house arrest. I had to go back to mom's house. I haven't been there since I was twelve."

"So where were you living before the accident?"

"I had an apartment. It was mine. I bought it when I was twenty-two. Scott, Dean and Lucy lived with me, but it was my apartment."

"Who is living there now?"

"I don't know."

"Have you violated your terms of house arrest?"

"No. I'm allowed out in my mom's backyard. I had lit the fire pit and my neighbor called 9-1-1. She came out and started yelling at me, but I never did anything to her.

"I get to go outside my house for an hour and a half every damn day. I wanted to go outside at nighttime and light the fire pit for a while. That is all I wanted to do."

"What kind of dancer were you?"

"I've studied all of it. Ballet, contemporary, ballroom, hip hop, jazz, and tap."

"Were you good?"

"I was ok," Max said.

"Are there video tapes of you dancing?"

"Yes, from every show."

"Do you have them?"

"They are at Sergeant Norris's house in one of the garbage bags she brought from my mom's house."

"I'd like to see some of those."

"Yeah, ok."

CHAPTER FIVE

The police were starting their own new investigation on Max's case. It was crystal clear that the night of her last dance performance there was no way that she could have stolen the items that were said to be stolen in the condition that Max left that night. There were now fifteen different suspects. Dean and Lucy were both at the top of the list.

A police detective stopped by Joanna and Grant's house. Max was outside going around the track. The detective watched her. Max pushed her wheelchair with ease and grace as she finalized the lap that she was on. She saw the person watching her and came up to the house.

"How are you doing?"

Fucking wonderful!

"Are you Maxine?"

Oh, boy, this guy deserves a cookie!

"Do you speak?"

"Yes. The sergeant isn't home right now."

"I know that."

"Am I in trouble? Because if I am, I swear I didn't do it."

"Well, that's actually what I came here to talk to you about."

"What do you mean? And wait a minute. Who are you?"

"I'm Detective Danial Starr."

"I've heard of you."

"Yeah. How is that?"

"You were in newspapers and you were on TV about some crime that you solved from twenty or so years ago."

"Right," he said.

Grant came to the door. "Max, who are you talking to?"

"I'm Detective Starr."

"Yeah, I know," Grant said. "Why don't you come in, so you aren't interrogating one of my children outside on my front porch."

"One of your children? Is Maxine related to you and Joanna?"

"Until everything gets squared away with Max here, as long as she is staying under our roof, she is one of our children."

They went into the house. "Can I go change?"

"Yes," Grant said.

Max went into the room and got a change of clothes. Then she went into the bathroom, where she showered and changed. She came back fifteen minutes later with wet hair.

"Maxine…"

"My name is Max."

"Ok," Daniel said. "So Max, tell me." He stopped. "Wait a minute," he said. "I was there that night. You were the dancer that was in the air. You took a hit like I've never seen before. That light and that rail just drove you right out of the other dancer's arms. And the way your body hit the stage floor…" he broke off. He wiped his eyes. "What can you tell me about that night?"

"The same that I have been saying all along. Rehearsals went phenomenal that day. Lucy brought in a new stage crew, who really didn't know shit about what they were doing. The rails…where the lights are hung from, must be super tight, but they kept bringing them down and then bringing them up and tying them off too loose, so there was slack on the line which is dangerous. Before we took our dinner break for the night, Elliot, Scott, Dean, and I tightened all the ropes in the rigging. The dance had been going so well until we heard a bang and a pop and then that rail came crashing down on top of all of us. Everyone was able to get away from it except for me."

"Do you still keep in touch with your teammates?"

"No. When I see them, they tell me that they can't speak to me."

"Do you know what was taken?"

"I was told, but I don't know what anything looks like. I didn't see anything. My bag was taken or moved before we started. I wanted to change, but I couldn't because my stuff wasn't there. Lucy told me to forget about it and to come on the stage and get ready. I lost the use of my legs that night and my home."

"Your home?"

"Yes, sir. I had my own apartment. It was mine. I paid for it all by myself. I let Lucy, Scott and Dean live with me."

"Are they still living there?"

"I don't know. I haven't been allowed out of my mother's house until Mrs. Stanley, the stupid neighbor, called the police on me and the fire department and then my wonderful mother kicked me out. True story.

"This is the closest I'll ever come to dancing again," Max said.

"What do you mean?"

"It's like a dance. Well-rehearsed by now. My story has never changed."

"Why didn't you tell that to the judge?"

Max looked away for the first time. "Because I couldn't. I didn't understand what was being said. My jaw was wired shut. I couldn't hear the questions. The lawyers stayed on my left side. I'm completely deaf on that side since the accident."

Joanna had come home. Seeing the added car in the driveway brought her in the house a bit faster.

"Your jaw was wired shut?"

"Yeah. Till two months after being at my mom's house. I was a dancer and now I am this. I have danced since I was five. I have been on my own since I was twelve. I was blamed for my parents divorcing. "The money" my mom would say. "The distance" my dad would whisper into the phone to his… he wouldn't let me come live with him and my mother wouldn't let me back in the house because at twelve I chose my father over her." Max wiped at the tears that rushed her eyes. "But this tale is my final dance. I talk about it over and over again. I close my eyes and see it over and over again. In my head, I hear the boom. I hear the pop. I hear myself telling Elliot to lower me. I am yelling it over and over. Lower me! Lower me! But it is so fucking loud. The boom was so loud that it vibrated in my head, in my teeth, in my chest – like a drummer just whaling on that drum causing so much friction that you can feel the vibrations going through you. Then I was hit. I was knocked hard with such force to the ground.

The nine others went scrambling. Someone kicked me in the head. My ear erupted like a volcano."

"Was your mother there?"

"No. She never saw mw dance since the divorce. My father was supposed to come with his wife and children. I don't know if he did or not."

"Did he come see you when you were in the hospital or in rehab?"

"I don't know. I never met his wife or children. Mom is thrilled that I won't be living with her anymore, so she can get her good kids back."

"What?" Joanna asked.

"You know. Her good kids. The ones that chose her. I'm tired. Can I go lay down?"

"Yes," Joanna and Grant said.

"No," the detective said.

Max was shutting down and Grant could see it. The detective asked her a question and she stopped hearing him all together.

"Ok! That's enough! She's done. Max, can you hear me?"

Max didn't answer. When Grant touched her, she seemed to wilt away from him. Grant pulled Max away from the table and then gently lifted her into his arms. He carried her into the bedroom. Joanna brought the wheelchair. When Grant put her on the bed, Max didn't move. Grant sat on the bed with her. "I'm going to sit with her for awhile," he said. "Is that ok?"

"Yes, of course."

Joanna came back in the kitchen. "Why are you investigating her?"

"It's my assignment, Jo."

"Well, you burned her out tonight."

"She's deaf?"

"Yes, in her left ear since the accident just like she said."

"And her parents?"

"I haven't had the pleasure to meet her father, but her mother… man that woman is a bitch. And the poor kid had to go stay there with her for all this time. The woman detests Maxine."

"Where's her father?"

"In Lees. I was going to go there tomorrow to meet him."

"Can I go with you?"

"Yep."

"I was there."

"You were where?"

"I was at that show. She was the brightest and the biggest on stage. She came on stage doing five front flips, she added two cartwheels, and then turned into six back flips. She was the most alive on that stage. It was so loud. My kids were complaining about the noise, but I couldn't draw myself away. Like she said there was a boom and then a pop and then it sounded like a train was coming through the building. They had all stopped. They were all looking up except for Maxine. The guy held her up as high as he could and then he went higher when he went up on the balls of his feet. That speed of the light hitting her, you could see it slamming into her with such force that she was knocked out of the guy's arms. Everyone starting yelling. The dancers were all running and scrambling like she said. The audience thought that it was part of their show until the stage was cleared of everyone except her. The house lights came on and the image of her… it will never leave me. Her left ear was facing the audience and it was pouring blood. She was calm. She was alert. Everyone had been screaming. She should have been screaming, Jo, but she wasn't. When the fire department had cleared her free of the bar and the light that had held her pinned tight to the floor, the medics moved quickly. They put her in a neck brace. They put the backboard on top of her. They straightened her legs. She didn't make a sound. She kept saying that her head hurt. She kept trying to grab her head."

He looked at Joanna. "Her mother…"

"No, she really doesn't want her back at her house. She wants to be free of that burden," she said.

"But she's still on house arrest?"

"Yes. But where the fuck is she going to go? When her energy is there, she can move like the wind and when it's done… well, you saw it."

Daniel left. He went to Maxine's mother's house. Music blasted from inside the house. He could hear people laughing and talking like nothing was missing from there. He watched the older woman come to her door, open it, look out, shake her head and then close her door. Daniel got out of the car. He went and knocked on the lady's door. She opened it cautiously.

"Hi, ma'am, I am detective Daniel…"

"Please come in. I can't really hear you with all that noise next door." Daniel went into her house. "Have you lived here long?"

"Yes. I have lived here for forty years. I am Mrs. Katherine Stanley."

"Did you know Maxine when she was growing up?"

"Yes. She was always dancing and moving about. She was a tall child. And skinny. Every time I saw her, I gave her a candy bar. And then when her father left, she was no longer around. Desiree said that she went to live with her father."

"Did you know her father?"

"Matt was always on the move. He would yell at Max when he had to take her to dance practice. He started sneaking out and sneaking around. When Matt and Maxine were gone for quite some time, Desiree said that it was Max that drove her father away.

"I had been out shopping when I first saw that twig of a girl on the streets. Max must have been fourteen or so by then. She was slimmer than a rail that one. I came home and told Desiree and she said that is where she belonged and that she wasn't welcome back in that home."

"Why did you call 9-1-1?"

"I saw the flames and smoke and Max was just there. I yelled for her to put it out, but she didn't. She is on house arrest because the street urchin that she is is a thief. I was yelling at her and she wouldn't… It was calm and nice here for like five minutes. As soon as Max was out of the picture, Desiree brought the others back to the house. And now it's like that most of the time."

"Did you ever see her dance?"

"I was lucky enough to see the show before her last show. The things that were claimed to be stolen were probably already stolen by then."

"Why do you say that?"

"There were these characters hanging around the stage door. Six of them."

"Did you see Max with them?"

"Now that ask that, no. I don't remember seeing her. There was an Asian girl (Lucy) with them and then a group of guys were there."

"Can you describe them?"

"I can do one better. I can show you them."

"How is that?"

She went to a drawer in the cabinet and pulled it out. Then she brought over a stack of photos. "Here you go," she said. "I took pictures that night.

Here is Maxie that night. So cheerful and bright. She lit up the whole stage that one. Then here are these shady looking guys by the stage door. There is one of the dancers chatting with them. That Asian girl. And then here are the guy dancers. This one." She was pointing at Jack. "This one." She now pointed at Mike. "This one." She pointed at Dean. "And these two fellows. This one is the one that held Maxie up over his head." Elliot. "And then this one." Scott. "And the other girl. I didn't get a good picture of her. She was blurry, but she's about five or six inches shorter than Maxie."

"Did you ever tell this to anyone before now?"

"No. No one has ever asked me. But these six guys... I don't know, but they seemed like trouble. They were sneaky and quick. Have you seen Maxie?"

"Yes."

"How is she?"

"You do know that she is deaf in her left ear?"

"Awe the poor thing. To go from being like that." She pointed to a picture that hung on her wall, "to what she is now and to be deaf to boot."

Daniel left a short time later.

Joanna and Daniel went to Lees to go see Matt. Joanna drove. When they pulled up to his house, two boys were running on the front lawn. They both stopped seeing the car pull into the driveway. One of them ran to the door, pulled it open and called for his dad to come. Matt appeared and came outside.

"Are you Matthew Brandon?"

"I am. What is this about?"

"Your daught..."

A woman came out of the house. She was just as tall as Matt. She put her hand in his. "What is going on?"

"Sir. Ma'am, we are here to talk to you about Maxine..."

"No!" Matt said. "She made her choice as did her brother when they were younger."

The woman lowered her head and then looked away. "Matt, she came here. She came after you. She saw us together and she ran away."

"When? When was that?"

"Right after the divorce."

"She came here?" he questioned.

"Yes. With her bags."

"No, Des said that the children chose to stay with her."

"Sir, Max lived on the streets since she was twelve. You didn't want her and your ex wouldn't let her come home after she went after you. When was the last time you saw your daughter?" Joanna asked.

"The day of the divorce," he said.

"Are you aware of the accident that she had?"

"Yes," he said.

"What accident?" his wife asked.

"Who had an accident?" one of the boys asked.

"Nobody," Matt said. "Go inside."

The boys ran in the house.

"So you are aware that your daughter is paralyzed from her belly button down," Joanna said. "That injury is between T10 and T11. That is where she suffered her injury."

"My house isn't accessible for a wheelchair or her needs," Matt said.

"No. We can see that," Daniel said. "We won't take up anymore of your time. Thank you, sir. Ma'am."

"Is she ok?" the woman asked.

"It doesn't matter," Matt said. "She's not coming here."

"Did you ever see her dance?"

"I saw enough of that shit that she did when she was a kid. Jumping around the stage. Running like a lunatic and I was paying for that shit," he said. "For her to act like a wild child with no direction. She would yell and scream and throw her body about. I couldn't take it anymore. The last time I saw her dance she was eleven. Maybe twelve."

"Well, thank you, Mr. Brandon. We don't want to take up much more of your time. Here is my card though if you would like to either see or speak to your daughter."

"Can she move at all?" his wife asked.

"Yes. She is paralyzed from the waist down," Daniel said.

"Is she in a manual chair or a power chair?"

"Manual," Joanna answered.

"Does she drive?"

"No. My husband is going to see about teaching her how to do that."

"Thank you for coming here and telling us about her," his wife said.

CHAPTER SIX

Matt Brandon's wife's name is Gwen. She is an attorney. She took Joanna's card when Matt flicked it out his fingers on the ground when Joanna and Daniel had left.

"Did you know about her accident?" Gwen asked.

"Desiree called me. Told me all the details."

"What are the details?"

"How Max is a dancer. The trouble she was into."

"What kind of trouble?"

"You know."

"No. I don't know. I've never personally met the girl."

"Max is thief and a druggy," Matt said. "I don't want her here. I don't want her around our boys. It wouldn't be fair to them. She would scare them."

"Have you seen her over the years?"

"No."

"Does she know that you have other children?"

"I don't know and I don't care. She made her choice."

"You are going to continuously punish and prosecute her for a decision that she made when she was twelve years old?"

"Gwen, this conversation and the topic of Max Brandon is shut."

Gwen nodded. "As you like," she said to him.

The next day, Gwen called Joanna to arrange a meeting between her and Max.

"Will it just be you?"

"At this time. Yes," Gwen said.

"Where do you want to do this?"

"Well, she is still technically on house arrest is that correct?"

"Yes."

"Has she violated her terms of house arrest?"

"Her mother did that for her."

"So she is in violation?"

"Yes."

"Then I'd like you to bring her into the station and I would like to meet her there."

"I'll call you back when it has been arranged."

"Thank you," Gwen said.

"When do you want to do this?"

"As soon as you can pull it together. Make it real, Sergeant."

"I will."

Joanna arranged it and called Gwen back with the details. Joanna would bring Max with her to work in the morning and then have someone come in and place Max under arrest. She would be led back into a room, where the meeting would take place.

"Max, you are going to go to work with me tomorrow," Joanna announced at dinner. Max didn't answer either way. She ate her dinner. She was quieter than she had been in the past few days. "Is everything ok? How did you spend your day today?"

"I had to leave her here by herself today," Grant said. "One of the boys got himself in a knot, so I had to go see what happened."

"So Max, what did you do today?"

"Made the bed. Went around the track for a few laps. I read through the driver's manual too. Oh, yeah and I prepared and cooked this dinner for us tonight."

"Well, thank you. It is very good. You made this?" Max smiled brightly.

"Did you hear from your mother or your siblings?" Grant questions.

"No. I'm currently not allowed to speak to them."

In the morning, Max was ready to go with Joanna. She hugged Grant goodbye. "Thank you for this breakfast. Can I hug you again? Just in case I don't see you again."

"You will see him tonight for dinner."

Grant hugged Max just the same anyway.

They went to the station. Joanna set Max up in the room again. Max was in the room for over an hour when an officer came in. "Are you Maxine Brandon?"

"Yes."

"You are under arrest for breaking your terms of house arrest."

"NO!" Max yelled. "I didn't do that."

"Come with me."

"No."

"Sergeant Norris sent me in here to bring you back."

"No!" Max said.

Joanna and the others weren't intending on Max resisting. Max pushed back from the table. The officer thought that she was giving in and that she was going to go with her, but instead Max put her hands on her wheels and started pushing herself as fast as she could. The officer reached for her but missed her.

"Stop her!" the officer yelled.

"NO!" Max yelled. Max went flying to the front doors of the station. She made it outside. Officers came running after her. Max made it four blocks away before she was caught. Gwen had watched. The initial officer who had told her that she was under arrest placed Max in handcuffs. Max's hands now sat folded in her lap as she was pushed back to the station. Her head hung down. "I hate my life," she said over and over again. Max hadn't seen Gwen when she was brought back into the station.

"Bring her in room three," Joanna said with annoyance in her voice. Joanna followed them into the room. "Where were you planning on going?"

Max didn't say anything.

"You know you can be locked up for that stunt you just pulled."

Max sat quiet. Until she couldn't hold the sob in any longer. Joanna heard it quake out of her. She watched Max shake as she sobbed. Her head came up. Her eyes were closed. She leaned her head back as she said, "I hate my life!" And then she cried and cried.

"If I uncuff you, will you stay in here?"

"I don't have anywhere else to go," Max said still crying and then lowered her head again.

Joanna released her. Max didn't move. Joanna left the room. Gwen had watched and heard everything. She now came into the room. "Hello," she said. "Are you Max Brandon?"

Max nodded her head.

"Can I sit with you?" Max shrugged. "Were you always in the wheelchair?" Max shook her head. "Can you talk to me? Oh, wait. Am I on your deaf side?"

"No," Max said. "You are my right side. I was answering you. If you'd been on my left side, I wouldn't have heard anything you said to me. This is my hell," Max said.

"What is?"

"This!" she said looking up. "Who are you?"

"My name is Gwen Quimby."

"Is that supposed to mean something to me?"

"No. So how did your accident happen?"

"Look. If you are here to know where the fucking drugs are or where the merchandise is, I still have no fucking clue. I never stole anything a day in my life. And God knows there were times when I could have and I needed to when I was younger, but I never took anything from anyone."

"Tell me about your life."

"My life sucks," Max said.

"Did it always?"

"No. I was a dancer. I started dancing when I was like five."

"Did your parents approve and encourage you along the way?"

"At first, but then Desiree got too busy to take me and Matt would make it miserable when he had to take me, but I didn't give up. I would go and dance. When I was dancing, nothing else in the world mattered to me. Not the fact that my father was having an illusive affair as was my mother.

"My parents divorce happened when I was twelve. It was finalized on the day of my last show of the season. Matt. That's my dad; he wasn't happy with the dance that I was doing in the performance. He came to the show and stayed in the back.

"He had told my brother and I to choose who we wanted to live with. I'm the oldest, so I let Logan say first. He chose mom, but I chose him. I had packed all of my stuff. After the recital, Matt grabbed me by the wrist. My arm was dangling in the air above my head. He told me that I couldn't live with him. He told me…" Max let out a sob. "He told me that he didn't want me. He couldn't have a kid flailing and jumping around like that in his new house.

"Because I chose him, Desiree wouldn't let me come back. I was twelve."

"Where did you go?"

"Alley ways. Coffee shops until they closed. I went to school like nothing happened. I still danced. I never told anyone that I was homeless. I hadn't lived or seen my mother since that day. Then we were dancing the final show and this happened."

"Did your dad ever come see you dance?"

"No. He has his gorgeous, handpicked trophy wife and he has their children. Desiree moved on too after Matt and her reminder of him had moved on. She too had other children. And then the accident happened, and I went to a rehab center. Neither of them came. No one in the family came and saw me. My team didn't come to see me. I was in rehab for six or eight months. Time ran together. They told me that my ride was coming and that I could wait outside. Only Desiree didn't come. In her place were the police. I was arrested and taken to jail."

"On what charges?"

"Theft, but I swear I never took anything. If things were taken that night from the show, there is no way I could have fucking done it. I went in dancing and I came out strapped down on a backboard."

"How did you lose your hearing?"

"I was kicked in the head by someone on my team as they all went running to get away from the danger on stage. I couldn't get away. I was pinned under it.

"I was supposed to meet her that night."

"Meet who?"

"My father's wife and their kids. I had set tickets aside when he called me out of the blue and said that they were going to come. I was so excited. I left tickets for them. They were at will call, yet they were never picked up. The unclaimed tickets were burned five minutes before show time. I had hoped that they would come, but in my heart and in my head, I knew they wouldn't. I hadn't met her or seen him in fourteen years."

"How did you wind up on house arrest?"

"I'm deaf in my left ear. My jaw was still wired shut since the accident. I couldn't hear what was being asked. I couldn't make it out. I was guilty of not admitting guilt and I was sentenced for seven or eight years on house arrest. I had to go stay at Desiree's. I called Matt to ask him if I could please come stay there. He didn't recognize the number calling him, so he hung up when I said "Dad". He called me back a few seconds later and told me to never call him again. He said that he had moved on and had forgotten all about me. He told me that he didn't want his wife or children upset and that I would upset them."

"Do you know his wife's name?"

"No."

"Did you ever see her?"

"I think so. Once. I went to their house when I was twelve. She was wrapped around him. He told her that she was the only thing now in his life and that his past life meant nothing to him."

"If given the chance would you want to meet her?"

"Yes."

"If given the chance would you want to see your father?"

"He couldn't accept me as a dancer, so he most likely can't or won't accept me like this. I can't change this. Though I wish I could."

The door opened. A young male officer came into the room. "Max, Grant is here to come take you home."

"I don't have a home. They took my apartment away from me…"

"Who took your apartment?"

"Lucy, Elliot, Dean, and Scott." Max started to just speak about them. "Elliot and I met when I was six. He came into the dance studio with tears sitting on his cheeks. He didn't want to be there. He was a shy kid. Skinny as ever. He told his mom that no one was going to like him. My dad after yelling at me that dance was shit, but it was the only thing that kept me from fighting with my brother 24/7, had just dropped me off. I found myself walking over to Elliot. He was looking up at his mom begging her to take him home. I took his hand. He stopped everything that he was doing and looked down at his hand. I asked him if he could maybe help me with a dance move. He said he didn't know how. I told him I would show him. I led him on to the dance floor. I never let go of his hand and we did a wave together. When it was over, the instructor came over and hugged me. Elliot ran back over to his mom and asked if he could stay but just for this class.

"We grew up together. We were there for each other and then this fucking thing happened and poof…They were all gone. I was the one who got injured and no one came."

Gwen nor Max had noticed that Joanna had come into the room. Joanna stood against the wall just listening.

"When I was twelve and homeless, Elliot's mom let me stay with them for a little while. I remember thinking how nice it was not getting yelled at every day. But in the end, Matt's words were right. I would go nowhere with dance. Dance would end my life, he told me that when I was I twelve. Dance would keep us apart. Those were his last words to me. He yelled it at me. "MAX, YOUR DANCING WILL DRIVE US APART. DANCE WILL KEEP US APART." Yeah, I guess he was right."

"Are you ready to go?" Joanna asked.

"Go where. I don't have a home. I'm as homeless now as I was when I was twelve. At least back then I had the team. Now I only have you and Grant until I fuck that up too."

"I want to thank you for talking with me."

"Yeah, I bet my stories blew your mind."

"Can I meet with you again?"

Max looked up at her. "I don't know why you would want to, but yeah. I guess so."

"Next time, you meet, you can see Max at my house," Joanna said.

"It was nice meeting you today," Gwen said. "Can I give you a hug?"

Max looked up at her again. "Yea…s. Yes."

Max moved herself for the first time since she was brought into the room. Gwen who had been standing now sat in the chair. She reached for Max's hand. Taking hold of it, she held it for a few seconds and then gently pulled her closer to her. She hugged Max. Max hugged her back. Max put her head on Gwen shoulder and cried softly now. "I wish my dad would have taken me in. I wish I would get to meet his wife and children one day. I wish that everyone didn't close and lock doors on me. I was twelve. I chose my dad. He told us to choose. I did. I chose him, yet he chose to throw me away. He's sees Logan. I don't know what I could have done that was so wrong. When I went back to the house, mom yelled at me that I no longer lived there. I chose him she kept yelling. You chose him over me, so you go fucking live with him. By then, there was no one. She smacked me across the face. Said I was ungrateful and then she slammed and locked the door in my face. I was only twelve."

Gwen tightened the hug. She rubbed Max's back. She held her in her arms. Max pulled away. "I'm sorry. You don't know me. I don't know you. I shouldn't have…"

"You are fine, Max." Gwen turned to Joanna. "When can I see her again?"

"Whenever you'd like."

"Yeah like never," Max said under her breath.

"No. I will come back and see you. I want to hear more about you."

"Why? Are you a reporter?"

"God no," Gwen said.

"Are you from the insurance company?"

"No, but since you brought that up, do you have medical bills?"

"I don't know. Desiree would know. Being on house arrest, she wouldn't let me see my mail if I ever got any. Going outside in the backyard from six to seven thirty in the evenings was my only freedom for the day. My only time to get real fresh air. All I wanted to do was see if the fire pit that Matt and I had put together and constructed when I was ten worked. I was just sitting enjoying watching the dance."

"What dance?" Gwen and Joanna asked together.

"Oh, the fire. It dances and it leaps. It falls and rises. It sways back and forth. It's always intense, but then it softens before it blows up bigger than life before taking it's final bow. It's how I used to be. Before this. Before I became stuck. Grounded for life. Well, here it is. I'm grounded for life. My flicker. My fire. My spark. They are gone. We told them that the rail was going to fall. We told them that they had to tie the ropes extra tight. We told them that someone was going to get hurt. We told them…"

Max put her arms on the table. She folded her arms and put her head face down on her arms. She was exhausted. She closed her eyes, and everything turned off. She slept. Joanna and Gwen left the room. Joanna closed the door. "I bet that's not what you wanted to hear."

"No. I'm glad she spoke to me."

"She really has no clue who you are?"

"No. No, she doesn't. I've never met her, and she has never met me. When can I see her again?"

"Whenever you'd like."

"Are her so called teammates and friends being investigated?"

"Yes."

"Has anything been found out?"

"My team is following up on leads."

"What about her siblings? I know that there are other children. Does she see any of them?"

"From what I gather, she hasn't seen any of them."

Joanna got one of the guys to go get Max. "Please be careful with her. She is sleeping." The guy that came in the room was tall and muscular. He went over to Max and hoisted her in his arms. Someone else came in for her wheelchair. Hank carried Max out of the station and to his own car. Gwen came outside. She watched Hank very gently and cautiously slide her into the front seat. He tipped the seat back and buckled her in. Hank straightened up. The other guy came out with her wheelchair. He gave it to Hank.

"Do you need me to come with you to help you get her out?" The other officer asked.

"No. I've got her."

"Where are you taking her?" Gwen asked.

"Back to Sergeant Norris's house. She is staying there."

"Would it be ok if I followed you to the house?"

"If the Sergeant oks it."

"Will you wait?"

"Yes."

Joanna came out of the station. "Hank, you got her?"

"Yes, Sergeant."

"Can I follow him?" Gwen asked.

"Yes. That will be fine."

"Will Grant be there?"

"No. My daughter Ashley will be there. She knows that you are coming. Please drive safe."

"Yes, Sergeant," Hank said.

"Hank, remember if she wakes up in the car, she cannot hear you. She is permanently deaf in her left ear."

"Yes, I know. I've got this."

He drove Max back to the house. Max didn't wake up. When he got there, he parked so gentle that it didn't seem like the car was driven. Then he went around and first took the wheelchair from the car. He brought it up on the porch and knocked on the door. Ashley opened the door.

"Is she ok?"

"She's sleeping."

"But is she ok?"

"I don't know her well enough to say yes or no, Ashley."

"Who is the woman?"

"She was in talking to Max. I don't know who she is."

"Excuse me," Ashely said stepping out on the porch. "Who are you? Why are you here? Does my mother know that you are here? Listen. I'm not particularly fond of Max, but if you are here to hurt her or cause her pain in any way, I will have you locked up. So come on and tell me who you are?"

Gwen stepped up on the porch. "My name is Gwen Quimby. I am a lawyer and after speaking with Max today, when I speak with her again, I am going to tell her that I would like to take on her case."

Gwen and Ashley both watched Hank ever so gently lift Max from the car. He carried her up on the porch and then followed Ashley to the room where Max stayed. When Hank put her down on the bed, it was the first time that Max moved. She whimpered.

"Are you hurting?" Hank asked. His hand was on her abdomen. He sat on the bed with her.

"Dean! Ell! Please stay! Please! I'm stuck! I can't move. Oh god, I can't move. My legs! My legs! They won't move. Please. Luc! Jack! Jack, please! Scott! I can't move my legs. I can't move my body. Why can't I move?" The scream that came rushing out of Max had both Gwen and Ashley running full speed into the room. Hank had her in his arms. He had tears in his eyes. He rocked Max.

"She dreams about it," Hank said. "I was at that final show. I saw her pinned down under the railing. I watched as the others ran as fast as they could to get away from the area. I had gone on stage to try to free her of that."

"Did you see which one of them kicked her in the head?"

"An Asian girl. She had lined up like she was going to kick a field goal. It was such a powerful kick that it was the first time Max cried out in pain."

Grant came home. Seeing the cars, he came running into the house. "JO! MAX!"

"Hi, dad."

"Where is your mother?"

"She is still at work."

"Where is Max?"

"She's sleeping."

Gwen's phone rang. It was Matt. "Are you getting the kids from school?"

"Can you get them today?"

"Yes. Will you be home for dinner?"

"Yes."

"Where are you?"

"Meeting with a new or potential client."

"Oh. Oh good. See you soon."

"Yes," she said and hung up the phone.

"You don't want your attitude to change towards your husband because of who were you meeting and spending some of the day with today," Joanna said to Gwen as she came in.

"I want her to wake up. I want to know that she is ok."

"We will let you," Ashley said. "We will call you and fill you in with the details."

"What time can I come tomorrow?"

"Whatever time you'd like," Grant and Joanna said together.

Gwen left. Hank stayed. Ashley stayed close so that she could watch Hank.

When Max woke up, she woke up with an attitude. She didn't know where she was. She woke mad and full of rage. She got into her wheelchair and went into the bathroom and then went outside and started to go around the track.

"Is she ok?" Ashley asked Joanna.

"I don't know. Anger is a good sign. Rage is another altogether."

As Max moved around the track, she threw her arms up in the air. She made them flutter like butterfly wings. She brought her chest down towards her thighs and pushed from that position. One push. Two push. And then she rose up with her body. She let her wheelchair carry her as she held her head back and her arms spread high and wide. And then she straightened and now she grabbed hold of the left wheel and the chair spun, once; twice, three times; and she broke out of the spin. She now pushed herself around the track. She finished another lap and then she started to move her body to make it flow. She looked like a waving flag hanging in the wind.

Grant, Joanna, Hank, and Ashley watched from inside. Ashley had grabbed her phone and recorded the dance. Max once again had her chest on her thighs and now she let her arms flutter again, but this time it was more like that of a bird's wings. And then she seemed to bow to an audience that wasn't there. She finished her laps around the track before coming into the house.

While she was out there, Ashley suggested to her father that they build Max a dance floor. Grant loved the idea. He could do it in the garage.

Their daughter Rebecca came over. "Hi," she said coming in. "Mario made pizzas, so I brought them here."

"Do you know what kind of floor a dance studio has?" Grant asked her.

"There is a snap and lock floor that seems to be really good. Why?"

"Dad is going to turn the garage into a dance studio for Max."

"Where is she?"

Max came in the house. "Can I listen to music? I miss music." Then she saw that there were others there. "Oh, I'm sorry."

"You are fine," Grant said. "Did you have a nice day?"

"Yes, it was ok. I was arrested for breaking my house arrest." That is when Max noticed Hank. "Are you here…" she swallowed hard. "Are you here to take me away?"

"No, angel," he said. "I'm here to make sure that you are ok."

"I…I remember you. You were there when the accident happened. You came on the stage. You tried to lift the rail off me. Then you sat with me. You held my hand. I don't think I cried. Did I cry?"

"No, angel, you didn't cry."

"Did you see who kicked me in the head. I know it was one of my team members, but I don't know who. I mean I think I know who it was."

"Who do you think it was?"

"Lucy," Max said.

"Why would Lucy kick you?" Ashley asked.

"Because she wanted to be the one that Elliot lifted up. She had been arguing with me for days. But Elliot and I rehearsed it so often that it was natural. The way he lifted me. It wasn't forced movement. It wasn't a lift. A pause. A hold. A pause. A move. A pause. And then down. With Elliot and I, it was just I was on my feet in one second and air bound the next and then back on my feet. We were smooth together."

"Yes, you were," Hank said.

"Do you know if my dad came that night? Did my mom come that night?"

"No, angel. After the audience cleared, it was only the fire fighters and the paramedics that were there."

"Did I black out?"

"No, angel, you didn't."

"You stayed with me when I went to the hospital. They gave me something. I remember I cried then. Things got fuzzy. I couldn't hear out of my left ear. People were rushing around. You held my hand. What is your name?"

"I am Hank Knowles."

"You saw me when I was pretty. When everything worked the way that it should," Max said.

"You are still beautiful."

"I'm not. When people see me out, they jump out of the way."

"Then they are assholes," Ashley said. "Do you like pizza?"

"Yes."

"What kind of dancer were you?" Rebecca asked.

"I learned all kinds. Ballroom, jazz, contemporary, tap, clog, hip hop and ballet."

"What was your favorite?"

"Hip hop I think." Max looked at Joanna. "Who was that lady today?"

"She's a lawyer. She's going to come here tomorrow to talk to you a bit more. There is a chance that she will take your case to try to get you off house arrest and to get the charges dropped permanently."

They had dinner together. After dinner, Max took a shower. She wanted to hear music. It was Ashley that went into Max's room, where she had just dressed in a pair of shorts and a t-shirt. Ashley touched Max's arm. Max turned to face her. "Here. I'm leaving this with you. Take good care of it ok."

"Are you sure?"

"Yes. It won't work as a phone, but it works pretty well as a radio and a camera."

"You should ask your mom first."

"I did. They both said that it was ok for you to have it. And here is an old pair of headphones. Only the right side works, so I thought that would be good for you."

"Thank you, Ashley."

"Are you ever in pain?"

"My ear," Max said. "But like deep inside my head. It hurts. Not always but sometimes."

"How hard did you get kicked?"

"Hard enough that I thought whoever kicked me detached my head from my body. But afterwards I felt pain. Like a driving sharp pain and then there was nothing. No sound. My left side was facing where the audience was. I could image that they were screaming, but I couldn't hear it and it was muffled on my right side because I had an earpiece in my ear to hear the music.

"Do you know what's going to happen?"

"What do you mean?"

"Like I'm homeless. My mom won't take me back. It's like being twelve years old all over again. My dad doesn't want anything to do with me and my mom won't let me come home, and my so-called friends stole my apartment right out from under me. Yet it's my name on the papers."

"I think everything will work itself out."

"I'll never dance again," Max said. She looked at Ashley. "Thank you for this."

Gwen came back the next day. She brought a notepad and pens. "I want you to write it all down. Write down the names of your team members, the coach. If you knew the name of the stagehands. Write down everyone who was involved in that final show."

People Involved In The Show

Name	Position	Present	Not Present
Scott	Dancer	Present	
Elliot	Dancer/Lead	Present	
Lucy	Dancer/Drama Queen	Present	
Dean	Dancer	Present	
Mike	Dancer	Present	
Genevieve	Dancer/Moron	Present	
Jack	Dancer/music man	Present	
Shawn	Dancer/controller	Present	
Brian	Dancer	Present	
Hannah Grace	Coach		Not Present
Paul	Stagehand		Not present
Cal	Stagehand		Not present
Mark	Stagehand		Not present
David	Stagehand		Not present
Troy	Stagehand		Not present
Dipshit # 1	Lucy knows him	Present	
Dipshit # 2	Lucy knows him	Present	
Dipshit # 3	Lucy knows him	Present	

		Present	Not Present
Dipshit # 4	Lucy knows him	Present	
Dipshit # 5	Lucy knows him	Present	
Dipshit # 6	Lucy knows him	Present	
John	Maintenance		Not Present
JP or PJ	Cleaning Crew		Not Present
Mr. McCoy	Stage Manager		Not Present
Lance Becks	Sound Director	Present	
Smith Connors	Set Crew		Not Present
Edward Drawl	Set Crew		Not Present

"I think that's everyone," Max said.

Gwen took the paper. "Why weren't the regulars there that night?"

"Lucy said that she wanted to try out a new crew to work with. Lucy swore that they were good, and they knew what the fuck they were doing, but they didn't. They kept going over to the rigging. That's what controls the rails where the stage lights are hung from. They brought rail after rail down. We kept telling them to stop. Then they would bring them back up, but you have to really secure the ropes or lines that they are on, but they kept leaving them with slack. Before we went for dinner, Elliot, Dean, Scott, and I made sure that all of the lines were tight. Then we went for dinner. When we came back my stuff was moved. I wanted to change, but Lucy said that there wasn't time for that, so I joined everyone on stage.

"We had started. We had a full house in the audience. A sold-out show. Well, minus four seats. My dad, stepmom, and I guess they are my brothers; anyway whatever, they didn't show up. We were flawless. We were having the best dance of our lives that night. And then we heard the boom and the pop, and the lights were getting brighter and brighter. I was high in the air above Elliot's head when the rail with the lights came crashing down hard and fast. It hit me in the back and then it knocked me out of Elliot's arms. They were all running to get away. I was trapped. Pinned tight under a light. It was in my back. I couldn't move my legs. I couldn't move at all and then someone went running by and kicked me hard in the head. The pain was excruciating and then there was blood. It was pouring out of my left ear and everything went muffled and then out. There was no sound and in my right ear, I had an earpiece to hear the music. It blocks out outside noise, so I couldn't hear anything. Then the house lights came on and people were running, and the fire department was there. Someone tried to pull the rail off my back. Then he sat with me. He held my hand.

"I wanted my dad. I wanted someone from my family to be there. I lay there abandoned by my family years before and now abandoned by my teammates. Even though dad yelled at me like all the time when he had to take me to dance, I wanted him there. He couldn't have done anything, but he would have been there. He would have seen me dance one more time, so his last impression of me dancing wouldn't have been from when I was twelve. But no one was there. I was surrounded by strangers.

"A neck brace was put on me. The rail was finally lifted off me. Then a backboard was literally put down on my back. My legs were straightened. Hands and straps were on me and then I was flipped so I was facing up. Someone pulled the earpiece out of my ear. They told me not to speak. They said that my jaw was broken. They said that I had extreme injuries. My head hurt. My ear hurt, but my back didn't hurt.

"I was taken to the hospital and the doctors were rushing around and then someone gave me something and it was lights out for a month. Maybe more. When I woke up, I was in traction. My legs wouldn't move. I went into a rehab center for like eight months, I think. The day I got out; I was arrested. My jaw was still wired shut. I think they said that I lost forty pounds. They took pictures of me. I was fingerprinted and then I was put into a cell. That happened on a Friday, so I was in jail through the weekend and it was a holiday weekend, so nothing was going to happen till Tuesday or Wednesday."

"Did your mom come see you?"

"When?"

"When you were in the rehab center?"

"No. Dad neither. The one day that I had to go for scans and x-rays, they told me that I had had a visitor, but I don't know who it was."

"Have you spoken to your father at all?"

"No. He won't take my calls. I haven't seen or spoken to him since I was twelve."

"What about Desiree?"

"Oh, she won't let me come back. Because I was on house arrest, she said that she was punished as well, and she had to send the others away to their fathers."

"Did you ever see them?"

"Only Logan. He would come over a few times. He'd bring pizza and beer. He would buy groceries, but he never came in the house. Mom would never let him in the house. She would let me go out in the backyard for like an hour or an hour and a half. She mostly kept me locked away. She did that for a long time. It was hell being in her house."

"Where is your ankle monitor?"

"Grant has it. He said that I don't have to wear it here. Why are you doing this?"

"Max, because I've seen all of the reports now as have the police. Your fingerprints don't line up on the things that were stolen. Though they were found in your bag and among your belongings, you are a very smart girl. See all of your things were nicely placed in Zip-loc bags. So the money, the jewels and the drugs don't have your DNA on them at all.

"As we speak right now, the true person of the crime is being arrested."

"Is it Lucy?"

"No."

"Was it any of the dancers?"

"No."

"Do I get to go back to my apartment?"

"Max, your apartment burned down," Joanna said. "Lucy, Scott and Elliot were lucky to make it out alive. More stolen items were found in your apartment."

"But I never stole anything in my life. I could have. Lord knows that there were opportunities, but the best thing that my parents did was put money in a trust fund for me. So when I was twenty-two I took out some of the money and I bought that apartment. But now without it, I'm just back where I was before then. I have nothing."

"Well, that's not true."

"I don't understand."

"Well, you are an extremely smart person as I said before. You paid for homeowners' insurance, you paid for fire insurance, and you covered your assets for that just in case moment." Max lowered her head. "Are you ok?"

"I...my brain doesn't process. I don't understand. It's like when I was in the courthouse. Everything ran together. Words go dancing across my mind. Excuse me please."

Max left the room. She went outside and went out on the track. She pushed herself to far side of it and started to yell at the top of her lungs. Max just screamed and yelled.

Gwen went running outside. She ran to Max. She took Max in her arms. Max tried to push her away, but Gwen wouldn't allow that.

"Since going deaf, my brain stops. I can't hear things right. That lawyer. He said things that I did, but I never did them and then he went on my left side and I couldn't hear anything. And then the pain comes back."

"What pain? Pain in your back?"

"No. In my head. Deep in my ear. It hurts so bad. Like on that day."

"Did you have pain when the rail hit you?"

"Yes, it broke my spine. I know that I screamed out, but then I was being driven hard to the floor and seconds later I was pinned down tight on the floor. There was pain. So much pain in my back and then there wasn't.

"Are you my father's wife?"

"What if I were?"

"Does he know that you are seeing me?"

"No."

"So what's your plan? To get to know me so that you can go back and report to him about how pathetic my life is?"

"Maxine, your life isn't pathetic."

"I was a free flying bird and now I got imprisoned twice. Did…did you and…and my dad know about the accident?"

"No. I didn't know anything about it until just a few days ago."

"How did you find out about that?"

"This wonderful woman came to our house and told your father and I?"

"Really? I just thought that he didn't care."

Matt had found Joanna's business card in the house. He saw the address printed on the back of the card. He called a sitter for the boys and then he came to the house. He didn't know what to expect. He walked up to the front door and knocked. Grant opened the door. "Hello. Can I help you?"

"I believe that my wife is here. Gwen Quimby Brandon."

"Please come in. I am Grant Norris. Welcome to my home."

"Where is my wife?"

"She is outside in the backyard with your daughter."

"Can I go out there?"

"Yes."

"The last time I saw her, she was a scrawny gawky awkward child. I punished her for wanting to stay with her mother."

"But she didn't," Joanna said.

"What?" Matt asked.

"She chose you. She wanted to live with you. She had packed her things to go live with you. You wouldn't take her, and your ex-wife wouldn't let her back in the house."

"No. I would call to speak to the Max and Logan."

"And which child never came to the phone?"

"Des told me it was because Max was upset about the divorce. Des would tell me that Max picked up another dancing class or that Max was out with her friends.

"When Logan would come for overnights, he would tell me that Max was grounded for telling off her mother or that she was busy studying."

"Your daughter was a street kid until she was twenty-two years old and she bought that apartment that someone torched while she was on house arrest for crimes that she didn't know anything about and had absolutely no involvement with," Joanna said.

Max and Gwen came back in the house. "What are you doing here?" Gwen asked.

"I could ask you the same question."

"Did you come here to get your wife, or did you come here to see me?" Max asked. "Make your choice. It could be your last." Max's upper body dropped to her thighs and she cried. "I was a child. I was just a fucking child. And I chose to live with you, but you had heard Logan say that he wanted to live with mom. Fuck. At twelve, I already knew that I was a disappointment. You told me that every time you drove me to my dance classes. But still I chose to live with you. I came to your house. I saw you two together. I was twelve, but not blind. I may not have ever met your beautiful wife, but at least I knew about her.

"Tell me, Gwen, did you think Max was his son? Maybe a beloved pet that he left behind with the bitch, who fathered him two children."

"Don't talk to my wife like that," Matt said.

"You lost your rights to tell me what to do. Did you ever come looking for me? I know that since the last time you saw me dance when I was twelve that that was the last time you saw me dance.

"Did you know that I had this incredible accident? Did Des ever call you and tell you?"

"Yes," Matt said. "She told me that you were thief and that you did drugs. She told me that there was an accident and that you were somehow injured in it. That was all I knew."

"When did your mother find out?" Gwen asked.

"When I had to go live with her while I'm on fucking house arrest I guess. I really don't know when the bitch found out."

"Did you take…"

"I've never stolen a day in my life. Not even when I was freezing cold and starving, I never took anything that didn't belong to me."

Matt moved so now he was on Max's left side. "You can't stay over there," Max said. "If you stay there, I won't be able to hear or distinguish what you are saying."

Matt looked at the others who were nodding.

"She is stone cold deaf in her left ear," Grant said. "I administered a hearing test to her to see if she would be able to hear frequencies and she doesn't hear anything."

Matt moved again. He sat on the couch.

"I…I can't be here."

"Max, you can't leave," Joanna said.

"But you know that I didn't do anything wrong."

"Well, until the judge clears your record then you are still on house arrest."

"I don't care. I can't stay here. I can't."

Max went flying to the door. She threw it open and went racing down the ramp and she took off as fast as her arms could continuously pump. Matt jumped up and ran after her.

"Max!" he called out.

"No! You turned me away. You didn't want me. You never came looking for me."

"I thought you were just being a difficult child."

Max stopped and sobbed and sobbed. "You called me and told me to reserve four tickets. You said that you were coming to see me dance. I was so excited. My dad was finally coming to see me dance and he was bringing his wife and kids with him, yet you didn't come. Why? Why didn't you come?"

"Maxine, I never called you for tickets. I don't know or even have a number for you," Matt said.

"Because you were still mad at a decision that your son made. Logan chose to live with mom. But that's not what you wanted. You didn't want me. You wanted Logan. You wanted your precious little good boy. Not your disappointment."

"Max, I'm sorry that I ever said that to you. I am sorry that I was always yelling at you. Your mother and I would fight or argue and then you would come in and say that you had dance."

"Where did you go? Where did you stay? Did your mother know?" Gwen said coming up.

"I stayed in places where I was accepted. Des didn't know. She had her life. You were gone."

"When did you leave her house?"

"My stuff was packed the day of my dance. I tried so hard to get your attention that day, yet I couldn't. I was in the room when you slammed the divorce papers on the kitchen table, and you told Des that it was finally over. You said that it was the biggest mistake you ever made."

"Max, I'm sorry."

A car pulled up. Hank got out of the car. "Where are you going?" Seeing Max crying, he went to her and took her out of the chair and into his arms, where he just held on to her and let her cry. "How about you be a nice guy and get her chair there, pal?" Hank carried Max back to the house. Matt came back in with her wheelchair. Gwen drove the car back to the house.

"Can we bring her home with us?" Matt asked.

"No," Joanna said. "There would have to be a transition period. Even though she is an adult. She is still on house arrest until the judge says otherwise."

"When will there be a hearing?"

"We are asking for a mandatory court hearing," Gwen said.

Hank now sat with Max on his lap on the couch. He held her ever so gently. Joanna saw him. "Is she sleeping?"

"Yes," he said. "I just want to hold her, Serge."

"I know."

"I couldn't that night." Matt and Gwen listened. "One minute she is sailing and making the pretties moves with her body that I have ever seen and then one of the guys had her. She was literally tossed from one guy to the other and then the leading man had her. He lifted her high into the air. Then there was a boom. Just like Max says," Hank took a breath and looked down at her in his arms. "She was hit and yet everyone thought that it was supposed to be part of the show. The force from the speed that the light and the rail hit her, she was driven hard into the floor. When I got to her on stage, I thought that she was going to be dead, yet she wasn't. I sat with her and held her hand. I went with her to the hospital. The first time she cried was when they gave her something to knock her out."

"Is there a video of it?" Gwen asked.

"Yes," Hank said.

"From that night's performance?"

"Yes," he said again.

"I'd like to see it. Matt, wouldn't you like to see it?"

He had moved when Hank was talking and now, he couldn't take his eyes off of Max. "Matt!" He looked up. "Wouldn't you want to see that?" Gwen asked.

Matt nodded his head because the words wouldn't come. He squatted down next to her and touched her head. He put his hand against the side of her face. Max startled. She opened her eyes. She pulled herself up on Hank's lap.

"We are going to have Max checked out to see why she fatigues so quickly," Joanna said.

"Can they come back and visit me?"

"Yes."

"I will definitely come back," Gwen said.

"I have to go to the bathroom," Max said. "Please don't leave yet."

Hank put her down in her wheelchair. Max went *running* off to the bathroom. She returned moments later.

"Max, are you hungry?"

"No thank you," she said to Joanna. "Can Ashley come back over?"

"We can call her," Grant said.

"Who is Ashley?" Matt asked.

"She is Joanna and Grant's daughter. She just makes me feel a little settled when she is here, and others come."

Grant called her and Ashley came. "She said what?" Ashley asked on the way over to the house. "Wait. Tell me again. I make her feel settled? Me? Dad, are you sure? Yes, I am listening to you. Yes. I hear you, but me? Really? Me? I'm pulling in now. Ok. Thanks."

Ashley came in the house. She automatically went into defense mode grilling Matt. "So what brought you here now?"

"I found your mother's business card."

"There is this wonderful invention. Maybe you have heard of it. It has been around for an exceptionally long time now. Are you thinking what it could possibly be? Oh, no throws out to what it might be. They are even small enough now to travel with us everywhere we go. Max? Max, can you help me out with this one? What would it be?"

"A telephone."

"See. Even the person, who can't have one and can't use one at this time knows what it is. You could have just called, sir. So why did come here?"

"I came here to see what brought my wife here?"

"Did you know that your beautiful daughter was here?"

"No," Matt said.

"Gwen, did you tell Matt here that your daughter was here?"

"No," she said.

Hank had found the recording of Max dancing. He and Grant together got it plugged in so it would show on their TV.

"You start like this," Max from the video said. "No. Like this. Smooth. Long strokes." She laughed. "Here. Let me demonstrate." Max stood in the middle of the stage. She then sat on the floor Indian style. She made herself appear like a ball on the stage. The music started and she moved with grace as she first unfolded her legs and then bent her knees bringing her feet to the stage floor. Then she arched her back and moved her arms gracefully. And then in a flash, she was on her feet spinning across the stage. She went from spinning to leaping in midair and then coming down on the stage in a front somersault. She twirled her body until she was in a standing position and then she stopped. "See. Just like that," she said with a smile that filled the camera.

It was an interview. "How long have you been dancing?"

"I started to dance as a toddler, but my parents signed me up for this academy when I was five."

"They must be so proud of you."

"I don't know. We are estranged."

"Oh, how awful. Do they know that you were in the service? And that you served this country for eight years?"

"No. They don't. They wouldn't."

"So who raised you to be this person that you are today?"

"Dance did."

"So your dance instructor?"

"No. Just dance. Dance itself until I was eighteen and then the service till, I was twenty-four. It was six years. Not eight."

"What branch were you in?"

Max watched herself. Gwen, Joanna, Grant, Hank, and Ashley watched Max watching herself.

"Do your parents or siblings come see you dance?"

"No. They haven't in a long time."

"You didn't answer what branch you were in."

"Oh, yeah. Sorry. I was in the Air Force. I was a pilot."

"And your parents never knew?"

"No."

"Do you think that they will see this interview?"

"I honestly couldn't tell you that. I would hope maybe that they do."

"So are your parents still together?"

"No, they divorced when I was twelve."

"Is it true that it happened on your birthday?"

"That doesn't matter to me anymore, but yes. Their divorce was finalized on my twelfth birthday. At least my dad saw me dance that night."

"And what is the new things that will be added in your upcoming shows? Can you show me?"

"Yeah. Let me just pull our lead guy out here." Elliot came on stage as did the others. The guys lined the stage staggered from right to left. Max took a few swallows of water and then walked over to Shawn, who started it. Shawn lifted her and twirled her around him and then he tossed her backwards to Brian. Brian danced with her and put her through his legs and then lifted her and tossed her forward to Mike. Mike and Max danced a Cha-Cha before Mike lifted her and tossed her back to Scott. Scott and Max danced a wickedly hot and steamy Tango. Then he lifted her up and tossed her sideways to Dean. Dean tossed her back to Scott and then the three of them danced and then Elliot had her. Elliot and Max danced with her bodies pressed together. They moved as one solid unit. And then he lifted her high into the air. Max stayed air bound for at least two minutes, before she ducked her head whispering to Elliot. Elliot then tossed her away, but no one was there to catch her, but the unseen trampoline was there. Max landed on her feet and then sprang into the air. She did flip after flip and flip before coming down again and then sprang up in the air for the second time. When she came down the third time, her body position changed and she now launched herself right into Elliot's arms.

The reporter dropped the microphone to clap. "When will that show start?"

"We do the final run throughs today, so it will start tomorrow. Excuse me one moment please." Max walked away. "Hey! What are you doing? Don't touch that. If you don't know how to use it then don't touch it. These lines have to be taut." Max is seen pushing one of the guys away and then grabbing the rope, putting her foot up on the rail that holds the ropes, and she pulled the line as tight as possible. "Don't touch it again."

"Max," a girl's voice calls. "Come on. It's time for dinner."

"Yeah. I'm coming." Max ran back over to the reporter. "Sorry about that. New stage crew today. I hope that we went over everything that you wanted to hear." Lucy is seen sneaking around the back of the stage in the curtain line and going over to the six guys, who are still by the side rail. She is seen paying them money and then she goes back the same way that she came. Max leaves. The camera guy with the reporter films the six guys messing around with the pulley ropes and system on stage right. They bring the rail that hits Max down and then bring it back up. They do this two or three times. They are heard laughing before they slap each other five and then take off to the other side of the stage.

Max had lowered her head. Another video comes on. Her final dance. With the lights flashing and the music blasting, the dancers moved as they had rehearsed and then Elliot had Max high in the air. And then there was clearly a BOOM followed by a POP and then a sound like the cross between a fast-moving train and a tornado. Then Max was hit with the light. Then she was thrown and knocked out of Elliot's arms. The other dancers, who were on the floor now all started to run and scramble. And there it was. Lucy coming rushing over. She stopped about a foot away from Max, brought her leg back like a kicker on a football team and then floored it right into the side of Max's head.

The scream came from behind all of them. They all stopped watching the TV and turned to see Max. She was bent in half just screaming. Hank, Matt, and Gwen rushed to her. Matt straightened her so she was upright and then he lifted her into his arms. He then sat on the couch with her and Gwen. The three of them cried together.

When Gwen and Matt left that night, Max was sure that she would probably never see them again. Matt and Gwen both copied the videos.

"Thank you, Ashley."

"You're welcome. Are you ok?"

"Yeah."

"So I make you feel settled huh?"

"Yeah. You seem to know what I want to ask, and it just comes flying out of your mouth. You make me feel safe."

"Can I hug you or will it hurt you?"

"Yes, you can hug me."

Ashley hugged Max. Max hugged her back.

Max went and spoke privately to Joanna. "Can I ask you something?"

"Sure."

"Can Hank stay tonight? Can he just hold me? Would that be ok with you?"

"Yes, Max," Joanna said.

"Do you think they will come back?"

"I don't know, but I hope they will. Would you want them to come back?"

"Yeah," Max said. "Do you mind me staying here?"

"Not a bit. It's nice having another person here. Do you mind staying here?"

"No. I like it here. I know that I'm still in trouble, but at least here I can breathe, and I'm not told every day that I am a burden."

Hank came in the kitchen. "Well, I'm going to take off for the night."

"No," Max said softly. Hank looked at her. "Will you stay tonight?"

"Serge?"

"Hank, you can stay here."

"Can I stay in your arms tonight?"

Hank looked at Joanna, who nodded before he answered. "Yes, Maxine, you can stay in my arms tonight."

That night when they all went to bed, Hank went in the room with Max. He pulled the bedding down and then he undressed to his boxers and a t-shirt that he wore under his clothes. Then he lifted Max and brought her down on the bed. He let her get herself comfortable and then he took her in his arms. He kissed her on the check. She turned her face to face him and he kissed her on the lips. She in turn kissed him back. They kissed for about ten minutes. When Max turned away, she felt things inside her body that she had never before. Twinges of currents. Currents cruising throughout her body. Max closed her eyes. Hank looped his fingers around hers before he too closed his eyes for the night.

CHAPTER SEVEN

Matt couldn't sleep all night. He watched both videos over and over. One of his boys came into the room. "Who is that?" his ten-year-old son Gunnar asked.

"Someone that mommy and I want you and your brother to meet."

"Wow! Look at the way she moves! That's awesome. Where do you know her from?"

"I knew her a long time ago."

"Is that from a long time ago then?"

"No. Just a couple of years ago."

"What does she do now?"

"Gunnar, it's getting late. You need to go back to bed."

"Ok, daddy." But he couldn't pull his eyes away from the screen. "She's really pretty and graceful. She looks like a bird in flight. Oh, does she land safely?" Gunnar asked and took a seat on their couch to watch.

"Gunnar, after you watch this last part, then you need to go back to bed."

He listened. He hugged and kissed Matt and then ran to his room.

Matt watched it again and again. Then he put in the other video and watched it. He shuttered as he saw Max getting hit.

Meanwhile when he was watching the videos, Gwen pulled up to see if she could find Max's service records. She was an Air Force pilot. She could fly planes, but she couldn't drive a car. Gwen found a report.

> Unknown female pilot flies mission and saves 148 soldiers. Though the conditions when returning to base camp were rocky and questionable, the female pilot landed her bird safely.
>
> The unknown female pilot has been identified as Maxine "Max" Brandon. She is just twenty years old. Her flying needs to be commended. She swooped in, took care of the business at bay, and then swooped out without any causalities left her in wake. - J. Stows

Gwen saw Max's picture. She was in full uniform with her helmet on her head and a smile on her face. It didn't appear that she posed for the picture. Gwen looked for other reports.

> F-18 female pilot takes to the skies and shows off her flying skills. It almost seems that she is dancing with her plane. Human and this Hornet of an aircraft seemed to be in an elegant tango in the sky. And when the dance was done, the pilot dipped her plane as in almost a bow to the audience below before she lit it up and tore off out of sight. This pilot's call sign is Elegant Dancer. And that was shown tonight. Her talented skills in the aircraft, were delivered beautifully. Max Brandon's parents should be extremely proud of this incredible young lady. – J. Stows

That night when Gwen went to bed, she did with a heavy heart. Though her job of proving that Max was not aware of the crimes and did not commit the crimes, she thought was going to be a slam dunk, she realized what they all missed out on. Matt climbed into bed with Gwen a few hours later.

"Are you asleep?" he asked.

"No."

"Gwen, I heard Logan say that they wanted to live with their mother. Well, that he wanted to live with his mother. He was seven when Des and I divorced. Max was twelve. I didn't realize that it was over on her twelfth birthday. I was constantly yelling at her. I told her things that a child should never have to hear from their parents. I barely paid attention to her. When she danced, she would move her body in ways that weren't natural, and she would grunt and yell. She would scream. I told her that she was a disappointment. I told her that I was embarrassed to be around her.

"I didn't know how she was doing in school. I didn't know her friends. I didn't know what her favorite color was. Des and I were in a tormented state and we apparently both took it out on this child.

"I never gave it a second thought why she didn't want to come to see us, or why she never came here. I was too wrapped up in my own life and the things that we were into to even care an ounce for my daughter. How do I make up eighteen years of her lifetime?"

"I don't know. I didn't know that you had a daughter. Even four years ago when she expected us all to be there, I never knew about her. Logan has never mentioned her. The girls and Harrison have never mentioned her."

"Only Logan would know who she is. The others weren't around to know her."

"Together, we need to go speak to Desiree. You both rejected a child for what? Because she was a pre-teen, and she was annoying?"

"I honestly couldn't tell you, Gwen. We've been together for eighteen years and married for sixteen of those years, but I don't know, and I can't tell you why I was so mad at my only daughter."

Gunnar had woken up early in the morning before his parents. He went into his father's study and found the videos that Matt had been watching the night before on the TV in the family room. He brought the DVDs into the family room and put one of them in the player. Then he sat on the couch and he watched the video. It was the video of the accident. Gunnar started to yell and scream. Both Gwen and Matt were ripped out of their sleep. They went running to see what had happened to their son.

"She's dead!" he cried. "Oh, my god. She's dead."

"No, baby," Gwen said taking her son in her arms. "She isn't dead."

"But she was hit so hard. Mommy she was hit and then it drove her to the floor."

Matt called Joanna. "Can we meet you and Max for breakfast?"

"Hank can bring her," Joanna said. "Where and when?"

"There is a diner in Lees."

"Le Café Diner," she said.

"Yes."

"What time?"

"At nine thirty."

"They will be there."

"Thanks."

Joanna came in the room. Max and Hank were still sleeping. Joanna woke them up. "Your presence is acquired at Le Café Diner in Lees."

"Who is going to take me?"

"Hank will. When are you done, please come back home here. You have your written driver's test on Wednesday, so you need to know the damn book."

"What time are we due there?" Hank asked.

"Nine thirty."

"Thank you, Sergeant."

"Hank, here in my house please call me Jo or Joanna."

He nodded.

When Joanna left the room, the two of them laid in bed together for a little while longer. They kissed again. Hank eased his hand under Max's shirt cupping her breast in his hand as he continued to kiss her. Max felt something pop inside the core of her and then there was a rush of warmth throughout her whole body. Hank took her nipple in between his fingertips and squeezed gently. When he did this, Max felt little explosions in her body. Hank deepened the sensation when he gently separated her and carefully slid his finger into her. Since her accident, this was the first sexual encounter that Max was experiencing, and she enjoyed the heighten sensations and the pleasures that were being released both within and out of her body. Hank kissed her, covering her mouth with his as she cried out with sheer pleasure. And then afterwards he held her.

"Thank you," she whispered. "Can we do it again?"

"Yes, but not right now. Now we have to get ready to go meet your parents."

They got up. Hank stripped the sheets off the bed. He found clean linens in the closet. He changed the sheets and made the bed. Then he too got dressed. Max had written down what she felt and what was happening within her body when it was happening. Hank had the Hummer. He lifted her into it and got her situated. Then he stowed her wheelchair, and they were off to Lees for at least the rest of the morning.

Le Café Diner, was a nice size cute diner. When they got there, Max decided that she didn't want to do this. "No. We are here. We are doing this."

"But…"

"Max, you already met them. The worst part is over. Come on," he said lifting her and putting her into her chair.

They went into the restaurant together. Max wanted to take hold of his hand, but she ignored her impulses. When they went in, she saw Matt and Gwen and then she saw two young boys.

"I don't want to do this."

"Max, it's ok. It's going to be ok."

Matt stood up and came over to them. "So our son Gunnar saw the videos of you. We were planning on meeting with you again today without the boys, but Gunnar wanted to make sure that you were ok."

"Which one is Gunnar?"

"The one with the autumn colored hair. He is ten. The other little peanut at the table is Jackson. Jackson is six."

"Has he seen the videos too?"

"No, just Gunnar."

Max watched as the boy rose from the table. He put his napkin down on the seat and then he came quickly over to Max. He put his arms out and Max took him into her arms. He sat on her lap. "Gunnar, no."

"He's fine, Matt," Max said.

Gunnar buried his face into her right shoulder and cried. "I'm sorry this happened to you," he said. Max was completely moved. She had never heard anyone say that to her. With Gunnar on her lap, she pushed herself over to the table.

"Hi," she said to Jackson. "I'm Max. So you must be Jackson."

He turned into Gwen. "How does she know my name?"

"I know your name because your mommy and daddy talk about you."

"Well, they have never mentioned you before."

"I know. I knew your daddy a long long time ago."

"How?"

"He was friends with my mom," Max said.

"Gunnar. Jackson, that's not true," Matt said. "Max, thank you for trying to cover for me, but I want them to know who you really are. Max is my daughter."

"WE HAVE A SISTER!" both boys said together. "AWESOME!"

"Are you related to Logan?" Gunnar asked.

"Yes. He's my brother too."

"He doesn't talk about you either," Jackson said.

"Yeah, I know."

"Gunnar, do you want to finish your breakfast?" Gwen asked.

"Can I do it from here?"

"Yes," Max said.

"Why are you in a wheelchair?" Jackson asked.

"I had an accident."

"Like a car accident?"

"No. I used to be a dancer, and something fell on me and it injured me."

"Are you ok?"

"Yeah, I'm ok."

"How come you don't come see us like Logan does?"

"Because I was away for a long time."

"Like where away?" Gunnar chimed in.

"Well, I have been all around the world."

"Really?"

"Yes. I was in the Air Force and I was an aviator. Do you know what that is?"

"You flew airplanes," Gunnar said.

"Yes, I did."

"Was it fun?"

"Yes, but it was also hard work."

"How long were in the service for?" Matt asked.

"Six years."

"Where did you go?" Gunnar threw in there as he popped a cut piece of French toast in his mouth.

"I went to Japan, China, Russia, Australia, Antarctica, South America, Canada, and other places too."

"Were you scared?" Jackson asked.

"No."

"Were you lonely?" Gunnar asked.

"At times."

"Did you write letters to your mom and to daddy?"

Max looked at Matt. "Yes."

"Daddy, did you get them?"

"I don't remember," Matt said. He had gotten them, and he had sent all of them back.

"Do you have feeling?" Jackson asked.

"In some of my body. So from my waist up I do."

"So you can't walk?"

"No. Not anymore."

"Do you miss it?"

"Every day of my life," Max said.

"Of course she misses it, Jackson. Sometimes you are so stupid."

"Gunnar," Gwen says through clenched teeth. "Don't call your brother stupid."

"But mommy that was stupid. She was hit by the thing..."

"What thing? What are you talking about?" Jackson asks.

"Please stop," Max pleads with them.

This was the first time that someone was standing up and fighting for Max; it came in the form of a ten year old boy, who literally just met her not even a half hour ago. It took Max's breath away. As he argued on and for her behalf, Max felt a twinge of love for the first time ever. Matt hearing his son fight for her made him regret never stopping his ex from turning his love off for a child whose looks are so similar to his own. Their hair color is exactly the same and always has been. And her hazel grey eyes that she got from him. She had his slim line figure and height as well. Matt stood at six' two, and so would Max if she could still stand. He recognized his younger self as he now looked at Max. He now sat across the table from her and watched his beautiful daughter looking at the back of Gunnar, who sat natural there perched on her lap. For maybe the first time since she was an incredibly young child, Matt Brandon felt love for his daughter. Gwen, who met and had fallen in love with Max just a few days before, she was proud of Gunnar and felt the boy's love for a stranger.

For his sister. Right there in the diner, Max was loved and being loved by her family. Max felt the love and it was terrifying to her at the moment.

The waitress came over and took their orders.

"Do you have a boyfriend?" Jackson asked.

"No."

"Do you have friends?" Gunnar asked.

"Um. Yeah. I have a few."

The waitress came over with Hank's meal, but nothing for Max. "I'm sorry, but is there a problem?" Gwen asked. "My daughter ordered as well as the gentlemen."

Mike came out from the kitchen. "I'm sorry, ma'am, but she can't be here, and she can't be served here."

"Gunnar, please go sit down," Max said. She spun around. "Mike! Please don't make a scene."

Mike took out his phone and called the police. "You always thought that you were better than the rest of us. Thief! Whore!"

"Hey, don't talk to her like that!" Gwen, Matt, and Hank said together.

"Oh, look who is a being a stand-up father now!" Mike said.

Jackson got out of his seat at the table and walked past Max, patting her arm along the way, he walked right over to Mike. He stood in front of him, looked up at him with sad eyes and then kicked him in the shin before turning and running back to the table and to Gwen.

Max left the restaurant. She was outside when the police got there. Mike came outside. "This thieving whore is on house arrest, so she shouldn't be here right now."

"Ma'am, is that true?"

"Yes, sir, but I am with a police officer and my lawyer, sir."

"She's a liar."

"No, sir. Gwen Quimby is my lawyer and Hank…"

"Hank? Hank is here?"

"Yes, sir. He was asked to stay inside by my lawyer, sir."

They came outside. Max didn't make eye contact with anyone. The officers had moved to her left side. Jackson watched everything that was going on. "She can't hear you." The officer began to yell at Max. "That won't help. She can't hear on her left side."

"Another lie," Mike said.

"No, it's true," Gunnar said, "Ever since the accident. The girl with the layered hair kicked her in the head."

Mike looked at Max. "I'm sorry officers. I made a mistake."

But the damage was already done. The captain of Lees pulled up. "Maxine Brandon, you are under arrest for violation of your house arrest. Let's go."

"Yes, ma'am," Max said.

"We will come," Gwen said.

Gunnar got so upset that he threw up.

Max was taken to the Lees police station, where she was put right into a holding cell. Gwen and Hank came. Hank called Joanna. Joanna and Grant came. Max was retrieved from the cell and brought into a room. The way things were set up, they were going to be on her left side.

"I am deaf in my left ear," Max said.

"Did anyone tell you that you can talk?" the captain asked. Max didn't hear her. "I am talking to you. So you speak out and then when you are spoken to, you don't say anything." The captain came really close to Max and she said, "WELL, TELL ME. DO YOU HEAR ME NOW?" Max didn't stir. "Bring her back to the cell. This girl is an absolute smart ass."

Max's wrists were grabbed. "NO! What did I do?"

"The captain was talking to you," a young officer said.

"When?"

"Just now. She was standing right next to you on your left side."

"I'm deaf in my left ear. I…" Max started to cry. "I can't hear anything on that side. I said that. I wasn't lying. I had permission to be here today. I was with a police officer and my lawyer, and my dad and my two little brothers."

"Until this is straightened out, take her back to the cell."

It took them a few hours to get everything straightened out. When Max was let out of the cell, she stayed quiet. Hank took her back to the house. They were alone and would be for the next two hours. They went into the bedroom. Hank lifted Max out of the chair. He placed her on the bed with pillows under her head, her back, and her shoulders. He laid next to her and began to kiss her again like he had this morning. He now sat her up and striped her out of her shirt and her bra. Then he eased her back down on the softness behind her. He kissed her again and put his hands on her breasts. He squeezed a little. Then he brought his mouth down to one of her nipples and took it deep in his mouth. He twirled his tongue around her nipple and sucked it. Max's body was definitely responding. He brought his hands down and now he undressed her completely. She lay there naked. He separated her legs and then he placed a firm hand over her pubic region. Then he started to separate her gently. Like he had done this morning. He now stroked her crack. Once. Twice. Three times and then he slid his finger deep inside her. Deeper than he had this morning. With his other hand, he repositioned her legs and then he brought his mouth down there. She was groaning and her pelvic area was answering him at every touch. He now separated her and put his mouth down on top of her and his tongue slipped inside her. Max felt pressure growing. Building and it was intense. Then Hank stopped. He took off his own pants. He slid his grown member into a condom and then he was on top of her and inside her. Max reached for him and Hank took her in his arms as he came inside of her. Max's pelvis butterflied and danced right along with Hank's. Max cried out as she herself exploded with pleasure. Max quaked right along with Hank. When it was over, they lay together. They rested for a little while and then they started again. This time Max rubbed Hank's member and it came to life. Max slid herself down on the bed and took Hank in her mouth. She pleasured him as he had pleasured her and when she was done, he then slipped himself inside of her again giving her another round of pelvic fluttering, sheet gripping, lip biting, sex. This time when they were done, Hank though he too was spent; he carried her into the shower. He washed her. Just having his hands on her body made her react. "Please," she said. With soap on his fingers, he slid them inside her vagina. Max put her head back as another raging gratifying orgasm empowered her.

"Did you feel that?"

"Yes," she said. "Something popped inside of me this morning."

"Why didn't you say anything?"

"Because it wasn't a pop. I've felt warmth throughout my whole body all day long and now it's tingly, but in a good way. That was the best I've ever had."

"How many men have you been with?"

"Before you; just Elliot. Will you be my boyfriend?"

"I would love to be your boyfriend," Hank said.

They went back into the room together and they both dressed. They stripped the sheets together and they went and found the washer, where they threw all the sheets in and washed them on hot water. Then they dried them. When they were done, they brought them back in the room and they made the bed together.

CHAPTER EIGHT

Max had never spoken to anyone about intimacy. She called Gwen. "I don't know if you can, but do you think you can come here?"

"Yes," Gwen said.

"Just you. Not dad."

"Yes, honey."

When Gwen got there, she and Max went out on the back porch. "What I need to tell you, I've never spoken about with anyone before."

"Max, you can tell me anything."

"Today is the first time that I've had sex since my accident. Gwen, something popped inside of me and I felt everything while it was happening."

"Have you ever been to the gynecologist?"

"Yes. In the past, but not recently."

"Have you been sexually active in the past?"

"Yes, but with only one person. Elliot and I were partners. Not really lovers. Like I didn't want to marry him or spend the rest of my life with him, but we were there for each other when it was needed or wanted. But sex with Elliot was nothing compared to what I experienced today."

"Did he take advantage of you?"

"No. Gwen, my body reacted to it. I felt things in my core." After a few minutes of silence, Max said, "I'm sorry if..."

"Thank you for telling me," Gwen said. "Wouldn't you want to tell this to your mother?"

"No. I know that we just recently met, but besides for Joanna, you are the only woman that I trust right now."

"Well, thank you for trusting me with this." Gwen cleared her throat. "I have a few questions for you."

"Sure."

"You told the boys today that you weren't scared when you were alone flying an F-18. Were you scared?"

"No. I was taught how to control and fly an aircraft. And every time, I climbed up that ladder to my plane, I knew I had a mission to do. I didn't have any distractions. I didn't have to worry about anyone back home or anywhere. It was just me and my bird up there. I took care of him the same way that he took care of me."

"Did you write to your parents?"

"I wrote to dad. He returned every letter."

"Do you still have them?"

"Yes."

"Could I maybe have them?"

"Yeah, if that is what you want."

"Did you ever write to your mom?"

"No. And then I was forced to go back there and live with her."

"How was that?"

"It was a prison hell. Jail would have been better than staying at mom's."

"Max!"

"No, I'm not lying, Gwen. At first, she kept me locked in my room. Then someone came to do a welfare check and she was told that house arrest means that I have access to the whole house. After that, because she was embarrassed, she removed the bedroom door. She would go to the grocery store and buy herself all kinds of food and she would buy me a loaf of bread and a jar of peanut butter. She would buy a box of cereal too sometimes."

"What did you have for dinners?"

"Usually nothing. She told me every day that I don't get to get luxuries because I'm supposed to be in prison. With me being on house arrest had her in jail too."

"Did she ever leave you alone?"

"Yeah. She went on a cruise for two weeks with Logan and the others."

"What did you do?"

"Rationed my food. I took a box of her crackers and when she came back, she called and reported that I stole a box of her crackers. Another welfare check was done. The lady asked me what I was served to eat for breakfast, lunch, and dinner. Mom tried to lie. She said that she cooks for me every day. The lady spoke with me privately. I told her that I eat peanut butter sandwiches every day for lunch.

"She asked what I had for breakfast and dinner. I told her that I hadn't had dinner since I left the police station. By the time the lady was done talking to me, Des had gotten herself good and wasted. When she's wasted, the truth just seems to flow right out of her. She told the lady that dinner was a privilege in her house, and I didn't deserve to get any privileges. After that, an officer would come to bring me breakfast in the morning and dinner at night."

Joanna came out to ask them if they needed anything. "Did you know how she was being treated while she was with her mother?"

"No."

"I think Desiree needs to be locked up."

"For what?" Joanna asked.

"Abuse to a disabled person."

"Well, Max isn't going back there. How did Hank do getting you back here?"

"He did great. We did the laundry."

Gwen looked at Max and smiled at her.

"Gwen, would you like to stay for dinner?"

"Yes, thank you."

"Max, did you eat today?"

"Yes. Hank stopped on the way back here. What is his name?"

"Whose name?"

"Hank's. What is his real name?"

"Trent Easton."

"Then where did Hank come from?"

He had come outside. "Well because I was a country buff," he said. "So they started calling me Hank. Jo, did you tell her my name?"

"I did."

"Why did you want to know that?" he asked.

"Well, say someone comes up to me…like Gwen here, who is a lawyer, and she starts asking me random questions…where have I been? Who I have been with? And then out of the blue she drops "how do you know Trent Easton." I can give her a confirmative answer and not be like…well, I don't know. I may know him, but I don't know."

Gwen laughed. "That was a great interpretation there." Max smiled. They could see how her jaw doesn't line up when she smiles. "So here is a random question. How come you never learned how to drive a car?"

"What would have been the point? I didn't have a car."

"But you can fly an F-18, and no one thought to teach you how to drive."

"Yeah, pretty much."

"Where did you spend your leave time?" Joanna asked.

"On base mostly."

"Did you ever have anyone come and visit you?"

"No. Elliot hooked up with Lucy when I enlisted, so he didn't want anything to do with me. Lucy was a bit jealous though because Elliot and I had sort of been together, but not serious."

Joanna laughed. "So you were friends with benefits?"

"Yeah, I guess. We weren't that active together though."

When Gwen and Max were alone again and no one was in ear shot, Gwen looked at Max. "So you did laundry?"

"What's that?"

"Is that what you are calling it?" Max threw her head back and laughed so hard. "Maxine Brandon!" Gwen said. Max continued to laugh. "Don't laugh. It's not funny." Max grabbed her stomach as she got a stitch from laughing so hard. Tears rushed from Max's eyes. "Stop it!" Gwen said. "Get control." Max laughed harder and harder. The more Gwen went on, the more Max laughed. She then went to Gwen and wrapped her arms around her. Max put her head on Gwen's shoulder, and she cried. Gwen wrapped her arms around Max. Max shook from sobbing so hard.

"No one wants me," she said. "No one has ever wanted me. Not my parents. Not my team. Everyone has always thrown me away."

"Oh, Max!" Gwen said.

"I'm sorry if I embarrassed you and dad in front of the boys today. What a wonderful fucking first impression. I meet my little brothers for the first time and get arrested. I'm…I'm sorry."

"I am going to get this all straightened out for you."

"And then what? And then I go back to being by myself with no one to give a shit what I am doing."

"It won't be like that, Max." Gwen held her tighter in her arms. "You can't lose me now and I won't let you go. Do you hear me?"

Max stopped crying. She pulled back from Gwen. "But what if the judge doesn't drop the charges? Then what? I will go to jail, right? I am violating my house arrest."

"The police know where you are. Your lawyer knows where you are."

Max lowered her head. "I don't understand."

"Understand what?"

"Why my dad was so mad at me. I don't know what I ever did. He yelled at me every day. Every minute he had to be with me, he would yell at me and degrade me. But I didn't know how to correct it. I didn't know what to do. He was never excited to see me. He was never happy to have to take me to dance. And then after the divorce, he never came looking for me. Des didn't either, but I didn't want her. I wanted my dad. I wanted him to know that I chose him. But no one came for me. Why didn't he come looking for me? Why didn't he ever want to see me again?"

"Max, stop this. Please. I will ask him."

Max pulled away from her and went into the house. She came back with a box full of letters. "Here. They are written to my dad and to you."

"To me?"

"You may not have known about me, but I knew about you. I didn't know your name, but I knew who you were. You were the one who made my dad laugh and smile. You made my dad happy. You changed him. He doesn't seem to yell at his kids now."

"Did he yell at Logan?"

"No. He would take Logan to the park. They would throw a baseball around in the back yard. They would play soccer together. Dad would take Logan fishing. He would take him, and they would do fun stuff together."

CHAPTER NINE

When Gwen left, she left with the box of letters and an extremely heavy heart. When she got to the house, she watched Matt playing with the boys. She told them that she was home, and then she went into her office with the box. She sat at her desk, opened the box, and took out one of the letters.

June 2008

Dear Dad,

Wow, it's been six years since I last saw you or heard from you. I am writing to you from Bootcamp. I enlisted. I chose to go into the Air Force. I am hoping to be a pilot.

We were told that we have to write home to family in case something happens. In my case, I know that you nor mom would care. Maybe you would shed a tear for me. Most likely you wouldn't. Well, I'll write again soon.

Your daughter,
Max

Gwen read the letter with tears in her eyes. She looked at the envelope seeing Matt's writing, where he had written return to sender. She put the letter back in the envelope before picking out the next letter. She opened it and read.

August 2008

Dear Dad,

Not that you would ever be proud of me, but today I graduated bootcamp top of my class. I will be on leave for two weeks, but because I am homeless without the service, I will be staying on base.

Hope this letter finds you and your wife doing well.

Others have cried and carried on that bootcamp is so hard and so tough. They cried because they were away from their parents for maybe the first time in their lives. I didn't cry. I have been on my own since I was twelve.

Bootcamp was like living with you all over again. You know with constantly getting yelled at and put down and degraded. It drives me though to do it right and to push harder. Well, I'll try to write again soon.

Your daughter,
Max

Gwen smiled as she read this letter. Hearing how Max had graduated at the top of her class. She read the lines *Bootcamp was like living with you all over again. You know constantly getting yelled at and put down and degraded.*

September 2008

Dear my dad's wife,

I'm sorry I don't know your name. I hope that you are doing well. I saw you a few times when I was younger, but dad never introduced us to each other. So here is my introduction. My name is Maxine "Max" Brandon. I am eighteen years old. Although, I was homeless since I was twelve, [That was when dad's divorce to my mom was over. He made Logan – that's my little brother – and I make a decision who we wanted to live with at that time. I let Logan go first. He said that he wanted to live with mom. Dad saw red. He slammed his hand down so hard on the table that he cracked the wood. I picked to live with him, but he didn't hear me. It was like his ears just turned off.] Oh, that day was my twelfth birthday. Happy birthday to me. Dad leaves forever and my mother threw me out of the house after she smacked me across the face. Hands down the worst birthday ever.

Maybe one day I will get the chance to meet you. Until then, take care and best wishes with whatever is going right in your life.

Your husband's girl,
Max

Letter # 2 to my dad's wife,

It is September 24th. I am scared, but I have no one to tell, so I will tell you. You don't know me, so you can't judge me or think poorly of me. I don't know what my father has told you about me. I wish I had a mom in my life right now. This is harder than bootcamp was. I wish I had someone on my side to tell me that they were proud of me.

You know I took dance since I was five. In all of those years, not once did my coach ever tell me how proud she was of me.

Well, getting back to why I am scared. I dreamt that I died, and no one was there. Will it be like that if something should happen to me? Will there be no one to cry from losing me.

Because I am an orphan, I will be deployed sooner than others. I am going to start aviation school in the beginning of October. I took the test, and I got the highest score. Maybe next time, I'll get a few wrong, so I don't make others feel bad.

Maybe it's stupid to say, but:
Love,
Max

Gwent left the letters sitting on her desk. She went to find Matt and the boys. Together they got the boys situated for the night. They read them a bedtime story.

"One day can Max come here and read us a bedtime story?" Gunnar asked.

"I'm sure she'd love that." Gwen said sweetly.

"Why didn't we ever meet her before now?"

"She had her own life," Matt said.

"Didn't she want to meet us?" Gunnar asked.

"Of course, she wanted to meet the two of you," Gwen said. "But you can't just show up to someone's house without being invited first, and we didn't know where Max lived so that we could have invited her. But after meeting you guys today, I'm sure she will be in our lives now."

"Was she bad?" Jackson asked.

"Bad?" Matt asked.

"Yeah. Was she bad? Is that why you didn't let us see her?"

"No, Jackson, she wasn't bad. Come on now. It's bedtime."

"I want you both to know how very proud of you your father and I are. The way you both reacted in the diner this morning. I am so proud of you both."

"I kicked that guy hard for the way he spoke to Max," Jackson said.

"I know you did," Gwen said with a proud smile.

"I liked sitting on her and being close to her," Gunnar said. "I like having a big sister."

"Maybe she will be better than Logan," Jackson said.

They each kissed the boys good night. Gwen looked at Matt. He didn't see her looking at him. They left the boys.

"Where did you go?"

"To see our daughter, Matt."

"Is she ok?"

"I don't know how to answer that. Why did you send her letters back to her?"

"Gwen, we had been out of each other's lives for a long time then. I didn't want it to end our marriage."

"Is that what you think? Do you think that by you and Desiree having that beautiful girl that it would have ended your marriage? That's a huge burden for one little child to bare. Did you always hate her?"

"No. She was my little princess. When she was three or so, Des and I had gotten into a heated argument and she told me that Max might not have been my child."

"What? So you took it out on the child? She was a goddamn baby, Matthew. So you started to yell at her and not play with her. You ignored her. And when you had to be the fucking adult parent and take her to dance practice, you would yell at her and degrade her.

"Well, it was you who prepared her for the service, Matthew."

"What?"

"She gave me the letters that she wrote to you over the years when she was in the service."

"I want to read them."

"No," Gwen said. "They no longer belong to you. She gave them to me, so they are mine now; I will not let you read them until I have read every last letter, Matt. Would you ever do what you did to our daughter to one of your sons?"

"No."

"When did you find out that she was in fact your blood? Because she is your child, Matthew."

"When she was ten, she had taken a bad spill at dance and had to go to the hospital. Because she was bleeding, I asked them to test her blood. I told them that I wanted to confirm what her blood type was. Both Desiree and I are O negative. I had asked them to do a DNA test on her. I took a paternity test and it proved that ninety-nine-point nine nine percent that she is my child."

"But you never changed the way you were with her, did you?"

Matt never looked away from her. "No. The damage was already done. Because I had the tests taken, Desiree wanted a divorce. Hell. I wanted a way out and then there it was in a form of a paternity test. My baby girl freed me from a marriage that I had felt stuck in since before Max was even born."

"Oh, Matt," Gwen said.

"I know, Gwen. And now look at her. That giant life of a little person has been knocked right out of her."

"She will be in our lives, Matthew. I want her in my life and in my sons' lives. Didn't it break your heart today seeing her hold Gunnar on her lap like it was nothing while we were at the restaurant. And the way she lied for you as not to hurt me or the boys. That's something. You hurt her for years, and yet she didn't want to hurt you or any of us. That means something. It speaks volumes about that girl. I'll be in my office for a little while."

Gwen returned to her office. She sat at her desk taking the next letter.

December 2008

Dear Dad,

I flew an actual plane today. We were working on take offs and landings. My superior officer says that I did a great job today. He said words to me today that I have never heard in my life. He told me that he was proud of me. He told me that I did a great job today. He said that my parents would be proud.

Would you though? Would you be proud of me? Even when I danced a flawless tango with Scott when I was nine, you never said those words. It had been raining and my new dress had gotten a little wet because I was so excited to be wearing it. It was the first time that you had bought me a costume for dance. I wanted nothing more than to show it off to you and for you to maybe once see me and smile like you did when you saw Logan. But you didn't. Instead, you yelled at me that money doesn't grow on trees and that because I was wearing the dress and it had rained, I had ruined it like I ruin everything else.

Do you still smile now when you see Logan? Would you maybe smile now if you saw me? Maybe. Probably not.

And I know that you must still be mad at me for something I am not aware of doing – that it drove you away – that it has kept you out of my life for all of these years. I know this because I got my letter back today. Well, even if I get all of them back, I will still write to you because the military told me to.

Hell, maybe your letter got returned because it's not the right address. Maybe I copied it wrong when I was twelve. I don't know, but I'll keep writing.

Love,
Max

December 2008

Dear Steppy,

I don't know your real name, so like I will gain a call sign when I get my bird, I am appointing you one. You are now Steppy. I wrote and told dad that I am really learning how to fly. We have been working on take offs and landings. My superior officer told me that he was proud of me. Somehow, though we don't know each other, I believe that you would be proud of me. I believe that you would be proud to say that Maxine "Max" Brandon is your daughter. FUCK! I'm sorry. I made myself cry. Ok. Bye for now.

Love,
Max

P.S. Merry Christmas to you and dad. Hope all is well.

January 2009

Dear Steppy,

I wanted to tell you a little more about myself. I don't know if dad talks about me or if he ever has. I was always fluttering around so when I was five my kindergarten teacher suggested to Des and dad that maybe I should be in dance.

I remember going to the studio. Des took me. She told me not to be shy and to do what I usually do. From the second that my feet touched the dance floor, I never

95

stopped moving. I covered that floor from one side to the other. Not leaving an inch untouched. Hannah Grace liked what she saw and that was that. I was signed up for dance. I remember I couldn't wait to get home and tell daddy. When he came in from work, I was jumping up and down and I started to tell him. He yelled at me to stop moving around so much. He pointed his finger in my face and told me to STOP IT! I should have cried. I should have thrown myself down on floor and cried for his attention, but I didn't. Instead, I spread my arms out as wide as they could go, and I tiptoed away from him. He never looked at me.

So after, dad left, and Des threw me out. The mark on my left cheek is from where her dangle bracelet had caught me when she smacked me across the face. It had made a slight gash in my face. It will forever mark the day that I became homeless. I consider it a birthday present. The only one I really got that year. Well, and a deep hole in my heart.

I continued to go to school. I was in the sixth grade when the earthquake that I call my life shattered. But I went to school like nothing had happened. I would go to coffee shops and do my homework. I made the honor roll. Straight A+s, but I had no one to share it with. I worked my ass off to maintain them all throughout school. Straight A+s. Even dad would have had to be proud of me for that. I graduated top of my class.

It was during an assembly that a recruiter came to the school to talk to the students about their futures. She said that going into the service would bring honor to not only us, but to our family as well. I was now eighteen and I thought this is how I would get dad to maybe see me and smile at me. Maybe hug me and not try to push me off or away so quickly. Maybe this was the way to make Coach Hannah Grace proud of me. Deep inside of me, I have the feeling that if you know me or is it knew me or whatever it is – that you would be proud of me and that you would tell me and let me know this. Maybe you would be the one to bring me back into my father's life.

I don't care about the rest of them. I just want my dad's approval. My dad's love.

Tomorrow, I will take the bird up for a twenty-minute flight. Wish me luck. With deep love although I am still a stranger. Love your daughter – MAX

January 2009

Dear Steppy and dad,

I GOT MY CALL SIGN TODAY. ELEGANT DANCER – my captain said that when I am flying my plane it looks like an elegant dance in the sky. I made it do spirals and then I tried to make it look like it was bowing before I landed it. I thought for sure that I would have been yelled at, but I wasn't. I GOT MY CALL SIGN. Well, I have to go. I have to go study. Love you both.

Love,
Max

March 2009

Dear dad,

Today was hard. I've been shipped out. I can't tell you my location, but it isn't pretty like home. The colors bleed together. Browns and greys. Tomorrow I will fly to see what my mission target will be. Would you be proud of me now? No. I don't think you would be. I think you would yell at me for this too.

MAX, WHAT THE FUCK ARE YOU DOING WITH YOUR LIFE? YOU ARE A DISAPPOINTMENT. WHY DO YOU DO THE THINGS THAT YOU DO? WHY CAN'T YOU JUST STOP AND STAY STILL? **MAX, FOR THE LOVE OF GOD JUST FUCKING STOP IT!!!!**

Your words are all that stay with me these days. Hell, they have always been with me. Ever since I could remember. They have drove me to get good grades in school. I thought maybe if…maybe if I did really well and you somehow found out about it that you would come get me. Well, I don't want to kill my happy mood here. With love. Love, Max

May 2009

Dear Steppy,

HAPPY MOTHER'S DAY!!! I know that you aren't my mom, but I don't write to her and I barely think about her, but I think about you and about dad.

Do you have children? I bet if you do that you are a wonderful loving and supporting mother. I dream of you sometimes. At least I think it is you, you know because we have never met. Anyway, in my dream you are holding me in a hug. Like a mother holds her child. Hope your day is wonderful because you deserve it. With love. Your daughter.

Love,
Max

"Christ," Gwen said aloud as she wiped the tears away. "Max!" Gwen looked at the nice row of letters that followed behind this one. She saw one that was much thicker. She filed the one that she had read right back in the order where it had come from and then she pulled out the thicker one. She gently opened the letter and pulled the letter out. When the letter came out, so did a medal. *FOR BRAVERY.* Gwen squeezed the medal in her hand. She read the letter that was addressed to her dated back to 2011. Instead of it reading: Dear Steppy, this one read: Dear Mommy. And then Gwen, though she was tired, she read the letter.

September 2011

Dear Mommy,

Yes, Steppy I am writing to you. Though my letters have mostly all been returned to me, I still will write to you and dad. Enclosed is a medal for bravery. I flew a mission under heavy fire and though my bird was hit, mom, I continued to fly. I completed my mission, and no lives were lost.

Mom, how I wish I knew you and knew your name. So today, I graduated you from Steppy to Mommy.

I dreamt about you again. About us together walking on the warm brown sand. I haven't been back state side in about a year now. I can't tell you or dad where I am right now, but after completing the mission, I will return home — well to the US for a month's worth of leave. I will not see family members or friends while I'm home. I hate being alone. I have always hated it. But it was my freedom. How I yearn to hug you and to get hugged by you. I think that you would take me in your arms and you'd never want to let go of me. How I would love that. And love you for that.

If by chance, dad keeps this one, would you please keep my medal for me until I am home for good. Also, maybe this sounds dumb, but would buy me a cuddly stuffed animal. Anything. Just something really soft and cuddly to hold and to squeeze. I love you Steppy — Mommy.

Love,

Maxine

Gwen now put the letter and medal back in the envelope and she put it back in the box. She decided to read one more. She picked the last letter in box that to her surprise was written to her. She opened it carefully. Inside this letter, she found a small plastic baggy with a chain inside. She found herself opening it and taking the chain out of the bag. She saw that there were two hearts attached that hung swinging from the chain. She saw that there was something engraved on both of them. Two simple words: Mother. Daughter. Gwen wrapped the chain around her hand and held the two hearts in the palm of her hand. She then closed her fingers around them as she took the letter out of the envelope and read the letter.

June 2014

Dear Mommy,

Six years has blown by. My tour of duty is done. I am not re-enlisting, so I will return home. This is the first time in six years that I am feeling complete and utter sorrow.

Coming home. To what? I do have a cute apartment. I bought it two years ago when I was on an extended leave. They said I had to take it and that I couldn't stay on the base for my leave time, so I came back to where all my past has been left behind.

I took the money out of the trust account. Not all of it, but a pretty decent lump sum and went and found an apartment. It's close to Lees. I know that is where dad and you live. I bought it on the chance that maybe one day, I would be out and possibly bump into you and dad. Of course, you wouldn't know me. Anyhow, I just bought the apartment and a few necessities for the time being and then I locked up my new place and drove back to the base. On the way there, I saw this woman and for some reason it made me think of you. She was running with a little boy of maybe two and pushing an empty stroller with three wheels. I was stopped at a light in Lees while the train went by and it just caught my eye. I stayed there watching them. The way they interacted together. The little boy would run ahead and then stop and wait and tap his little foot on the ground. After the train went by I found myself pulling over to watch them. The woman was tall with dark hair and highlighted shades of autumn brown in it. The little boy's hair was that beautiful tone of brown. Not too dark, but not blond either. Well, anyway, that was two years ago. I guess I brought it up because maybe I will see them again when I am now home for good.

Home! That word is foreign to me. I haven't truly had a home since I was twelve. The apartment will be dirty. I haven't been back since I bought it. I don't have luxury things. I don't have a phone or TV or even a proper kitchen yet in it. I will have to do a lot to it when I get back.

I have thought over the years of how nice it would have been to have known you. I tell myself that your love would make you proud of me. My service days have to come to end, which saddens me because it makes me think if I will continue to write to you and dad. Thank you for being there even if it was just in my head for the past six years. You have helped me in more ways than you could have known, and I am grateful. Though this is my last night here and tomorrow I will board a plane to come home, I know in my heart that you won't see this letter, for all of my letters in the past six years that I have been writing to you and dad have been returned to me unopened. I will stow them away in the box that I made for them with the hope that one day you will get the chance to see and read these letters.

I am so afraid to come home. At least now when I do, I will have a roof or ceiling over my head and four walls to keep me safe and warm, but I will be alone again. I hate loneliness. Six years ago, when I started to write dad and then to you, I thought maybe there would be a chance that I would die during this time. Well, I'm glad to report that that didn't happen.

I hope when I come home to maybe see that woman and child again. He is two years older. Two years taller. And she is most likely two years more beautiful. Well, I am signing off for the last time. I have to finish packing my things. Sending you love.

Love always,

Elegant Dancer
Maxine

Gwen put the letter and chain with the hearts on it back into the envelope. Gwen put her hand over her heart, for Max had in fact seen her and Gunnar that day. The woman and the little boy that Max described were them. Gwen hugged herself. She wanted to be hugging and holding Max right now. She got up from her desk, turned off her desk lamp. And then she carried the box over to where there was a wall safe and she opened it and stowed the box inside. Then she went to check on the boys before going to bed.

The next morning, Gwen got the boys ready for the day. "Are you going to go see Max?" Jackson asked.

"Yes."

"Here. I want her to have this," he said. He handed Gwen a little transformer.

"Why this one?"

"Because it can be changed to do other things. And I want her to have it."

"Well, if you are sure," Gwen said.

"Yes, I am sure."

Matt came in the kitchen. "Hi, daddy!" both boys said.

"Hi, guys."

After the boys left the kitchen, Matt looked at Gwen. "Can you bring her here?"

"No not yet. Like Joanna said yesterday there will be a transition period."

"Are you ok?"

"Matt, I just can't believe that you never read any of her letters. You sent each and every one back to her. She didn't only write to you though. She wrote beautiful letters to me as well.

"Maybe I'm a little dense when it comes to how things were between you and Desiree, but Desiree didn't suffer. Logan didn't suffer, but Maxine… God, Matt, with all that was happening, she made straight A's in school. Imagine Gunnar in two years all alone, out on the street with no one to turn to. With nowhere to go."

"I can't imagine that."

"But that is what you and Desiree did to your only daughter. I know it was a long time ago, but the hurt, the guilt, the blame; it is all there. And yet it's not you or her mother who are experiencing that. It's our thirty-year-old daughter."

"When did Max become our daughter?"

"The second I saw her. The second I met her. When I took her in my arms and held her while she cried. She cried for you, Matthew. After all of these years, she is still crying for her father's love and support. That is when she became *my* daughter."

"When can I read the letters?"

"When I have read through all of them."

"Are there a lot of them?"

"There are six years of them. She wrote a letter a month. Sometimes two letters a month. There must be close to one hundred letters in the box. I'll take the boys to school and then I will be gone all day long."

"Ok. I'll pick them up and get dinner."

"Thank you," she said. She went to him and wrapped her arms around him. He encompassed her in his arms.

"Can I come with you?"

"Not today."

Gwen took the boys to school. "No fighting! Do you hear me?"

"Yes, mom," they said together.

Gwen left them at school and then she made a stop at the children's store. She went in. "Do you have stuffed animals?"

"Yes."

"What is the softest one that you have."

A girl in her twenties brought Gwen back to where the plushies were. "The softest plushy that we have in the store is this elephant." The girl looked at the price. "Let me see if there is anything cheaper."

"No, that's ok. I will take it. Do you gift wrap?"

"Yes, ma'am. Is it for a girl or for a boy?"

"It is for my daughter," Gwen said.

As Gwen was leaving, Logan came into the store. "I thought that was you," he said to her. "How are you doing?"

"I am fine. How are you?"

"Good. Do you know where Max is staying?"

"Why do you want to know?"

"Well, there is reward money being offered for whoever turns her in."

"Is there something wrong with you, Logan?"

"No. What do you mean?"

"When is the last time that you have seen your sister?"

"God, I don't know. I was seven. She was twelve. What's that? Eighteen years ago."

"So what makes you think that you can locate her to turn her in so that you can get rewarded?"

"Well, mom thinks that she deserves the money. You know with her losing wages for the time that Max was staying there and not contributing to the bills or anything."

"Have you ever contributed to the bills, Logan?"

"Well, no, but that is different."

"How is that different?"

"I had to move out when she went to live with mom. As did Caitlin, Leah, and Harrison. We all got displaced because Max is a crook and thief. She's probably faking being paralyzed, so her ass doesn't go to jail."

"Logan, don't you ever say that again. When was the last time that you really saw her?"

"I don't know. I was a little kid, I guess. Mom said that she ran way and joined the circus. She said that we were no longer allowed to talk about her or bring her up, so I didn't. Maybe I'll go see dad. I'll see if he will give her up to us."

She wanted to tell him that he made her sick, but she didn't. "Well, I have to go to work."

"Do you think that dad will turn her in?"

Matt was suddenly there in the store. "Turn who in?" he asked. "What are you talking about?"

"Well, mom believes that she is entitled to the reward money that is out there if Max is turned in to the police."

"How much money are we talking about here?"

"Like twenty thousand dollars."

"And you and your mother are going to split this money?"

"Well, yeah," Logan said. "I had to move out when she moved in. Caitlin, Leah, and Harrison haven't been able to see mom in years because

Max is crook and thief. She lies and steals. She is probably faking being paralyzed so that she wouldn't go to jail. She stole drugs, jewels, and money."

"Where did you hear that?"

"I read it in the papers. I saw it on the news. She made mom cry."

"I'm sure," Gwen said.

"You, nor your mother is going to collect reward money for turning your sister over to the police."

"Why not?" Logan asked.

"Because it's not right," Matt said.

"Like it was right for her to just up and bail after you and mom divorced. She was an embarrassment to you. She was yours and mom's biggest disappointment. Your biggest mistake. And now the little bitch is claiming she is deaf. That's rich," he said. "It is so she doesn't have to hear the truth about how much mom was hurt when she left."

"Tell me something," Gwen said. "Did your mom leave Max's room for her?"

"No. Why would you she? She turned it into a gym for me. It was my playroom. I had so much fun in that room when I was growing up. The house was so much quieter without her there. No more of her dancing over every inch of the house. No more of her screaming and throwing herself from here to there like an idiot."

"What would you do, if you saw her?" Gwen asked Logan.

"I'd make her prove that she is really and truly paralyzed. Then I would make her give me the money that she stole."

"Logan, that is enough of this bullshit." Matt reprimanded.

"So are you going to tell me where she is?"

"No," both Gwen and Matt said.

"But you know where she is?"

"Logan, get some compassion," Gwen said. "Your sister…"

"I don't care about her. She never cared about me," Logan said. "She left all of us. She didn't want me in her life. She just wanted to be a martyr and have people cry over her because you moved out. Parents divorce all the time. You stayed in my life over the years. She didn't. Where the hell did she go?"

"That's a great question. Where the hell did she go? You had someone taking care of you, right?" Hank asked.

"Who the hell are you?"

"Come with me, you little punk," Hank said.

"Dad! Gwen!"

Hank took Logan by the shirt and brought him out to his Hummer. "Get in."

"What are you going to do with me?"

"Don't make me arrest you." Logan climbed into the Hummer. "So what is this bullshit that you were saying to your stepmother and your dad?"

"I think that mom is entitled to the reward money for Max."

"Why?"

"Because mom lost wages while Max was staying with her. She had to pay her ex-husbands child support for their children because Max managed to get herself on house arrest instead of going to jail. I saw the way she was at the trail. When someone was on her left side, she played and made like she couldn't hear them. She was trying to go for the insanity plea. With her jaw… Wait, was her jaw really wired shut?"

"Yes."

"Why?"

"Your sister…no wait. Let me enlighten you," Hank said.

They went to the police station. "Are you arresting me?"

"Are you in handcuffs?"

"No."

"Then I guess you answered your own question. Come with me." Hank brought him into a room with a TV. He put a disc in the player and there was Max. She was laughing and sitting on the front of the stage and then she was up and dancing across the stage. Then it was the show. Logan watched.

"I've never seen her dance on stage before," he said. "Wow! She's beautiful." He watched as she went from one guy's arms to the next until she got to the lead guy and then he hoisted her high up in the air. Logan heard the boom. He jumped. "What the hell was that?" Followed by a pop and then a sound like a rushing bullet train and a tornado all at once. He saw Max get hit. "Oh, Christ!" he said. And then he watched and cringed as he saw her laying on the stage floor pinned under the light. He watched the others in the crew run away. "What is that girl doing?" he asked about Lucy and then he saw her drive a kick like a field goal right to the left side of Max's head and face. As the girl ran off, Logan saw the blood spewing out of Max's ear. "I never saw this."

"Did your mother?"

"I… I don't know."

"That first hit crushed her back. That kick to her head deafened her permanently in her left ear and broke her jaw. It was wired shut when she was on trial. She couldn't answer the questions. Your mother mistreated your sister from the time that she was in the house with her on house arrest.

"When your parents divorced, Logan, you chose to stay with your mom."

"Yes, I remember that. Dad was mad."

"Yes, well Max chose to go live with your dad."

"Why though. He was always yelling at her. Anytime he had to do something with her or for her, he would go off on her like a drill sergeant. It was vicious and intense. I didn't want him to yell at me like that ever. That's why I chose to stay with mom," Logan said.

"Well, your father thought he heard that you both wanted to stay with your mother, so he was incredibly angry. Max wanted to live with him. When she came back after being rejected by your father, your mother threw her out. She wouldn't let her come back to live there."

"I remember him being angry. I thought he was going to turn into the incredible hulk or something. It was Max's birthday," Logan said. "She was twelve. I know because I was seven. For most of the year, she is five years older than me. That was the last time that I saw Max. Mom said that we couldn't talk about her anymore and if dad asked where she was when I went for a visit, I was to say that she didn't want to come, so I did. He never really pressed the issue at first and then all together no one ever discussed Max. Gwen didn't know about her. I think she found out about Max when Jackson was born, so that was six years ago, but she never met her."

"How did it come out?"

"Gwen said that she wanted a girl and dad said that he has a daughter. That she is his oldest child. Gwen wanted to know where she was, why she never met her, and like so much more and dad couldn't tell her anything. So it was more like Max was a family pet that we lost.

"How did my mom mistreat her? I would go by the house with groceries for them. Mom wouldn't let me in the house or even see Max, but there was plenty of food."

"How many loaves of bread did you buy?"

"Three a week," Logan said.

"What went with the bread?"

"Peanut butter." It just hit Logan. "What? That's all she was eating? But there was so much more food than that. Chips, crackers, steaks, chicken breasts, rice, corn on the cob, pasta and a shit load of veggies."

"Well, Max never got any of those. She had cold cereals and peanut butter sandwiches."

"What about dinners?"

"No."

"Because dinner is luxury," Logan said.

"What?"

"You had to show that you worked hard to get dinner."

"Did you, your siblings and your mom go on a cruise?"

"Yeah. We went on a two-week cruise. Then like a month or so later, mom took all of us to New York City for just under a month. Oh, shit! Max was alone with no food. Mom said that she had shut off the phone."

"Did she shut anything else off?"

"The power too I think."

"And no one questioned about Max?"

"No. I guess because we never talked about her. It's normal for mom to do that while we go on family vacations, so no one thought any different. Plus the others don't know her."

"Did anyone go and check on Max?"

"Not that I know of."

"Come. I will drive you back to your car. Do I have to worry about you trying to hurt Max?"

"No," Logan said. "Has mom seen that video of her?"

"I don't know."

"Has dad?"

"You would have to ask him about it."

"Did she do it?"

"Do what?"

"Steal those things that were said to be stolen that night?"

"Logan, how did your sister leave the theatre that night?"

"In an ambulance."

"Right. So where was she going to put all of the stolen belongings?"

Max was quiet in Joanna and Grant's house that day. She kept to herself. She read the driver's manual for the second time. Hank had left last night after kissing her goodbye and telling her that he would see her soon.

The feelings that Max had felt yesterday: burning, traveling, and exploding in her body were gone today. She felt nothing. This saddened her.

Gwen changed her schedule because she hadn't wanted Logan to follow her to Joanna's house, so she went into the office and worked from there for most of the day, but she freed herself to go get the boys from school. They were excited to see her.

"What do you have there, Gunnar?"

"I made a picture of Max for Max."

"That is very sweet of you."

"Did you see her today?"

"No, Jackson. I didn't get to go there."

"Is she going to be forgotten."

"No. Why would you ask that?"

"Because she has been my sister all of my life, yet we didn't know about her," he said.

"Is dad afraid of her?" Gunnar asked.

"What?"

"Yesterday, when we met her. Dad seemed like he was scared of her."

"No, he isn't scared of Max."

"But this morning, dad didn't want to talk about Max with us."

"Well, dad and I don't know all of the answers to your questions just yet. Come. Let's go home."

Matt hadn't known that Gwen went to go pick the boys up from school, so when he got to the school and the boys weren't there, panic set in. As he paced the front office, he called Gwen. She answered right away. "Hi."

"Hi. I'm at the boys' school, yet they aren't here. Please tell me that you got them."

"Yes. I did. I'm sorry. I forgot to call you."

"Did you go see Max?"

"No. I'll go there tomorrow."

"Ok. I'll see you soon."

When Matt got home, Gunnar met him at the front door. "Are you going to forget Max?"

Matt went down on his knees in front of Gunnar. "Have you been thinking of this thought all day long?"

"No. But are you going to forget about her?"

"No, Gunnar."

"Are we going to see her again?"

"Yes, but it may be some time."

"Why? Doesn't she like us?"

"She loves you and your brother."

"Does she love you and mommy?"

"That might take a while longer."

"Why?"

"Well, mommy and I like you and your brother have to really get to know Max."

"Will we?"

"Yes, Gunnar."

"Can we call her and speak to her?"

"Maybe not tonight, but yes."

"How does she do things?" Jackson asked. "Does she sleep in her wheelchair?"

"No," Gwen said. "How about we let daddy come in."

Matt got up. "Look I drew a picture for Max," Gunnar said. "When can I give it to her?"

"In a few days," Matt said.

The boys went off to play before they did their homework. Gwen and Matt spoke in the kitchen as they prepared dinner. "Have you spoken with her today?" Matt asked.

"No. I went to the office and I was going over her case again. I don't know how she was charged with anything."

Just then the phone rang. Matt answered it. It was Logan. "Can I come over?"

"Of course."

"Can I bring anything?"

"Whatever you'd like."

Logan went to the store. He bought brownies and ice cream. Then he went to the house. Gwen put a movie on for the boys in her and Matt's room and closed the door. She, Logan and Matt sat at the table and spoke. "Did you know about Max?" Logan asked looking at Gwen.

"You know the answer to that question. If I would have known about your sister, I would have put out a search party until we found her and then I would have brought her here to live with us."

Logan lowered his head. "I saw the video of her accident," he said. "She's lucky to be alive. And does anyone know who the girl is that field goaled her right in the head?"

"Yes," Gwen said.

"Well, what's happening about that?"

"We are building a case."

"How long does that take?"

"It takes time."

"I feel bad," Logan now said. "I found out the way mom treated her while she was there with her."

"What do you mean?" Matt asked.

"Mom kept Max locked in her bedroom until a check was done and she was told that she couldn't do that. Then mom was only letting Max eat twice a day. Plain cereal and peanut butter sandwiches.

"Again, I feel bad. Mom hadn't seen us in awhile, so she took us on vacation. Max was left in the house with minimal food for two weeks while we were on a cruise and then when mom had taken us to New York for about a month. She left Max with no power and no phone and food that probably only should have lasted about a week.

"Mom used to yell at Max just as much as you did," Logan spoke freely. "You both told her what a disappointment she was. You never played with her like you played with me. You'd play ball with me and we would ride bikes together. When Max wanted to join, you would yell at her to go practice her dances and then you would yell at her to stop dancing.

I know that she was older than me, but she too was just a kid. You and mom's divorce went through on her birthday. That was the last day that she was at the house. Mom hauled off and smacked her across the face. Mom's bracelets cut Max's cheek. Then mom pushed her out of the door, slammed the door and locked it. Max left bleeding. She was gone for a long time after that. Well, until four years ago. If she didn't have the accident, she'd still be out there."

"How come you never told me that your mother hit her?"

"Mom said that we weren't allowed to talk about Max. She said that Max was no more. She said that she was like a fairy. Here and then just gone. Gone for good."

"Jesus Christ," Matt said.

"Max wanted to live with you," Logan said. "I'm sorry that I said I wanted to live with mom. Max probably blames herself for you and mom divorcing, but I blame myself for driving Max away. You didn't want her, and mom didn't want her. It's not like we had aunts or uncles or even grandparents for her to retreat to until everything settled down.

"Max was in middle school, and I was in elementary school, so I never saw her. Where was she sleeping? Where was she staying and eating? You and mom had paid for her dance school for two years. I know that you and mom argued about it."

Gunnar came into the room. "The movie is over. Hi, Logan."

"Hi, Gunny," he said and then he picked him up and hung him upside down by his ankles. He gently swung him back and forth. Gunnar laughed.

"Are you going to meet Max? She uses a wheelchair. Something fell on her back and hurt her and then someone kicked in the head so hard that it made her deaf."

"How do you know that?" Logan asked lowering Gunnar to the floor and then reaching down and picking him up.

"I saw the videos of her dancing. She was a beautiful dancer, Logan. When she danced, she was like a bird or a butterfly. I wish I could have seen her dance on her legs for real."

"Gun, where is your brother?"

"He's sleeping. I want to go see Max again. That man in the restaurant had her taken by the police."

Logan looked at Matt and Gwen. They both nodded.

"Was she hurt?"

"No," Gwen said.

"She put her head down and she was like Shane at school."

"What does Shane do?" Matt asked.

"She tries not to cry. She tries not to let anyone see if she does. Max did that yesterday. She stayed strong because she didn't want to scare us away. She didn't want us to be afraid of her."

"Why would you be afraid of her?" Gwen asked.

"Because she's not like us, but I'm not afraid of her. She let me sit on her lap. And then the guy came out of the kitchen and they wouldn't bring her breakfast," Gunnar told Logan. "He made Max go outside and then the police came. I cried when they took her away," he said now crying. He went to Gwen and cried in her arms. "It's my fault that happened," he cried. "I wanted to meet her. I saw the video and I had to see that she was ok after that thing hit her and pinned her down on the floor." Gunnar now cried harder. "I didn't know that I had a sister. I want Max, mommy. I want Max. Please. I want to tell her that I am sorry. I didn't mean to get her in trouble."

"You didn't get her in trouble," Matt said.

"Where can we find her, mommy? I want Max."

Matt was devastated to see how torn up his ten-year-old son was. He went into another room and called Joanna. "Is it possible that Max can come here for just a little while? Gunnar really wants to see her."

"We will be there within an hour," Joanna said.

"Is she ok?"

"She's really quiet today. She hasn't eaten much today."

"Will she be ok to come?"

"I believe she will." Joanna went to go see where Max was. She was in the room laying on the bed. Just staring straight ahead. "Max, your dad is on the phone." Max didn't hear her. Her left ear was up. Joanna stood in the room. "She's not getting up."

"Should we come there?"

"Yes, I think that will be best."

"We will see you soon."

Joanna noticed that Max shook from crying. Joanna went over to the bed and sat with her. She put her hand on Max's shoulder and Max jumped. She turned her head up to look and Joanna saw the tears just flowing.

Ashley had come over. She stood in the doorway and watched Max. Her heart broke for her. "How is she today, dad?"

"She's been quiet. She hasn't eaten anything all day long."

"Did something happen?"

"Yesterday, we took her to Lees to meet her little brothers and the owner of the restaurant wouldn't let her be served and then he called the police. She was arrested in Lees and held for violating her terms of house arrest. She was arrested in front of her father, Gwen, and their two sons."

"Mom couldn't stop it?"

"Mom isn't a law enforcement agent in Lees, sweetheart. We had to let it happen. It took hours to get it all straightened out.

"Gwen told her that she was going to come today, but she didn't."

CHAPTER TEN

Within an hour, Matt, Gwen, Gunnar, Jackson, and Logan were at the house. Grant let them in. "Who are you?" he asked Logan.

"I'm Max's brother Logan."

"Listen kid, if you have any reservation of being a fuck and calling the police on her then you can leave right now. We were told about you this morning."

"Maybe that was my plan for this morning, but now I just want to see my sister. I haven't seen her in eighteen years. The last time I saw her, I was seven."

"Where is she," Gwen asked.

"She's struggling today. She's in the bedroom."

Gwen didn't ask permission to go in there. She went into the room. Max had cried herself to sleep. Unfallen tears sat in perfect drops on her eye lashes. Gwen got down on her knees on the side of the bed and she softly touched Max's cheek. She saw the scar that Desiree had left her with. Gwen slid her fingertips over it. Max twitched and then opened her eyes. She pulled her head back. She wiped the tears off her face. "Hi, Gwen." Max moved her head so she would be able to hear her.

"Hi, how are you today?" Max sat up. "Are you doing ok?"

Max lowered her head and shook it a little. "I'm embarrassed," she said.

"Why?"

"Because you, dad, and the boys saw me being taken away. The boys probably never want to see me again."

"No, sweetheart. We are here because Gunnar wouldn't stop crying that he wanted to see you. He had to know that you are ok."

"They are here?"

"Yes."

"Dad probably didn't come though. Again, I disappointed him."

"No, angel, your dad is here too."

Max got up out of bed. She went into the kitchen with Gwen. Gunnar went to her first. He held his arms out, his head was tucked from him crying. Max took him in her arms. She pulled him on her lap and the two of them cried together. "I'm sorry," they both said together.

"Why are you sorry?" Max asked Gunnar.

"It's my fault that you got taken away yesterday."

"No, Gunnar. You can't do that. You can't take on that kind of responsibility. It wasn't your fault."

"But I wanted to meet you."

"I'm glad that you wanted to meet me."

"I had to know that you were ok. I saw the accident," he said still crying.

"I'm ok, Gunny. Can I call you Gunny?"

"Yeah."

"I'm ok." She held him and swayed with him in her arms. "You are an amazing boy."

"But I got you in trouble yesterday. I'm sorry, Max."

She kissed him on the cheek. "It's ok. I love you."

"I love you too."

She kept him in her arms for a little while. Matt took him from her after he had been asleep for quite some time. When he did, Max saw someone else standing in the room. He was six foot two and muscular. "Who are you?" Max asked him.

"You wouldn't remember be. The last time we saw each other, it was your twelfth birthday, and I was just a seven-year-old twerp," Logan said.

Ashley stood close. She was becoming very protective over Max these past couple of weeks now.

"You're Logan," Max said. "Wow! You're all grown up."

"Can I hug you? Is it ok?"

"Yes."

Logan went to her. He got down on his knees and then he took her into his arms. "Hi, Max," he said. "I may not have been able to talk about you over the years, but damn have I missed my big sister. Did you ever think of me?"

"Every day," she said.

Logan let her go. Matt hugged her now. He kissed her on the cheek. He held her firm in his arms. "You have made a lasting impression on my children's lives, Max, and I can't thank you enough. To see my ten-year-old not only have compassion, but to show it. He has wanted to come see you all day long today. He couldn't have gone to bed tonight without personally knowing that you are ok."

"Max, honey," Ashley said awhile later. "You need to eat something. What can I make for you? What would you like?"

"I don't want anything."

"That's ok, but you have to eat something." Ashley made a pasta dish. Max ate it. She genuinely enjoyed it.

"Thank you, Ashley."

"Are you ok?"

"I feel lost."

"How do you feel lost?"

"I guess because now my dad and Gwen know where I am. Logan too. I should feel happy and relieved. I have wanted this to happen since I was twelve, but I am so afraid right now."

"Afraid of what?"

"Of them getting to know me and not liking me. Abandoning me again. My mom did it." Max was quiet for a few minutes. "Who chooses me?" she said. "When will I be the chosen one?

"Lucy was always jealous when Elliot chose to dance with me. He is a great dancer, but he's not all that if you know what I mean. I mean he's good looking in his own way. But if I didn't know him, I wouldn't be missing anything. All he talks about is dancing and who does what better than the other. It's stupid.

"They never came to see me after the accident. As my once abled body was turned off for good, I had to deal with it alone. No one came. Well, no, there was a guy who would come and sit in the room with me, but we didn't talk," she told Ashley.

"What was it like living with your mom?"

"It was rough. I didn't want to be there. She didn't want me there. For awhile she kept me locked in a room. I only got two meals a day the whole time I lived there."

"Did she take your siblings on vacation?"

"Yeah. They went on a two-week cruise."

"Did they go anywhere else?"

"They went to New York for a month."

"And what conditions were you left in?"

"In the dark. Mom had the power turned off and the phone. I had bread and peanut butter."

"Did your supply run out?"

"Yeah."

"What did you do?"

"The neighbor noticed that mom's house was dark about three weeks after they were gone. She called the house, but the phone was shut off, so she called the power company and told them that the power was off in the house next door and that a disabled person lived in the house. She gave them mom's number. The power was left off, but the neighbor brought me warm meals for dinner.

"It was the first time that I had a warm meal in a long time. I'm used to not eating though. As a kid from the time that I was younger, I wouldn't eat a lot of food. It would piss off my dad when I had to eat with him, so I would just choose not to eat around him."

Max didn't know that Ashley is a psychologist. As Max was speaking to her, Ashley was jotting things down. "Tell me about the trial? Where did you go when you left the rehabilitation center?"

"I was arrested."

"Yes, I know that, but where did you go until the trial?"

"I was in a cell at the police station because I had special circumstances and the women's prison is on the second floor with no elevator. I was held for months. Then one day, they came and they got me and said that I was going for my hearing."

"Had you met with legal representation?"

"No."

"Did anyone come see you while you were locked up?"

"Your mom would come often to see how I was doing. She would bring me a book every once in awhile. But like the hospital and rehab no one came to see me."

"So how was it in the courtroom?"

"What do you mean?"

"Where was the witness stand?"

"To the right of the judge. So my left side was facing the judge."

"Did you hear any of the questions?"

"No. And even if I did, with my jaw wired shut, I couldn't answer them anyway. Then the big guy with his booming voice went and spoke to the jurors. I heard him then. But it didn't make sense to me what he was saying. I was so tired. I was hungry and thirsty. I didn't want people looking at me."

"At anytime did you hear him mention money…jewels…and drugs?"

"Yes," Max said. She put her head down on the table. "But I couldn't tell them that I didn't know what he was talking about. I couldn't tell him that I didn't understand. And then he went back on my left side so I moved to face him so I could try to see his lips and read his lips, but the court officer came over and straightened me out. He told me if I moved again that it would be over. I told him that I couldn't hear anything from my left ear.

"And then the jurors left the room. They came back an hour later. I heard them say guilty. The judge made me look at her. I saw her say house arrest and seven years. Then mom was there in the courtroom. Cuffs were put on me. Two officers took me out of the courtroom. I was put into a van and driven to mom's house. They got me out of the van, and they wheeled me into the house. Renovations had been made to accommodate the wheelchair. Ramps on both the front and back door. The bathroom door was made wider. The tub had a bench across it so I could shower.

"Mom said TV, the kitchen and outside were luxuries. My childhood bedroom wasn't there anymore. It was a gym. My room was a room I didn't recognize. The locks were on the outside of the door. There was a commode for when I had to go to the bathroom. After I had gone into the room when she left, she locked the door behind her, so I was locked in.

She would bring me cereal for breakfast and peanut butter sandwiches for lunch and then just water."

"How long did she keep you locked in your room?"

"I don't know exactly. There were no windows in that room, so I didn't know if it was day or nighttime."

"You basically were in solitary confinement at your mother's house?"

"Yeah," Max said.

"Did you tell anyone about this?"

"Who? There was no one to tell. At least not until the lady came to do the welfare check. She saw the conditions of where I lived at mom's house. It was supposedly reported."

"Tell me what happened after you exposed her of keeping you locked in your room."

"She was mad. She yelled at me that I'm worthless. I must have heard that I am hers and my father's biggest mistake and disappointment just about every day.

"She removed the bedroom door. I now had free roam of the house, but I still couldn't go in the kitchen. Even if I wanted to, I couldn't manage it. The way the fridge is positioned. The door is backwards."

"What do you mean?"

"Like here the door opens to the right because the freezer is on top. Mom's is the same, but the door opens to the left, but the wall is there, so I could never go see what was inside the fridge or get anything from it. She would leave the peanut butter on the counter with a knife, and a loaf of bread. There would be a bottle of water next to it."

Joanna had been in the other room listening. Grant too. Together they took wonderful notes. They allowed Max to talk to Ashley for as long as she wanted to.

"What was it like meeting your dad after all of these years?"

"I was scared."

"Scared of what?"

"Of how he would have reacted. Of what he would have said to me. I was afraid that he would have walked over to me and smacked me across the face. Like mom had done when I told her that I wanted to live with him when I was twelve. She left me this beauty, then she pushed and shoved me out of the house before she slammed and locked the door on me."

"What did she hit you with?"

"Her hand, but she always wore these dangle bracelets and one of them had prongs on them and that is what she got me with. It made a gash on my face."

"Tell me, where did you go when you left your mom's house?"

"To a coffee shop until they closed and then I went into an alley and stayed hidden between two of those giant trash bins. I had my sleeping bag and my elephant, so I felt safe. I wasn't in the dark. In the morning, I went to school like nothing had happened."

"Did anyone ask you about your cheek?"

"No. No one really cared. When school was over, I went to dance practice. It was the first time that I had gone by myself. It was the first time that I hadn't been yelled at in seven years. I went in there that day and I danced like I'd never had in my life. Hannah Grace, she's the coach, she was so impressed. Then I went to the local pool and took a shower and changed. After that I went to the coffee shop and did my homework.

"The coffee shop owner was the first to realize that I wasn't going home when I left her shop. But I made it through about five months before anyone noticed and no one came looking for me. The dance academy was paid for, so I went to dance every day, and I went to school. I had signed up for summer classes, so I kept my routine the same.

"I had won a scholarship for the dance academy two years later. The lady in the coffee shop gave me a job washing dishes and cleaning the shop at closing time. Sometimes she brought me home with her. She would make sure that I had new shoes when I needed them and new clothes too. She drove me when I had to take the SATs in Lees."

"What did you get on them?"

"I got a perfect score. On the ACTs too."

"So how come you didn't go to school?"

"Because I didn't have anyone to take me for the college tours. I had gone to one, but I was turned away because I was by myself. They said that I needed a parent with me. Then this woman came to talk to the school about going into the military. She named all the branches. She said that hard work would pay off and be rewarding. So I went and enlisted before I graduated high school. And I left for bootcamp a few weeks later. I sailed through bootcamp. I would do whatever I was told to do and run the drills by myself if I didn't do so well the first time around. I had taken an interest in the planes, so after bootcamp, I went to aviation school and then I started to fly for the Air Force."

"What did you do on leaves?"

"I stayed on base. I told my superior officers that I was an orphan, and I didn't have anywhere to go. It wasn't a lie. I would read and run drills every day. They made sure that I was eating.

"When others got care packages and mail from loved ones, it was the only time it really bothered me. The only thing I ever got in the mail was the returned letters that I wrote to my dad and to Gwen. But I didn't know her name back then, so I called her Steppy and then after awhile, I started to call her mom. I thought that maybe if we met that maybe she would or could convince dad to let me come live with them. I wrote to them for six years and I got every single letter back."

Ashley wiped a tear. "Did you keep the letters?"

"I gave them to Gwen yesterday. I doubt that she will read them or even show them to dad, but they are theirs anyway.

"Do you know what will happen to me?"

"No, Max. Not yet."

"I've still got four and half years left of my house arrest terms."

"Well, that's being looked into. What did you think about seeing your brother Logan tonight?"

"I was nervous. I think that he will try to turn me into the police so he and mom can collect the reward money."

"Max, you live with the sergeant of the police force right now and mom and dad and I won't let anything happen to you. What's going on. You seem sad."

"No. I'm ok. Will I have to go back and live with my mom again?"

Joanna and Grant came into the room. "No. Never," they said together.

Ashley looked at her parents. "If it's ok with you, I'm going to stay tonight."

"Yes, of course."

There was a knock on the door. Hank had come. Joanna let him in. "How is Max?"

"She's having a hard day today."

"Why what is going on?"

"Gwen had said that she was going to come today and then she didn't come. I think that Max was upset that you left. She was quiet most of the day. Ashley finally got her to eat a little while ago. Gwen, Matt, the two boys and her brother Logan came here this evening. Gwen said that Gunnar had to make sure that she was ok. He is the first one in the family to show her a sign of love. She is excited about it and scared all at once."

"I think Gwen loves her too."

"Max doesn't know how to handle this. She doesn't know how to wrap her head around it."

"Can I go see her?"

"Yes."

"Can I stay with her overnight again?"

"Yeah. That would be ok."

"Thank you, Jo."

Hank went and found Max. She was back in the room. She was staring out the window. Hank went to her. He got down on his knees next to her before he tapped her on the shoulder. She turned to see what it was. Seeing him, she smiled. She wrapped her arms around his neck. He wrapped his arms around her. Then he stood up with her in his arms. Max never let him go.

That night, when they got in bed together, Hank held Max. Sadness poured out of her and she cried. Hank rocked her slowly until she was asleep.

CHAPTER ELEVEN

Gwen read almost all of the letters that Max had written to both her and Matt. Max had sent home a total of six medals. Gwen was going to make sure that she had those back. Those were her honors and hers alone. When she finished reading the last of the letters, she brought the coffin like box into their bedroom. Matt had put the boys to bed, showered and now came into the room. "What is that?"

"These would be the letters from our daughter, Matt."

"The box?"

"She made this box on her one of her leaves so that she would have a place to store the letters that by then she was more than sure would be sent back to her from you. Matt, Max is a brilliant woman. She scored perfect scores on both the SATs and the ACTs. She graduated top of her class in high school, and yet there was no one there to celebrate it with her.

"The way she feels deprived, Matt, I do too. I only knew that you had Logan. You never once mentioned Max until Jackson was born. But why wouldn't you tell me? You are my best friend and I thought I was yours too."

"You are Gwen."

"But then how could you not tell me about this angel in your life."

"Because I never saw her that way. I saw her as my trap. And then when Des said she wasn't mine; I was relieved but hurt all at once."

"Matt, I am going to fight for this girl's rights, and I will fight to have her in our lives as well."

"Tonight, I didn't want to leave her, Gwen. She was so torn."

Matt stayed up all night reading every single one of the letters that Max had written. He placed each one back in its envelope and back in the order that he had found it in. When he picked the letters with her medals in them, he held them in his hand and squeezed it. He wondered why she would have written to them, but he was now grateful that he had read them.

In the morning, he had called the school to inform them that the boys wouldn't be there for the rest of week. Then Matt cooked breakfast for the family. As they trickled into the kitchen, he told them to get dressed, but not for school. When Gwen came in, Matt told her that he wanted all of them to go spend the day with Max at Joanna and Grant's. Watch movies, have a meal with her. Celebrate her.

"I want to give her back her medals," they said together.

"Then she should have them," Gwen said. "Did you ask Joanna and Grant about us spending the day with Maxine?"

"Yes, last night. They said it would be fine."

They went there. Gwen wanted to wait to give Max the plushy and now her medals until it was just them. When they got to the house, Max was going around the track. She didn't know that they were coming. Both Gwen and Matt watched her do lap after lap. "Is she ok?" Matt asked.

"She's better than she was," Grant said. "Yesterday, before you came, she wouldn't get out of bed. She just seems so lost, and we are at a lose of how we can help her."

"She's still not free to come and go on her own accord," Gwen said. "Since she has been out of rehab, she has been in jail and on house arrest. For a person who was a pilot and a dancer, this must be like hell and torture."

"Not to mention that now she is wheelchair bound for the rest of her life." Grant said.

Max came back to the house. She came in a bit winded. She saw them. "I…I didn't know…" she took a deep breath. "I didn't know that you were coming."

"We wanted to come spend the day with you," Matt said.

"Will you have to leave to get the boys?"

"No. The boys are with us."

"Let me go change and I'll be right back."

Max went into the bathroom, where she took a quick shower and then she got dressed. Her hair was wet when she came back into the kitchen. Max's hair was down. They saw how long and wavy it was. "Can I brush it for you?" Max was taken back by that. No one had brushed her hair since she was little.

"Yes," Max said. Her voice was small. "I'll go get the brush." Max left the room. She went in the room and came back with her hairbrush. Max handed it to Gwen.

"Have you always had long hair?"

"They make you cut your hair for bootcamp, so I had short hair then. It had to be neck length."

"How long did you fly for?" Matt asked.

"Five year and half years."

"Did you think of becoming an airline pilot?"

"No. I wanted to go to college."

"For what?"

"Psychology."

"You didn't want to be a dance instructor?" a little voice asked from behind them. Gunnar came around and hugged her. She picked him up and sat him on her lap. "You can still teach it if you wanted to," he said.

"I probably could," Max said.

"Would you like to watch a movie with us?"

"Yes, that would be so much fun."

"Go stay with Jackson for a little while longer and we will come in."

"Ok, mommy."

Gwen brushed Max's hair. She ran her fingers through it feeling the thickness. She brushed one side and then the other. She put her hands on Max's head and she could feel the depression on the left side of her head. As she now looked down at her from behind her, she could see where her jaw sunk in a bit on the left side. She now pushed Max's hair back to see the permanent indent that is a visible spot right above her ear. "Does that hurt?" Gwen said leaning down on her left.

"She can't hear you," Grant reminded her.

"What? Oh shit. Right. Damn."

"It's ok," he said. "She wouldn't know."

Gwen went in front of Max. She sat in a chair, so they were almost eye level. "Does that hurt?"

"My dent you mean?"

"Yes."

"Sometimes."

"What about your jaw?"

"Yeah. It hurts. Because of my situation, I couldn't get the follow up surgery."

"What?" Matt asked.

His tone startled Max. "And your back to yelling at me."

"No," Matt said. "No. What kind of surgery?"

"I don't know. To line it up a bit better I guess."

"What would have to be done for that?"

"Probably having it wired shut again."

"We will find out about it." Matt said.

"Can I press charges against Lucy?"

"Let's talk legal issues when the kids aren't here," Gwen said.

"Yeah. Of course. Right. I'm sorry."

"It's fine, Max," Gwen stated.

They went into the family room, where the boys were busy at the moment putting together a puzzle. Max went over joining them. They finished the puzzle twenty minutes later. "Let's watch a movie," she said.

The boys picked Top Gun. "No," Matt said.

"It's ok, dad. I don't mind."

"Will you sit with us on the couch?"

"Yes, Jackson."

They all watched Top Gun. "Did you ever fly your plane upside down?" Gunnar asked.

"Yes."

"Can planes fly backwards?" Jackson asked.

"There are some planes that can fly backwards, but no. My plane did not. It flew vertically though."

"What does that mean?"

"Well, usually planes fly horizontal, so it's like you are looking at the horizon line, but the plane that I flew, I could take it straight up and climb high into the air that way."

"Cool!" both boys said.

"Could you make it roll?" Jackson asked.

"Yeah. I did that."

"Did you ever have to jump out of it?" Gunnar questioned.

"My plane? No. But yes, I have jumped out of a plane."

"What was it like?" Gwen and Matt inquired together.

"Fast," Max said.

"Was something wrong with the plane that you had to jump out of it?" Jackson asked.

Max laughed. "No. It was just for training, so if I ever had to do it, I would know how."

"Was it fun?" Both boys asked with smiles on their faces.

"Ah. Yeah, but it was work. It takes a lot of training sessions and a lot of practice. It's like dance. The first time you get on the dance floor, you just can't suddenly start to boogie. It takes being taught and practicing it. It was a lot different in the service, but the same. You have to practice so that you know what you're doing. Nothing else can matter when you are behind the controls of a powerful jet like that. Distractions cause accidents to happen."

"Is that how your accident happened?" Jackson asked.

"No. My accident happened because someone wasn't trained right in using something that is very important to know how to use. Because of that, I got hurt."

"Did they get into trouble?"

"I don't know."

"Why did you get into trouble?"

"Because someone lied."

"When the truth comes out, will you not be in trouble anymore?"

"That's the plan," Max said.

"Who helps you with that?"

"Your mommy does."

"Are we related?" Gunnar asked playing with his hands.

"Yes."

"But how?"

"Because your daddy is my daddy."

"But mommy isn't your mommy."

"Yes and no," Max said.

"How can that be?"

"Because your mommy is married to our daddy, so though your mommy didn't have me like she had you two," Max said tickling them. "She is my mom though. It's called a stepmom, but your mom is too wonderful for the step part." Max said looking and smiling at Gwen.

"Will you ever call mommy mommy instead of Gwen?" Gunnar asked.

"I hope to maybe one day."

"But daddy is your daddy too?"

"Yes, Jackson. Your daddy and my daddy are the same person."

"What's your mommy like?"

"Let's change the subject," Gwen said.

"But mom," Gunnar said.

"My mom is set on how she is. She is different from your mommy. Your mom is wonderful and does wonderful things for other people."

"Ok," both boys said.

They went back to watching the movie. When it was over, Gunnar looked at Max. "What's your favorite movie? Max, what's your favorite movie?"

"I don't know," she said.

"Did you have a favorite TV show that you used to watch with daddy when you were my age?"

"I don't remember, Gunny. That was a long time ago."

"Come on guys," Gwen said.

"Are you leaving?" Max asked anxiously.

"No. We are going to have lunch together," Gwen said to her.

"What is your favorite lunch?" Jackson asked.

Max transferred into her wheelchair. "Cool," the boys said together. They went into the kitchen.

"Do you know how to cook?" Gwen asked.

"Yes," Max said laughing. "I lived by myself for quite some time. I picked up on a few things."

"Ok, smart ass," Gwen teased.

"Do you have a favorite stuffed animal?" Jackson asked. "I do. His name is Dillon the doggy. And Gunnar still sleeps with Ludwig the Lion. He keeps it tucked under his pill…"

"Shut up, Jackson."

"No, don't tell him to shut up. It's ok," Max said. "I still have something from when I was little. I sleep with it every night. It's old, but I still love it."

"What it is," Matt asked.

"The elephant that you gave me for luck when I started dance. Do you remember that?"

"Yes," he said. "You took it with you everywhere you went."

"Did it go with when you went to the service?"

"Yes, Gunnar. It went with me everywhere. It's lost its softness over the years. It would be cool to get another plushy to have, so I can hold it, hug it, squeeze it when I have not so great days."

The boys went running out of the room and chased each other around Joanna and Grant's house. This left Max in the kitchen with Matt and Gwen. They were preparing lunch.

"Do you have those?" Gwen asked.

"Yeah. I wasn't good yesterday."

"Why? What happened?" Matt asked.

"Sadness, dad. Sadness is debilitating. It's crippling to me with this already crippled body. There was a time when I would get sad and I would dance it out of me, but I can't do that anymore. Hell, I can't leave the confines of this house or this yard. But at least I can breathe here. I am not caged here as I was at mom's house.

"I don't understand what I've could have done that was so…"

Jackson came into the room and threw his arms around Max. "I love you." Max picked him up. His knees were on her thighs. She was supporting him as he threw his shoulders and head back. He threw his arms out wide.

"Jackson, no, you will hurt her!" Matt said.

"No. I'm ok. He's ok. I've got him." Jackson then straightened and looked at her. Then he leaned into her putting his head on her shoulder. He wrapped his arms around her. Max hugged and held him. "Will you always be my sister?"

"Yes, Jackson. I will always be your sister. And you will always be my baby brother."

"Logan has a little brother too."

"Yes. He has you and Gunnar."

"No," Jackson said. "There is another boy. He's younger than me. Is he your brother too?"

"Yes."

"Have you met him?"

"No."

"Have you met the snobby mean girls?"

"No," Max said. "I've met you and your adorable older brother," Max said tickling him.

"I'm so happy that we got to meet you."

"I am too."

"But will you leave again?"

"No, Jackson. I can't leave."

"Well, I don't want to ever leave you," he said.

He was so sweet. It made Max feel good about herself.

"Jackson, can you go find Gunnar please and tell him that lunch is almost ready. And then can you find Joanna or Grant and ask them where you can wash your hands?"

"Yep!" he said. "Ok. I have to leave you now, but it will just be for a short time." He kissed Max on the cheek and then tore out of the room.

Matt looked at Max. "So have you met your siblings? Max!"

Gwen looked up from cutting the meat. "Matt! You are on her left side. She can't hear you."

"Dammit!" he said. "I fucking did it again."

Grant came into the kitchen. "Everything ok in here?"

"Yeah. Fucking wonderful," Matt said. "Just the fact that I forget that she can't hear me."

"Only when you're on her left side."

"Is it a game that she is playing?"

"MATT!" Gwen yelled.

Max looked up and looked at them. She smiled at them. Then she lowered her head and went back to shelling edamame from their pods.

"No, Matt, it's not a game," Grant said. "I had her hearing checked. Even the highest sound frequency she couldn't hear. Now in her right ear, she heard a paper clip dropped, but on her left side, nothing."

"It's not nice to talk about someone in front of them," Gunnar said. "Even if they can't hear you."

"Where did we get this one from?" Matt playfully asked.

Max had a pain in her head and then her left ear started to bleed. "She's bleeding," Gunnar said.

"It's ok. Go stay with your brother please," Gwen said.

Grant grabbed a towel. "JOANNA!"

She came running in the kitchen. Max was trying to grab her ear. Blood ran from her ear. Gwen went behind her and put her arms around Max. "Mommy has you," she said softly in her right ear. "Mommy has you. Try to stay calm."

"It hurts."

"What hurts?"

"Inside. Oh, it hurts."

"Come on. We will take you," Matt said, and he lifted her in his arms. "Would you mind watching the boys?"

"No," Joanna said.

Gwen drove. Matt held Max. He held the towel against her ear. When they got to the hospital, they both ran in with her.

"She's deaf in her left ear," Gwen said. "She was fine and then she got a pain in her head and her ear started to bleed.

They gave Max something. "NO! I DON'T WANT TO BE PUT DOWN AGAIN!"

"What did she say?" a doctor asked coming into the room.

"NO. THIS HAPPENED LAST TIME TOO. I WAS GIVEN SOMETHING AND I WOKE UP A MONTH LATER. NO!"

"Max, it won't be like that this time." Gwen said.

"I'm sorry. I won't..." and she blacked out.

"Can someone please explain that to me?" the doctor said.

"She was an exquisite dancer," Matt said. "And then there was an accident that not only paralyzed her, but also made her lose her hearing in her left ear."

X-rays and scans were taken. A sist in her ear that had probably been putting pressure there for a long time had erupted. It was emptying out. The doctor wound up lancing it.

"Now she just needs to sleep off the sedative."

"Can she do that at the house?" Matt asked.

"Will that happen again?"

"It could. She will need to be on antibiotics for at least the next ten days. She has a wicked inner and middle ear infection. Has she been complaining about being in pain?"

"Not until the blood started to run out of her ear," Gwen said.

"That's Max Brandon," a woman said.

"Yes," Gwen said.

"It's so sad what happened to her. I was there that night. She seemed a little distracted before the show started. Almost as if she were waiting for someone or looking to see if she saw someone. But then the lights went out and when they came on again, she was ready to go. I had been to the show before. That night everything was perfect. She was flawless. And then there was a boom and it felt like the ground shook. Then the pop came and then a sound that I wish to never hear again in my life. She was high in the air and Elliot Berk was high on the balls of his feet. The other dancers had stopped. They were looking up, but Max couldn't look up. And then that thing with the light hit her with such force, it knocked her right out of Elliot's arms. Her body hit the stage floor with a thud. She wasn't yelling in pain. She just kept saying that she was trapped. The other dancers went running, but Lucy came back. With her back to audience, she kicked Max in the head. Her ear was bleeding almost like it was when you brought her in.

"The doctors had to cut her head because of how badly her skull was fractured. They inserted a plate in her head. She might have gotten some of her hearing back if not for her skull being as fractured as badly as it was. Her jaw was wired shut for about a year. Her lower spine was fused together. If it would have fallen on her leg or legs, they would have amputated her leg, but of course they could not amputate her lower torso. She was kept in an induced coma for eight weeks. When she woke up, she was moved the rehab center."

"How come her parents were never called?"

"You. You're her mother," she said talking to Gwen.

"No. I'm her stepmother."

"Well, her mother was called. Yet, she never came. A tall bulky man came just about every day to check on her. He would sit with her and hold her hand. He would move her legs for us."

Hank came into the hospital. "Is Max ok? Why is she knocked out?"

"Her ear exploded," Matt said.

"My god! Is she ok?"

"It's you!" the lady said.

"What?" Hank asked.

"You are the one who came with her when she was injured. You came and saw her every day. You would hold her hand and you would stretch her legs. You never missed a day while she was here. What is your name?"

"Trent," he said.

"When she woke up, before she was moved, she asked for you. She asked for the man that held her hand when she was brought in."

"Does she have to stay overnight here?"

"No. She will need to take it easy for the next few days, but she can go home."

Trent came in the room and lifted her into his arms. The three of them walked out with her. Matt now got into the driver's seat. Gwen sat in the backseat. Trent laid Max on the seat. Her head resting on Gwen's lap.

"I'll follow you back to the house and then carry her in if you like."

"Yes, thank you," Matt and Gwen said together.

"We need to fill her prescriptions."

"Ok," Matt said.

He glanced back seeing his daughter and he envisioned her younger. Smaller. Laying across the backseat going on and on about a new dance move. Speaking about a little girl named Lucy. "She's jealous," he heard Max say. "She's not bendable, daddy." He had yelled at her that the word was flexible. Max clammed up and didn't say anything else.

"Matt?"

"Yes."

"Are you ok?"

"Yes. I was just thinking back."

"What about?"

"To Max. She was probably Jackson's age. She had been telling me about a girl who couldn't do a new dance move. Gwen, I yelled at her so badly. She didn't cry, but she stopped talking to me. I should have made things right with her."

"You still can, Matt."

"But all of those years are lost."

"She is still looking for your love, Matt. For your acceptance."

"At the house, you told her that mommy is here."

"Yes, I did. You read the letters. You know that if I would have known of her, her life would have been different."

Matt stopped at the pharmacy. Gwen stayed in the car with Max, who slept soundly. Hank came and sat in the front seat with them.

"Did she tell you about the letters that she wrote to her father and I?"

"Yes. How they were returned to her."

"She gave them to me the other day. I read all of them."

"I wish I would I have met her before that day," Hank said.

"I know what you mean."

Max cried out in her sleep. Hank jumped out of the front seat and opened the backdoor. Max said, "Mommy."

"I'm here, sweetheart," Gwen said. "What's wrong?"

Max opened her eyes. "I'm going to be sick. I'm going to throw up."

Hank got her out of the car. He held her crouched over as Max heaved and retched. Matt came out with the medications and saw that she was sick. Gwen was standing right next to her. She was rubbing Max's upper back.

"Here. Max, you need to drink," Matt said. He kicked a pile of dirt over the mess on the ground. "Max, you need to drink, honey." Matt opened the bottle of juice. "Small sips."

"Mom," Max said.

"I'm right here." Gwen took her in her arms. "I'm right here, Maxine."

"I want to run and dance right now."

"She's high," Hank said. "Let me call Jo and tell her that we can't bring her back to the house. Can we bring her to your house?"

"Of course," Gwen and Matt said together.

"I WANT TO RUN AND DANCE RIGHT NOW? WHY CAN'T I DO IT? WHY?"

"Max, it's going to be ok," Matt said.

"IT WILL NEVER BE OK, DAD. I WANT MY BODY TO WORK AGAIN. I WANT…" Max passed out.

"Max? Max?"

"She'll be ok, Matt. It will wear off. This has been coming for almost four years now. She has been caged inside her own body and within your ex-wife's house. She needs to let the emotion, the anger, and everything else that needs to come out of her come out. She needs to say whatever needs to be said. No matter what," Hank said. He called Joanna. "They gave her something at the hospital and now she is starting to come off of it stoned."

"Are you fucking kidding me?"

"No, Sergeant. She's stoned. She's puking. She's loud. She just passed out."

"Grant will come. I will keep the little ones here. I will call Ashley and Rebecca to come over."

"We are going to take her to Gwen and Matt's house."

"Grant is coming now."

"We will see him there."

"Keep me posted."

"Sure."

They took Max to Matt and Gwen's house. Max came around. "NO. I DON'T WANT TO GO BACK THERE."

"Max, honey, this is dad's and my house."

"NO. HE DOESN'T WANT ME. HE HATES ME. I TRAPPED HIM. I WAS HIS FUCKING MISTAKE. I WAS HIS FUCKING DISAPPOINTMENT."

"Max, I'm sorry that I ever said those words to you."

"DID YOU EVER FIND OUT."

"Find out what?"

"AM I REALLY YOUR GODDAMN KID?"

"Yes, Maxine. You are my only daughter."

Max let out a long scream and then passed out.

Some of their neighbors had heard what was going on. "Matt? Gwen? Is everything ok?"

"Yes," they said together.

"Should we call the police?"

"No. No please don't do that."

"Well, then can you keep her from yelling?"

"Yes."

They brought her in the house. They put her in a bed. Sweat beaded on her body.

Round three of the yelling started at two in the morning. "I WANT TO RUN AND DANCE. WHY CAN'T I DO IT? WHY WON'T MY BODY WORK. WHY DID THIS HAPPEN? I WANT TO DANCE. I WANT DAD TO SEE ME DANCE."

One of the neighbors called the police. They responded with no lights or sirens. Grant and Hank explained the situation to them. "She needs plenty of fluids to flush it out of her system."

"We are giving her fluids," Matt said.

"Do you know what they gave her?"

"I think it was a sedative," Gwen said. "She's paralyzed. She used to be a dancer and now she can't."

Max woke up again. "PLEASE END MY LIFE," she cried.

"What?" Everyone in the house said together.

Gwen went to Max and took her in her arms. Max screamed and cried. Gwen held her the whole time. Max threw her head back screaming and crying. "No one was there for me. I had to do this all by myself and then I had to go live with that cunt of a mother that I was granted to have. I HATE MY LIFE. WHY DOESN'T ANYONE LOVE ME? I WAS TOSSED AWAY LIKE A PIECE OF FUCKING SHIT TRASH. The dead turtle got a better send off then I did."

Max got the chills that shook her to the core. Gwen called Matt to bring in an extra blanket. She bundled Max up. She stayed with her all night long. Giving her fluids and making sure she was comfortable. Matt had come into the room at five in the morning when Max was wide awake.

She stared up at the ceiling. He sat on the bed with her and took her in his arms. Gwen had fallen asleep.

"When…"

"Shh. It's going to be ok, Max," Matt said. He turned the soft light on above the bed. He pushed Max's hair back off of her forehead. He felt the track line scar from where her head had been cut opened for them to put a plate in her head. He bent his neck and kissed her. Then he read a book that he would reluctantly read to her as child. He read her *Where The Wild Things Are*. Max was quiet. She listened.

"You used to tell me that I was your wild child."

"I read your letters that you wrote to me and Gwen."

"Can she be my mom too?"

"Yes, Max."

"Dad, I want my life back. I want to dance and run. I want to climb and fly through the air. I want to be free. I don't know the things that were taken." Max cried. "It didn't make sense what he was saying that I did. And then he went on my left side." Max brought her hand up and smacked herself in the head.

"No. Don't do that."

Max cried. "She kicked me so fucking hard that my skull vibrated, dad. Everything rattled. My teeth and jaw felt like they were knocked out. And then the blood started to come out of my ear. Everything went muffled and then there was nothing. I can't hear the music anymore on my left side. I can't…" she sobbed.

"Max, you have to look at the things that you can do."

"What though? I can't do shit because they fucking lied. I swear, dad, I never took anything." Max brought her hand up to her head and pulled her hair up revealing the line that ran from her temple, over her ear, down the side of her head and around to the other side. "Dad, they kept fucking with the lines. Elliot, Scott, and I tightened them an hour before the show. Everything was weighted correctly."

"What were you looking for?"

"What?"

"That night. Someone told us that you were looking for something. What were you looking for?"

"You. I left tickets for you, Gwen and the boys."

Max drifted off to sleep and she slept soundly until one in the afternoon. She got up and got into her chair. She went into the bathroom, where she peed for the first time in over a day. Then seeing the bench in the shower, she undressed and took a shower. She stayed under the water for a long time. When she was done showering, her fingers were as wrinkled as prunes. She went into the room, where Gwen had laid out clean clothes for her. Max dressed and then went exploring the house. She found the boys' room. They shared a room. Then she found Gwen and Matt's room. Max just looked in from the doorway. After that, she went to go find them.

"Can I please have something to eat?"

"Yes. What would you like?"

"Anything," she said to Gwen.

"How are you feeling?"

"My head feels loopy."

"Here. Drink this and I'll make you something."

"Oh, what about the boys?"

"They are with Joanna."

"They must think that I am a freak."

"No, they don't think that," Grant said. "When's the last time you were stoned or high."

"What do you mean? I've never done drugs."

"Max, come on. Tell the truth."

"Grant, I am. The first time I smoked pot, I was in the service. I did it one time and that was enough for me."

"Have you been taking the random drug screenings?"

"I didn't know about that," Max said.

"What will we tell the judge about your conditions of the agreement to your terms of house arrest, Maxine?"

"What terms? What conditions? My conditions sucked worse than jail. I know. I was there for four months after being arrested. At Desiree's I was locked in a room. Not my childhood bedroom. No. That was turned into a gym after I left. Instead, I was locked in a room with no windows and a fucking commode to use if I had to go the bathroom. I was given cereal and peanut butter sandwiches to eat and that was it.

"I didn't know if it was day or night. I didn't know if it was sunny or raining outside. I lived that way for like six months. Maybe more. Then she takes the family on vacation… ok, I'm not stupid. I knew I couldn't have gone with them…but she takes the family on a two-week cruise leaving me just enough food to last till they get back, then the cunt takes them for a fucking month and leaves me with no phone and no lights. The bitch left me with no power. And there was nothing I could do. Nowhere I could go. No one I could call.

"After that, what can be worse? The streets weren't even that fucking harsh and I know because for six years I lived on them. She told me that she was going to make my worthless life hell, and she proved it.

"And now Logan after all these years wants to come see me. He probably wants the goddamn reward money for turning me in. I know that there is a bounty on my head. Grant, you are the one who took the ankle monitor off of me. I didn't remove it."

"Max," Matt asked. "What accommodations need to be made for here?"

Max looked at her father. "What now?"

"What renovations need to be made so that our house is accessible for you?"

"I don't know," she said with a small voice.

"How was the bathroom? Does it need to be larger. More room to maneuver your chair in?"

"Maybe." She lowered her head and tried not to cry, but the tears came.

Gwen sat in a chair and gently pulled Max closer to her and then took her in her arms. "You cry all you want," she said to her. Max put her face toward Gwen's neck and cried hard. Matt, Grant, and Hank left the room. They left both women sitting there hugging each other and crying.

When Max was brought back to Joanna and Grant's house, she went to find the boys. "Are you ok now?" Gunnar asked. "You had blood coming out of your head."

"I know," Max said. "Was it gross?"

"We just learned about volcanoes in school and it looked like the one that bubbles up and then pours out."

"What?" Max asked. "I've got to see this."

"Come. I'll show you," Gunnar said taking her hand and pulling her into the kitchen where Gwen was talking to Joanna. "Excuse me please," Gunnar said rocking on his feet but never letting go of Max's right hand. "Can I please use your phone to show Max something."

Gwen had turned to her son. "What do you want to show her?"

"What her ear looked like yesterday, so she will know, mommy."

Max sat him on her lap when Gwen gave him the phone. He went to the search engine and typed in *Types of Volcanoes* and then he found the one that he had mentioned and played it for Max.

"What?" Max said. She shifted Gunnar so he was now looking at her. "This is what my ear looked like yesterday?"

The boy laughed and laughed.

"Mom, did he answer? I didn't hear him answer." Gunnar was laughing so hard now. "Are you telling me that is what it looked like?"

"Yessss," Gunnar hissed out through his state of laugher.

"What does it look like now?"

"An ear again," Gunnar laughed out.

"Hey, didn't you promise me a piece of your brownie yesterday?"

"Yes," Gunnar said.

"Well, what the hell happened to it?"

"I ate it. It's in here," the boy continued to smile and laugh all at once. "It's in where?"

"Here," Gunnar said pointing to his belly.

"Here? This particular spot?"

"Yep!" Gunnar said.

Max put her hand on that spot and tickled him. Laughter filled the house. Max played with Gunnar awhile longer. "So it's here?" she asked pointing to another spot.

"No," he said. "It's right here."

"Oh, so it's here?"

"Yes," he said still laughing and having the best time. Max tickled him again. Gwen and Joanna were laughing as well. Then Gunnar got on his knees. He turned on Max's lap and he hugged her. The embrace was settling for Max. "I love you to infinity," Gunnar said. Max had never heard that. She hugged her young brother. Gunnar snuggled into her arms and closed his eyes.

Matt, Hank, and Grant had been watching the whole thing as well. Gunnar had nestled himself right into Max's arms. He closed his eyes. They watched Max bring him to a sitting position on her lap. His head now rested on her chest. His hands sat atop her shoulders. Max held him in her arms.

CHAPTER TWELVE

A trial date had been set. Gwen had taken the boys to school and then she came to see Max. She brought the bag with her, for it was the first time that she was alone with her since the first time she met her. Gwen wore the necklace with the two Mother and Daughter hearts on it. Max was still in bed when she came. Dale was at the house because his parents both had to go to work and with Max being on house arrest, she couldn't be left alone in the house. Dale was on his computer when Gwen came to the house. He was working from home that day. Gwen knocked on the door. Dale answered it.

"Am I not at the right house?"

"No. You are. My parents had to go to work and Ashley is out of town for the next few days. I'm Dale."

"Hi, Dale, I'm Gwen."

"The lawyer slash stepmom."

"Yeah, that's me. Where is Max?"

"She's in the bedroom. She's in bed still."

"Why?"

"Dad put the monitor back on her ankle today."

"Dammit!"

"Yeah, that's what I said too," he said. "I mean I understand she's on house arrest, but where the fuck is she going to go. With it on, she can't go beyond the front or back doors."

"Why did he do it?"

"Mom told him to."

"But why? Was she talking about leaving to go anywhere?"

"I don't know the particulars other than mom told him to do it and he did and now she's staying hidden away in the room. She's spunky. I like her. Also mom found out that she had…um well you know. That's not permitted."

"Can I see her?"

"Yes, of course."

Gwen came into the house. She went into the bedroom. She put the bag down on the bed. "What are you doing, Max?"

"Nothing."

"Get up. We have things to work through."

"I can't get fresh air anymore."

"Max, it won't be long."

"Joanna," Max said with anger and tears. "She came in this morning and she was screaming at me."

"Why?"

"Because they saw us on the cameras."

"What?" Gwen sat on the bed.

"There are cameras. Grant was watching the tapes before he deletes them or does whatever he does with them, and he saw Trent and I having sex. He showed it to Joanna, and she came in here yelling at me. Then Grant came in and said because I didn't know how to behave the monitor is going back on." Max saw the bag that Gwen had brought. "What's in the bag." Gwen gave it to Max. Max pulled out the new stuffed elephant. She looked it over and then she hugged it tight. She reached for Gwen, who moved closer. They hugged each other. "You really read my letters. And you're wearing the necklace that I got for you. Thank you. Thank you, so much."

Lucy, Scott, Dean, Mike, Brian, and Shawn met.

"I wouldn't serve her," Mike said.

"She used to be our best friend," Dean said.

"We need to come clean," Shawn stated. "We need to the tell the police that Max is and always was innocent."

"I'm not going to jail for that bitch."

"No, you would rather have her take the fall and get locked up for what you started, Lucy."

"Shut up, Scott."

"No one was supposed to get hurt," Brian said.

"Hurt. She could have been killed. We were her friends. We had been there for her when she got kicked out of her mom's house and when her dad didn't want her either," Scott said.

"Were we really?" Lucy questioned. "Max was thrown out and living on the streets and no one fucking knew that for almost a year. I was the one who went to her mom's house to drop off something Max left behind. Her mom told me that Max no longer lived there. We didn't know. Hannah didn't know."

"She knew about the heist," Shawn said.

"Everyone knew except for Max. Miss goody too shoes wouldn't steal a fucking candy bar if she were starving. She thought she was better than us," Dean said.

"Well, Lucy brought the crew in?"

"They said they knew what they were doing, Mike."

"Well, did they, Lucy?"

"Why did you kick her in the head?" Shawn asked.

"I thought it would knock her out."

"You made her go fucking deaf," Mike said. "Were you trying to decapitate her?"

"How would I sink her? We weren't on the water."

"No, not capsize her you idiot. Decapitate her."

"What the fuck does that mean?"

"LUCY! Take her head off."

Elliot and Genevieve showed up. "So the groups all here now," Genevieve said. "Lucy, we need to move the money again and then switch where the drugs are too."

"Why do we still have it after all these years?" Elliot said.

"NO ONE WAS SUPPOSED TO GET HURT!" Brian said again.

"I'll move the money and the goods tomorrow," Lucy said. "Brian, get over yourself."

"You purposely hired that crew, Lucy."

"You're right. I did. The regular crew would have never gone for it."

"But why wasn't Hannah there that night?"

"She had asked that we not preform that night," Elliot said to Shawn's question.

"Why not?"

"One of the tramps wasn't working right. If Xine would have gone down on it, it could have broken her leg."

"Then she wouldn't be paralyzed or deaf right now," Genevieve said. "Elliot, why didn't you tell us?"

"Because I was mad at Max."

"Why?"

"Because she was a slut!" Lucy said.

"She never slept around, Luc. I did, but she didn't. Max was choosing to leave us to go off to college. I didn't want her to go. She was insistent. I wanted to hurt her."

"You two damn near killed her," Brian said. "We can't continue to let her take the blame for this shit."

"Well, I'm not doing time for a prank," Lucy said. She crossed her arms over her chest.

"She was our friend. We were all like family," Dean said.

"She left us for six years," Lucy stated. "She never came home when she was on break."

"Leave."

"What?"

"It's leave. Not break."

"Oh my god, Mike. Shut up!"

"Get a brain, you stupid ass."

"Fuck off."

"No, Lucy, you did all of this to Max."

"We are all involved, Mike. We all planned the heist. Get the money, the drugs, and the jewels. Xine had no clue what was going on. She would come into rehearsal and just be ready to dance. We would come into rehearsal looking for the payout. The only one who ever made money off of us was Hannah. And the only one who never seemed to mind was Xine. Xine would come in even when she was having a bad day or whatever and come in and dance her heart out. She always came in to dance.

"Her parents divorced…she danced. Her mom cut her face and threw her ass out…she danced. She graduated top of our class…she danced. She enlisted in the fucking Air Force…she danced. She came home and rejoined us…she danced."

"She used it as an out," Jack said coming into their meeting.

"Where have you been?" Elliot asked.

"Around."

"Did you see her?" Brian asked.

"No, man, I don't know where she is."

"What do you mean? She's at her mom's house on house arrest." Shawn stated.

"No, bro, she's off that now." Mike said.

"What?" Jack asked.

"Bro, my diner is in Lees. She was there. I wouldn't serve her. I threw her ass out of there. I called the boys in blue and they came and took that tramp away."

"Could we get busted for burning her apartment into the ground?" Genevieve asked.

"That wasn't supposed to happen," Brian said.

"Well, man, the unthinkable things happened. Xine was paralyzed and we couldn't afford to stay in her apartment without her," Jack said.

It was Genevieve, who had gone to the police station and turned herself in. "Who is dealing with the Brandon case?" Joanna looked up from her desk. "Is it you?"

"Yes, I'm on that case," she said. "Who are you?"

"I…I used to dance with Xine," she said. "My name is Genevieve Dawsonboroson but Dawson for short. I'm Genevieve Dawson"

"Let's go talk in a private room."

Genevieve carried a bag of some of the stolen jewels, money, and drugs into the room.

"What do you have there?"

"It was a prank that night," Genevieve said. "No one was supposed to get hurt. When the lights went out prior to us starting, we went around and stole things."

"Was everyone involved?"

"Everyone but Xine. She didn't know. It was going to be her last dance with us for awhile, but we didn't know. Only Elliot knew that. Xine was going to go to college. The trampolines weren't working right. Hannah told this to Elliot. He never told us that. He said that we could dance anyway."

"How was it a prank?"

"The rail was supposed to come crashing down, the lights would go off, everyone would run away. The stuff was already put in Xine's bag, but it was only to get her to stay with us and not leave us again."

Jack came into the police station. He too turned himself in. One by one they came in. Dean, Scott, Mike, and Brian. Then Shawn came in too. The only two who hadn't come in were Elliot and Lucy. They told the same story in different versions.

"When the light and the rail hit Xine…Maxine, that's when the shit got real," Mike said.

"Did Max know about it?"

"No. If she did, she would have never been there that night."

"Did your coach know about it?"

"I don't think so," Mike said. "She knew that there was something wrong with the tramps, so she told the usual crew that the show was going to be postponed. Elliot told us different earlier in the day. Lucy got the new crew. She said that they worked with her brother on projects before, but they came in and didn't know shit. Maxine told them to stop messing with the ropes. She was hungry. We went to eat after running it through one more time. It was perfect. She was flawless. We went to eat. When we went back, she wanted to change, but if she would have, she would have found the loot in her bag. She would have been major pissed off.

"I don't want to go to jail for this."

"Who did it?"

"Lucy and Elliot. Elliot had asked Max to marry him, and she said no. Lucy was jealous because Elliot wanted Max, yet Lucy wanted Elliot.

"Elliot wanted to show Max that we were all family and that family sticks together."

"Where did you keep the stash?"

"At Max's in the first hall closet. The plan was for Max to find it a few days later and then touch everything. We all stayed in the apartment. Lucy split up the goods so that there were now multiple bags. They were scattered about at Max's.

"There was a sweep done by the police. A bag with the loot in it was found in Max's original bag. Then we heard that she was out of rehab and that she had been arrested. She couldn't speak because her mouth was wired shut. She couldn't hear anything on the left side because of what happened. She had problems keeping her head up. The lawyer kept going on her left side as if testing her to see if she turned her head to see if she was messing around. She had started to cry. The judge said house arrest."

"So were you all there?"

"No. I was though."

"Why now?"

"Why now what?"

"Mike, why come forward now?"

"Because I saw her. I watched her. It's Max. She still there inside there, but she's different. But she still has that heart of gold, and compassion, and kindness. It was a prank," he said. "No one was supposed to get hurt." He looked at Joanna. "Lucy and that crew did that to her. Lucy wanted to be the one in the air, but she's not and never has been as graceful as Max."

"Thank you for coming in."

"Wait! I can go."

"For now," Joanna said.

She had to let him go though she didn't want to because the case was still open. Joanna met with her captain, who had been listening. They all had been able to leave. Genevieve came back. "Can we see Max?"

"No," the captain said. "Max cannot have visitors at this time."

Mike came back in as well. "Can we see Max?"

"No," the captain said again. "Max cannot have visitors at this time."

"Did she get into more trouble?"

"Well, son, she violated her terms of house arrest."

"But her mom kicked her out," Mike defended her. "Max lived on the streets for six years of her life because her parents divorced and her mom threw her out. Who throws a twelve-year-old kid out? I begged my parents to take her in. She was such a great kid, but they didn't want to get involved because of her mother. I think it was the same with all of us. But the thing about Max, no one knew about her circumstance for like six months or longer.

"I feel so awful what I did to her in Lees," Mike said. "I was or am mad that Max got hurt. I shouldn't have taken it out on her though. I had her arrested in front of her family. I don't know the last time she saw them, but I felt bad, so I didn't want to look at her," he said.

"Listen. You and your friends might want to get legal assistance."

"Yeah. Right. Thank you, sir."

Mike left. They all left. "What did he say?" Dean asked.

"To get legal assistance," Mike answered.

"But you saw her right Mike?"

"Yes."

"How did she look? Is she deformed?"

"Yeah, Gen, she is deformed. She can't move her legs. She can't walk and she's fucking deaf in her left ear from Lucy driving a steel toed shoe right to the side of Max's head as if it were a recycled metal can."

Elliot and Lucy were arrested later that day. The merchandise was all turned in now by the others. Though they would be marked as accomplices, they were all complainant and wanting to do the right thing. It was found out that Lucy was the fire starter to Max's apartment. She thought that she was going to destroy all of the evidence not knowing that Elliot had moved everything out of Max's apartment and to the studio. There were other things that were now in evidence that there was no way Max could have or would have known about. Lucy's stash had dated back to when they were kids. Things had gone missing, and no one ever thought that the adorably cute little Asian girl was responsible. Necklaces, rings, watches, earrings, neck ties, cufflinks, charms, awards, team jackets from competitions. There was a slew of evidence. Things that Max had been blamed for. Things that Matt had yelled at her for taking, and yet Max hadn't had a clue what he was even talking about.

When Gwen told Matt, he cupped his face. "I would angrily search her bag, Gwen. She started dancing at five. Hannah Grace stopped me one day and she told me that a pink my little pony watch had been stolen from another girl. They thought that maybe Max would have taken it. She had her bag on her shoulder. I tore it off of her shoulder. I pulled her jacket off her in front of everyone. I ripped her jacket going through her pockets and the lining. She watched big eyed. She watched me destroy her stuff looking for a watch that was never found."

"It's been found now," Gwen said.

"A few months later, Hannah came to Desiree and told her that a butterfly pin had been taken. She was told that Lucy saw Max with it and saw her tuck it into one of her socks. That night, I spanked her for stealing and for lying. She didn't know what I was referring to. By then I was yelling at her constantly and not listening to her or hearing what she was saying.

"In that little kid's way, she tried to tell me that it wasn't her."

Max took pencil to paper and drew an elegant dancer with her arms spread high above her. As she drew the body, she made it in a wheelchair. There was no face on the dancer. She left it sitting on the table. Joanna saw it when she came in that evening. Dale was still at the house.

"Where is our house mate?"

"She had a visitor today. The lawyer slash stepmother. She stayed awhile and then Max and I watched some of a movie together. She asked for paper and pencil. She sat at the table a long time. For the most part, she has been quiet though. She's in the bedroom now."

"Did she eat today?"

"Yes, mom. I made sure she ate today."

Joanna went to the table and looked at the picture that under it read: *JUST A FUCKING DREAM!* Next to the picture there was a letter to her and Grant.

March 2021

Sergeant Norris and Grant,

I am so sorry that I disrespected your hospitality. You took me in, and I am most appreciative. I know that if you hadn't, I would be locked up somewhere.

I am not an infant, who needs to be watched every minute of the day. I will not leave your house without permission. I never left my mother's house although there were times when I really and truly wanted to. I have done everything that you have asked or told me to do.

As for having sex in your house, I am not sorry. It's the first time that I have been in the arms of a man since the accident. I've missed that part of my life along with dancing. I know that you have heard Lucy and Mike both refer to me as a slut, but I was never. Prior to sleeping with Trent in your house, I have only ever been with one other person and that was Elliot. We were never in the traditional relationship. We were friends who satisfied each other in times of need. I stopped fooling around with him when I found him with Lucy.

I am thankful for the hospitality and kindness that you have showed me. I truly lived with a Nazi warden, who abused her power of detainer. I am grateful for all that you both are doing for me. I am scared of what will happen if and when my house arrest days are over. Where will I go? Who would want to be around me? Will my dad bail again? Will they close this chapter and move on with their lives without me? What will become of me?

I have said over and over, and I will keep saying it until I am truly heard. I have never taken a thing in my life. Even when I was in the service and someone's family sent a care package (which I never received one) of cookies or brownies and everyone was told to help themselves, I never indulged. It wasn't mine. It didn't belong to me. I didn't touch it.

My whole life has been a form of a punishment. Being born to save my parents relationship. (I couldn't do it.) Becoming a dancer. (It only pissed my father off even more.) And then I ultimately punished myself from my family at twelve. I took myself right out of their equation and though I was alone and I was lonely, I was free. I went into the service and I became even more free. I could then fly. Just me and my bird. Oh how we danced high up in the clouds together. But when it came down to it and time for business, I was there full force. Full on. And then my six years was up. I made the decision to come back and try to put myself back into a world I left behind. I hooked back up with old friends, who were supposed to be my family. And then BAM! The accident happened and WAM! I'm all alone again. There to pick up the pieces of myself. There to figure out what the fuck is going to happen next. I get through rehab. Life is looking up again and SLAM! I'm in jail. Then court. Then back to the mouse trap I knew as home once upon a time, but it's not my home. Instead, it's my cage. It's my hell. You freed me from there, and I am ever so grateful.

You didn't have to yell at me. I am sorry that I disrespected you both in your lovely, comforting home, but again I am not sorry for having a heated and exquisite rendezvous with Trent. It was heated and passionate and it made me feel something deep within me.

I am forever grateful.

Maxine Brandon

Joanna went into the bedroom. Max was sleeping. Joanna sat on the bed and woke her up. Joanna undid the ankle monitor. "Get up and come with me." Max did without speaking. Joanna knew that Grant wanted to be the one to show her and to give her a present, but Joanna didn't think it could wait. She brought Max out to the garage, where Grant had installed a dance floor.

Grant pulled in just as they were getting ready to go in. Joanna stopped Max. They now waited for Grant to join them. Grant took the opportunity being on Max's left side to speak. "What changed your mind?"

"I'll show you when we go inside," she said to him.

They went into the garage together. Grant flipped on the light switch. A lite-up radio glowed neon blue on a table. There were two large speakers on the floor on either side of the table. Grant tapped Max, so she turned to look at him. "It's also a CD player, so you can play whatever you like."

"Thank you so much," she said. "This is wonderful."

"The doors are always unlocked until the last person is in for the night," Grant said to her. "So you enjoy yourself for as long as you like."

"Oh, thank you. Thank you so very much."

Grant kissed her on the head before he took Joanna's hand and they left Max to be alone in the garage. Max turned backwards and pulled back on the wheels going backwards around the space. Then she turned and started to move in circles before she went into the middle of the floor and she let out a piercing scream and she sobbed a hardy cry. She had her head back and her arms hung spread apart pointing down and she just cried and cried. Max cried till the tears stopped coming. She cried her tear ducts dry. She wiped the moisture off her face and then she started to try to move this way and that way and in patterns. Forming shapes and lines.

She hadn't known that Matt and Gwen came to the house that evening. They both now stood in silence and in complete awe as they watched Max flutter and glide with elegance and grace. When she was done, she heard the clapping. She spun around and saw them watching her. She put her hands on her wheels and pushed herself hard and fast over to them. Matt reached for her though she was hot and sweaty. He lifted her into his arms and then he and Gwen just held her together. They hugged her and they all three cried.

"You are beautiful," Matt said.

"You are breathtaking to watch," Gwen said.

Matt put Max back down in her chair. He looked at the dance floor. He walked to the middle of it and held out his hand. "Maxine Brandon, can I have this dance?" Max pushed herself to join him on the floor. Matt took her hand. Max was looking up at him. She closed her eyes and envisioned herself standing there in his arms. It was her first ever father-daughter dance. As they danced, Matt was aware of the tears that sat like dew droplets on a flower on his daughter's cheeks. She slowly opened her eyes and blinked at tears that clouded her vision. When the dance was over, Matt got down on one knee and took Max in his arms. She cried softly in his arms. He heard her thank him and say how she has always waited for her father-daughter dance.

The trial started on a Tuesday. Jurors were brought in and chosen to hear the cases. This would be two cases bundled together. The jurors would be sequestered for the length of the trial. Max was questioned the very next day.

"Please state your name for the record," Gwen asked her.

"Maxine Josephine Brandon, but I go by Max."

"Please tell us for the record about the last night that you danced."

Max went through all of the details. She told about their coach being mad, but she didn't know exactly why. She told about the new crew and how incompetent they were. She spoke about how Elliot, Dean, and herself had yelled at them numerous times to stop playing around with the lines. She brought up how her bag had been moved prior to the show starting. And then she spoke about that incredible unforgettable moments that altered her life forever. She heard the gasps and winces as she went on with her story.

"Max, do you know who kicked you in the head?"

"Yes, ma'am," Max said.

"Please tell the court who is responsible for doing that."

"It was Lucy."

"Do you know Lucy's last name?" The judge asked.

"Smutbrook I think."

There was laughter in the gallery. "That's enough everyone," the judge said. "Young lady, is that really her last name?"

"Yes, your honor," Max said.

"Is Ms. Smutbrook in the court?"

"Yes, your honor."

"Can you please point to her?" Gwen said.

Max looked and pointed right at Lucy. "Please stand up and state your name for the record," the judge said.

"My name is Lucia Smutbrook, your honor. I go by Luc or Lucy."

"Thank you. You may sit down. Please continue on Ms. Brandon."

Max became a bit emotional. "I was pinned down on the stage. I knew that by back was crushed. I knew that I was paralyzed, for I should have been in pain. I should have been screaming and crying from the pain, but there wasn't any pain. I was on my stomach, pinned to the ground by a light and the rail that held it. Everyone went running. Lucy went running, but then she came back and with her back to the audience, she stopped about a foot away from my head. Then she brought her right leg back like a field goal kicker does and she kicked me as hard as she could right in the side of my head. I felt instant pain in my head. In my ear and then there was a popping inside my head and after that blood started to flow from my ear. I went deaf right there on that stage."

"Max, did you ever see stacks and stacks of money?"

"No."

"Did you ever see lost jewelry?"

"No."

"What about the drugs? Did you ever see drugs?"

"No."

"Were you ever blamed in the past for taking lost or stolen items?"

"Yes," Max said.

"When?"

"When I was five or six and just becoming a dancer. Another girl in the group had had a pink watch and after practice it was no longer in her bag. Some of the other kids said that I took it."

"Could you describe the watch?"

"I thought I did," Max said. "It was pink."

"What color pink?"

"I don't know."

"What was printed on the watch?"

"Printed on it? I don't know."

"What color pink was it?"

"It was pink. That is all I know."

"Were you also accused of stealing a pin?"

"Yes," Max said. "But I never knew what it was. Other than being a pin, I never saw it."

"Did either girl ever get their stolen items back?"

"I don't think so."

"Max, when was your parents' divorce finalized?"

"On my twelfth birthday."

"Was something taken from you that day at dance practice?"

Max had never said anything about this. She looked down at her hands. "Max, can you please answer the question?"

"That morning, my dad had given me something that belonged to my grandmother. She passed away when I was a baby, so I never knew her. My dad gave me a string of her pearls. I was so proud to have gotten them. At dance practice, our coach Hannah Grace made me take them off. She had taken them off of me because I couldn't do the clasp. She had put them in a private place. After practice was over, I went to her to get them and they were gone. We searched for them, but they never turned up."

"To the best of your ability can you please describe them to the court."

"They were opal in color. There was a charm of a dancer in the middle that hung a little. Then there were twenty pearls on both sides of the necklace, so there was a total of forty pearls. The dancer was gold. Her legs were together, but her arms were spread way above her head. Her arms are what held her on the necklace."

Matt had had a picture at the house of Max holding up the necklace. A bright big gappy smile plastered on her face. She had lost the last of her baby teeth on the bottom, so she was missing some teeth. She was an adorable young girl. As Matt listened to Gwen questioning her and Max speaking freely about this, his heart broke a bit.

"What happened to the necklace?"

"I don't know. I never saw it past that day. I had gotten it that morning for my birthday and it was gone within a blink of an eye."

"Did you tell your father about it?"

Max lowered her head. "I couldn't. When I got home from dance that night, he had permanently moved out. He had left without saying goodbye to me."

"Max, after the accident had happened and after you had gone through rehabilitation, what happened?"

"I was arrested for the theft of the stolen things that night."

"Did you know about them?"

"No."

"Then why wouldn't you voice that at the hearing?"

"I couldn't because of my jaw being wired shut." Max was losing her steam. She was drained. She was getting antsy. "Your honor, I have to go to the bathroom."

"Oh, yes. Let's all break for lunch and come back at two o'clock."

Max went to the bathroom. She put her head up against the wall and just leaned into it. Joanna knocked on the bathroom door. "Max!"

"Yes. I'll be out shortly." Max finished in the bathroom and washed her hands before leaving.

"Are you ok?"

Max went close to the wall and leaned into it.

"Max!"

Hank came over. "Max!" She lifted her head up to look at him.

"How much longer is this going to be?"

"Awhile longer," Joanna said. "Come. Let's go get something to eat."

They went to get something, but Max didn't eat. She played with her food. "How did Gwen know about the necklace?" Max asked not looking up. She had picked up the fork and had stabbed it through a French fry. "I...I never told anyone. Only Hannah, me, and the person who took it knew. How did Gwen know how to ask about that?" Max trembled. She shivered.

"Max, are you cold, honey?" Joanna asked.

"I never got to tell anyone about the necklace," Max said torturing the poor French fry.

Grant reached over and took the fork out of Max's hand. "Everything is going to be righted."

"But how do you know?"

"Max, sweetheart you just have to have faith. Please eat something."

"Am I going to go home with you tonight?"

Joanna and Grant looked at each other. "Well, where else would you go?"

With tears in her eyes, Max said, "County lock up."

"No," Joanna said.

"But I violated..."

"It's really going to be ok," Grant said.

"No one has ever said that to me." Max was antsy. "I don't want to be inside. I feel like I can't breathe. I feel like I'm in a box. Can I just go outside? I promise I won't go anywhere."

"Hank, take her outside for a few minutes. I don't have to tell you not to let her out of your sight."

"No, Sergeant," he said. "Come on, Max."

When they went outside, Max sucked in a deep breath of the cold fresh air. "It's the first winter in four years that I have been outside."

"Come on. We have to go back inside."

"Just one more minute. Please Hank?"

"Fine, but then we really need to go back inside."

"Will you let me just run around for that minute?"

"No."

"Please?"

"No. Let's go back inside." He took hold of Max's hand. She pulled away. "Max!" He took her hand again and again she pulled away. "Don't do what you are thinking right now. I will cuff you."

"That's the only way I'm going back in there," Max said. She pushed fast away from him. He grabbed hold of her five feet away. He put cuffs on her. Max lowered her head to her chest. Hank brought her back into the courthouse.

"What the fuck is going on?"

"She tried to run."

"I just can't sit still anymore today. I can't breathe in here. I just wanted to go for a little run. I wasn't going to leave. Fuck! Where would I go anyway? I don't have…" she started to cry. "Can't we ask the judge if we can come back tomorrow? Please?"

Gwen saw her crying. She came rushing over. "What's going on?"

"I don't want to do this anymore today. Please, Gwen. I can't sit still anymore."

"Why is she in handcuffs?"

"She was trying to take off," Hank said.

"Where the fuck is she going to go?" Gwen said. "Take those off her."

"No, they stay on," Joanna said.

"I swear I wasn't going to leave. I just want to move around a bit. I know that I am sitting like all the time, but I can't stay in one place all that long. I go stir crazy."

"Let's go back upstairs."

Once in the elevator, Hank removed the handcuffs. Max moved herself as close to the elevator wall as she could possibly get. Grant got on his knees next to her. He was on her left side. He touched her shoulder, so she looked at him. "Do you have faith, Maxine?" Max shrugged. "Everything is going to work out." They went back in the courtroom. The judge had been observing Max for the past hour.

"Ok, we are going to call for a recess until tomorrow morning at ten." Max never wavered. She kept her head turned down. Lucy and Elliot were smiling like idiots on the other hand. "Now nothing that was spoken of today can be spoken about. Ms. Brandon, do you hear me?"

"Yes, your honor," Max said barely moving.

"I need a minute with her alone," the judge said. Max was brought into a room behind the courtroom. The judge came in taking off her robe. "What are you afraid of, Max?"

"Being forgotten," Max said looking up.

"That's hard to do."

"It's been my life. First my parents, then my so-called friends. It's hard for me to be in the same room as Lucy, your honor. It's because of her that all of this…" Max waved her hands from the top of head all the way down her body. "That all of this happened."

"I want an honest truthful answer right here. Right now."

"Yes, ma'am," Max said.

"Did you know about the heist?"

"No, ma'am. I am a veteran, your honor. I served and protected. I wouldn't turn around and steal, cheat, and lie, your honor."

"Ok. I got it," she said. "Come on. We will pick this back up tomorrow."

"Thank you, ma'am."

"Max, is there video from that night's performance?"

"Yes."

"Do you have a copy of it?"

"Yes, your honor."

"With you?"

"Yes, your honor. Well, they are in the courtroom."

They returned to the courtroom. Max gave the judge the discs. Joanna and Hank were waiting for Max in the back of the courtroom. When she got closer to them, Hank reached out and took hold of her hand. This time, Max didn't pull away. "Can you pick me up so I can stretch?" Max asked him. They were still in the courtroom. The judge was still on the bench. She watched as Hank picked Max up into his arms and as she put her head against his chest and closed her eyes. Joanna pushed the empty wheelchair. By the time they had waited for the elevator, Max was sleeping in Hank's arms.

The third day. Thursday. By the end of the morning, Lucy, who hadn't stopped watching Max in the past two days had an absolute outburst. She stood up in the gallery, pounded her hands down on the top of the wooden row of pews in front of her and said, "Oh I can't take it anymore. It was just a prank. I wanted to hurt Xine…"

"Who?" the judge asked.

"Xine." Lucy pointed her pointer finger towards Max. "I wanted to hurt her, so I did it. I paid theses six dudes who didn't know shit what they were doing to come in and screw with the rails and the lights.

"I was mad. I was jealous. I wanted to be the one in Elliot's arms. He asked her to marry him. But I wanted him. It should have been me that he was lifting that night. It was me for the six years that she left us to go be a guy and fly a plane. Whoopi doo! But then the slut came back, and Elliot took her back. He chose her over me. He chose the beauty princess with her honey brownish red hair and her hazel cat like eyes." Lucy gripped the top of the bench in front of her. "Not to mention her streetlamp pole height. And…and she is graceful and elegant without even trying. It's not fair. It wasn't fair."

"Miss Smutbrook sit down," the judge said.

"Oh, no please your honor, do let her go on," Gwen said.

Lucy took a bow in Gwen's direction and then she smiled and grinned really big.

"I was the one who took that stupid pink My Little Pony watch all of those years ago. I smiled and laughed as her dad angrily grabbed her. He ripped her bag and jacket off of her. She stared at him wide eyed, and yet she didn't cry. She never saw the damn watch. The way little Nancy paraded around the studio with it. Showing it off to everyone who would stop and take notice. Well, I took notice. I saw the light and hot pinks of that watch. I saw the pony inside the face of the watch. Our coach made little Nancy take it off and put in her cubby with the rest of her stuff and I swayed my little self over to that cubby and snatched it and no one noticed. And then I blamed it on Xine. I told our coach that I saw Max with it, yet Max never saw the damn thing to begin with. But I still smile and laugh at how she watched her dad violently go through her things and the way he tore up her jacket like that." Lucy clasped her hands together. She brought them under her chin as she smiled and looked up as if seeing it happen all over again…"

"Did you wear the watch?"

"Wait! What? Why are you interrupting me?"

"Did you wear the watch?"

"Yes. But never to dance."

"Did you show it off to anyone?"

"Did I do what now?"

"Did you show it off? You know like the little girl…"

"Nancy!" Lucy snapped. "It was Nancy's pink My Little Pony watch. And yes, I showed it off in the cafeteria to everyone at school and at recess too."

"Why did you blame Miss Brandon?"

Lucy looked at Max and gloatingly smiled.

"Miss Smutbrook, please answer the question," Gwen said. Lucy never stopped smiling and glaring at Max. "Your honor!"

"Miss Smutbrook!" Lucy looked at her. "You are trying my patience. Please continue."

"What the hell was the damn question?"

"Why did you blame Maxine Brandon?"

"It was easy to blame her. It was fun to blame her. I loved getting her into trouble. Her dad had been constantly yelling at her and mad at her like all the time. And we all knew that her mother not only despised her but detested her too. Oh, I would get great joy when her dad jerked her by the arm or dragged her twig like self to the car." Lucy cheered and stomped her feet as she went on. "How he pounded his fists against the roof of the car. How he always looked like a heated pot that was over boiling. And when I took the butterfly pin. Max again never saw the damn thing. She always came into the studio, put her shit down nice and tidy like and then she would go out on the dance floor. Oh my god how it drove me crazy. So I told our coach that she put Julie's pin in her sock and that she tucked it down deep in her bag." Lucy laughed. "Yet, she never had it. I just liked to get her into trouble. I thought her parents would have ripped her out of dance for stealing.

"But the best. My joy came on November twelfth. When she turned twelve. She came into dance class that day with a bright smile. She wore a necklace. They were pearls. Opal in color. They were small pearls. There were a lot of them. And in the middle of it there was a golden charm of a dancer. And it was doing Max's signature move." Lucy threw her arms up in the air. "Xine loved this stupid goddamn pose. She started every class with that fucking move and she ended every fucking class with that same fucking move." Lucy seemed to brush the frustration away from her face and then she continued. "I saw it immediately. She went right over to the coach, who told her that she had to take it off. She said that it was a birthday present from her father. The same guy that for past seven years had brought or picked up Xine and he'd be mad as hell at her. Like the second he saw her, his face would distort; he would just grow madder and madder by the minute. Yet he gave his daughter this stunning gift. Hannah made her take it off and she put her in a secret place." Lucy put her hand to side of her mouth like she was going to tell a secret. "She put it in her desk drawer for safe keeping. Yet it wasn't safe. I got it and I swiped that thing in a heartbeat. Then I just sat there watching her grow more frantic by the minute. The next day she came to practice with a gash on her cheek. I just assumed that it was from her having to tell her monstrous father that she lost it. That it was stolen while she was at dance practice, but that little bitch never said a fucking word about it. It was never mentioned again. This made me both mad and sad all together.

"We were thirteen when we learned that pretty little dancing princess was homeless. Awe! The poor baby! No one wanted her. Not her anger boiled dad and not her jealous love thriving mother; they just tossed her aside. I mean man, you should have seen her mom. She'd come to the studio in her tight ass skirts and tops that were like two sizes way too small for her, and she would throw herself at all of our dads. Or should I say the dads that showed her an ounce of attention. She didn't come to see Max dance. What the fuck did she care? But Little Dancing Princess caught her mommy sneaking around with some of the dads and she threatened to tell her daddy, but her mom threatened to put her out for good if she ever did. She got the ultimate present from both of her parents. They just closed their doors on her like she no longer existed. How awesome was that? Like

I said. We were thirteen when we learned that pretty little dancing princess was homeless. Oh, boo hoo hoo!

"When we were fourteen, my hatred grew even deeper for Princess Beauty Maxie. She and Scott had gotten into a fight in school that I started." She hugged herself. "Oh, I love this one. I told Scotty that Xine said that he sucked royal ass as a dancer. And then I sat back when they got into a rip-roaring fight right in the hallway. I thought for sure that Scotty would have kicked her skinny little starving ass, but he didn't. She fought back just as hard he fought her. When we went practice, our coach punished them both big time. Punishment for Coach Hannah Grace was having to take off your socks and shoes and stand on the hardwood dance floor on the balls of the feet for the whole fucking practice. They had to do this for a week. But Xine never whined or complained. Man, how I hated her.

"Shit! I thought for sure that child services would have come in and taken her skinny little ass away. But NO! She got to stay.

"And then in high school. Little miss A+s graduates top of our fucking class. But then it happened. My prayers came true, she was gone for six years.

"I had my brother call her portraying to be her long absent father – saying how he was going to come with his wife and children to see our show." Lucy stood up on the bench seat and clasped her hands together again. "It was the best distraction that I could think of. Oh, you should have been there to see her. She was so anxious and just so distracted. I moved her bag right in front of her and she never noticed. Of course, she didn't see me put the loot in her bag.

"She didn't involve anyone in the TV interview that she did. It was all about the Air Force Pilot Dancing Princess." Lucy now attempted to do a pirouette on the wooden bench and stumbled and fell out of it before falling off the bench. "AH SHIT! Fuck!" People in the gallery laughed at her. Lucy death gripped the top of the bench in front of her again. "I had to hurt her. I had to punish her. Those guys were dumb as rocks. They had no clue what they were doing. I paid them money to take down the middle rail, which I knew that Max would be right under neath it. But they couldn't follow directions either. It was a prank. The rail was supposed to come down right above her as she was in midair. It wouldn't have happened if she weren't so damn fucking good all the time. Elliot and her, they were smooth together. But I just couldn't stand it any longer. She had to get hurt, so that I could slide into her place again and be Elliot's forever partner. I was his forever partner for the six years that the slut left us for."

"I will not have that kind of language spoken in this court room. Do you hear me?"

"Yes, your honor. And I can hear you out of both ears. I am sorry that she became paralyzed. I didn't intend for that to happen. Maybe for her to get a broken leg or arm or something. So I am sorry that she became paralyzed." Lucy now directed her full attention to Max. "But I'm not sorry. You were an easy target. You always were. I had to make it, so you weren't always so fucking perfect anymore."

"Why did you kick her in the head when she was pinned down?" Gwen asked.

"Because I finally could," she said with a smirky smile on her face. "But no. Really. I did it because I wanted to end her pain. I wanted... I wanted to finally knock the perfection queen out.

"And then when the police came to our apartment and they found her duffle bag with the loot in it, we all thought that we were cooked for good then, but that didn't happen. We heard that she was arrested, she was being held until the trial. She was in a wheelchair, she's permanently deaf in her left ear, and her mouth was wired shut. She couldn't hear, she couldn't speak, and when she was pushed into court for those four days, she could barely keep her head up." Lucy laughed. "Then we all heard her sentencing. She was sentenced to eight years of house arrest and she would have to go back to the queen bitch villain in her life." Lucy then sang a verse of a song. "You're going down. We're calling timber." The judge finally stopped her from saying anything else.

"That's enough!" the judge said. "I think that we have heard all we need to hear to proceed with this case. Miss Smutbrook, sit your ass down and don't get out of that seat again. Bailiff, please go place Miss Smutbrook in handcuffs."

"But... But..."

"Not another word!" the judge demanded.

"But Max is guilty." Lucy laughed. "Guilty of being so trusting and so innocent. She wouldn't steal a damn thing. Even when she saw money laying in the street when she was on the streets and homeless, she never would pick it up." Lucy mocked Maxine. "Oh, no. I can't. It doesn't belong to me." She smiled and laughed at herself. "Shit! Do you think I gave a shit that things didn't belong to me? If they were there, I was fucking raking it in. I have quite a collection from over the years and it was all there in Max's place and yet she never noticed it. She never saw it. She was too distracted learning and striving to be fucking perfect to hopefully get her daddy's attention. Oh, boo hoo hoo! He doesn't love me! Hell, none of us love you. That's why we never came to see you after you got hurt. We didn't want to be around you!"

"Do not address Miss Brandon directly again. Do I make myself clear, Miss Smutbrook?"

"You were kind enough to leave us not only the keys to your apartment, but your apartment as well. But the shit had to go down just like you had to go down." Lucy laughed. "You went down though, and it went up. Fire and smoke rise."

"Miss Smutbrook!" The judge reprimanded for a second time. "Do not directly address Miss Brandon."

Lucy put her hand over her heart. "I am guilty of loving Elliot and I would do anything in my power to get him away from her over the years. You see, I already told you how Coach Hannah Grace served out punishments in dance practice. Well, she started that goddamn shit when we were children. And when we got punished, everyone would whine and cry and carry on because it was…it was hell. And then you have Princess Slut Dancer over there." Lucy pointed at Max again. "She would get punished. A lot. Because of me over the years. Oh, the joy. To watch her have to sit out and not be able to dance. Well, stand there in the middle of the floor. Barefooted. On the balls of her feet; god forbid you put your fucking heels down on the floor to relieve the pressure and tension in your calves, your legs, your back, your butt, your neck, your arms. Everything tingled. Everything hurt like hell, and yet when Max would get punished, she would just… She would just…well do it. God, how it drove me crazy. If you put your heels down, you got another hour added to your already day of punishment. She never whined, cried, whimpered, or made a fucking peep. Oh, how it drove me crazy.

"Practice when we were teenagers lasted from three to seven at night each day. And Max and Scotty had to stand there for four hours each day. Monday through Saturday on the balls of their feet in the middle of the floor. Scotty whined and complained. He cried a bit too, but not the stoic slut over there. She would hold that pose from exactly three o'clock on the dot until seven oh eight when practice was over. It took eight minutes for all of us to gather our things. I always tried to push it out longer if I could. And still, she would stand there. On the balls of her feet. Her toes were close to being blue by then. And then when she was released from this pose, and she was able to put her heels down, she wouldn't fall to the floor like Scotty or the rest of us did. She would just stand there on her feet for a few minutes and then she would take the agonizing walk to the wall where her stuff was; she would gather her things and then limp out." Lucy grinned. "Our parents would come and tell Coach Grace that that was a form of torture, but poor little Xine didn't have anyone coming to stand up for her."

"I said that that is enough from you, Miss Smutbrook!" the judge yelled.

"Your honor, if I may question this suspect?" Gwen asked.

"She opened the door, so go ahead, Mrs. Brandon."

"Suspect? Who's a suspect?" Lucy jumped up and down as if throwing a child's temper tantrum. She pulled herself together before saying, "Like she's the guilty party that has brought us all here together again. Hooray! Let's party!"

Gwen ignored this. And went on with her questioning. "So your parents would come and tell your coach how unjust this punishment was right?"

"Yes. I said that," Lucy spat out. "I thought the only semi-deaf person in the room was Maxine!"

"Miss Smutbrook!" the judge reprimanded. Lucy looked at the judge. "Enough of that!"

"Oh, yeah, stick up for her," she said throwing up her arms and rolling her eyes.

"So your parents came? And the other parents came right?"

"Yes," Lucy snapped.

"And did your coach stop that form of punishment then?"

"No! Not until we were out of high school. When we became adults. When we joined the adult world," Lucy said. "Then the poor little homeless girl, left us for bootcamp. We all made wages and bets for how long the little slut would stay in it for. And she lasted six years. She was homeless for six years. And then she was a flying fucking soldier for six years. I couldn't let her keep me from Elliot for another six years, so I had been thinking of this plan for two years since she came back. How I could hurt her. How I could break her. And then when we moved from the studio to the theater space six months before the accident. I knew then. I watched the stagehands load things in and load things out. I watched them bring down the rails."

"What was the accident date? Do you recall the day and date, Miss Smutbrook," Gwen asked.

"Why yes. Of course. It was our last show for the season. So it was a Saturday night performance. And the date was May twenty-eighth. I was giving myself the best twenty-seventh birthday present ever. I was taking the best of us out of the equation. I was eliminating her from our family. Just like her family had done to her all of those years back." Lucy looked up. Almost gloating. "I'd like to think that I had part in that," Lucy said.

"How would you have had a part in that, Miss Smutbrook?"

"Well, her dad was already constantly mad at her. Her mother didn't seem to give a shit about her either. I was constantly getting her in trouble and feeding into why her dad was always mad at her. So like that was my doing back then, so was this my doing at our final show of the season. That BITCH had to go down!"

"We are done now," Gwen said. "Thank you, your honor for allowing this to go on as long as it has. Thank you, Lucy. I mean thank you, Miss Smutbrook."

"Oh, yeah. You bet," Lucy said and then she willing sat back down since getting up and starting her rant and outburst.

Matt had been in the courtroom. He listened to all of this as everyone else had. He hadn't been able to draw his gaze away from Maxine. He found himself getting up and going to her and taking her warm and snug in his arms and holding her as she quietly cried. He held her safe, warm, and shielded wishing that he done that all of those years back. He wished that he could have looked through the red wall of anger and seen his beautiful daughter.

All charges were dropped against Max before the end of that day. Though Max was thrilled by this, she was scared too. She didn't know what she would now do with her life.

Lucy was sentenced to premediated attempted murder while the crew was sentenced to attempted murder. Also, Lucy was sentenced with reckless endangerment, theft, conspiracy, negligence, and the attempt to sell drugs and stolen items. The judge backed her theft charges all the way from the time that she was a child, so twenty-four years of attempting to run a theft ring. She was also charged with libel and slander against Max. Lucy was sentenced to two consecutive life sentences with no chance of parole.

Elliot confessed that he knew of what was planned, but he honestly thought it was a prank and that no one was going to get hurt. Elliot confessed to the knowledge and whereabouts of the stolen merchandise. He was sentenced to knowing the plans for premediated mischief that led to bodily harm. The others were sentenced to two thousand days of community service, which is roughly five and half years. Elliot was given a ten-year sentence plus the four years that Max lost, so fourteen years with no chance of early release or parole prior to his term being up.

Mike took a plea deal, so he was only sentenced to five hundred days of community service.

It was two hours a day that they had to do something within the community. Max's sentence for the so-called prank was a life sentence. She couldn't do it for a little while every day and then step away from it or push it aside. She was going to be paralyzed for the rest of her life. She was going to be deaf for the rest of her life as well.

CHAPTER THIRTEEN

Max was free for the first time in almost four years. She could now come and go as she pleased. Joanna and Grant had taken her back to their house. Gwen, Matt, and the boys came. They celebrated with a catered in dinner. At the end of dinner, there was cake and coffee.

"Can I have a beer?" Max asked.

"Yes," Grant said.

"I'll have one too," Gwen and Matt said together.

"To my first beer with my daughter," Matt said.

"Can I take the boys into the garage to show them the dance floor?

"Yes. You can go wherever you like now. You don't need permission."

"It's your house and I am still a guest in your house, so I will still ask for things before I do or take anything."

"Who taught her that?" Grant asked.

"Definitely not her mother or I," Matt said.

Max took the boys into the garage. She picked Gunnar up first and told him to stay on his knees. Gwen and Joanna had followed. Gwen recorded what was going on. How Max put her hands on her wheels and pushed off gliding them across the floor. How Gunnar listened and kept his knees on her thighs and his hands firmly gripping her shoulders. The way she brought her hands around him supporting his small frame. And then how she gently with one hand brought her hand to the rim of the chair and with the smallest effort tugged a bit and the wheelchair moved off in that direction. Matt now came and stood with them. They all heard and listen to Gunnar as he said, "Weeeee." Or he cheered. "Look. I'm flying," he said as he bravely balanced and put his arms out. When Max turned again, she slightly grabbed him reassuring him that she was going to be there at every turn. When it was over, Gunnar sat back on his calves and looked a breathless Max in the face. Then he rose on his knees again wrapping his arms around her. Max put her arms around him. She squeezed his sides lightly and he started to laugh. She laughed with him.

"So can you come now and visit us whenever you or we want?"

"Yes," Max said.

"Can I tell you a secret?"

"Yes."

"I love you," he said.

"Look. I can teach you how to sign that," Max said to him. He sat back on her legs again. Max showed him. He followed what she did.

"What did I say?"

"You said… we said I love you."

"Cool," he said with a smile.

Gwen hadn't stopped recording the interaction. There were twenty years between the two of them and yet she didn't speak down to him. She spoke to him. Not at him.

"I have to pee," he said. Max threw her head back laughing.

"There is a bathroom right through that door. Go on."

"Will you wait for me?"

"Yes, of course," she said. Gunnar ran and used the bathroom. "Gunny, wash your hands."

"Oh, yeah," he called from the other side of the door. Max laughed again.

"Jackson, do you want to try it?"

"Yeah," he said.

"I'm going to try something a little different with you ok."

"Yeah. Ok," Jackson said.

She picked him up and sat him on her shoulders. He wasn't a heavy six-year-old. "Now you have to remain seated the whole time." Jackson smiled so big. "Keep your hands on my shoulders ok."

"Yep!"

Max moved the wheelchair slowly. As she moved, she swayed side to side moving him with her. Then she stopped. She brought him down and around to face her like she had done with Gunnar. And then she danced with him. She tickled him when it was over. He laughed and then he started to cry. "What happened? Did I hurt you?"

"No," Jackson said.

"Then why are you crying?"

"Because it just seemed so pretty," he said. "I watched our shadows behind us, and it was so pretty." He put his head on her shoulder. She sat him on her lap and held him as he cried. "I don't want you to go away."

"I'm not going to go anywhere. Why would you think that I would go away?"

"Because you can now," he said. "Like when Logan comes. He says that he will come back, but then he doesn't for a long, long time."

"I won't do that, Jackson. You will see me."

"Can we have you meet our friends?"

"I would like that."

Gunnar came over to her. He stood next to her. Matt and Gwen both saw how he trusted her enough to lean into her. She wrapped her arm around him.

"Can we go watch a movie now?" Jackson asked.

"Boys, we have to get going."

They all three looked at Gwen.

"But we want to stay here, mommy," Gunnar said.

"I know you do, but it has been a long day. We will come back. You both have to get ready for school tomorrow."

"It's ok," Max said. "I'll see you both..."

"Tomorrow?" Gunnar and Matt asked together. Max looked at Matt.

"Yes. I can see you tomorrow," Max said looking back at Gunnar and Jackson. "But you have to go to school and do good in school tomorrow."

"You can come home with us," Jackson said. "You can come live with us."

"Well, that needs to be discussed with your mommy and daddy first, but I love that you want me to come live with you, Jackson."

"I want that too."

"I know you do, Gunnar."

"Can you?"

Max looked at Matt. "I don't know yet," she said. "But I will come see you both tomorrow." Max never took her eyes off of her father this time. "I will see you tomorrow for sure."

They left after a round of hugs were exchanged. Max stayed in the garage and she moved around the space. Max went into the middle of the room. She closed her eyes and she envisioned herself dancing like she had danced all of her life. She saw herself barefoot, dancing a contemporary self choreographed piece. She swayed gently back and forth and then she heard a door close. It jarred her out of her thoughts and memories. She swiped at the tears that had fallen. She went to see what was going on. Harrison stood on the porch. He knocked hard on the door. Max went towards the house.

"Why are you still here?" he asked. "It's not like you live here. Why don't you go live with your own parents? These are my parents," he said. His breath reeked of booze.

"Did you drive here?"

"Like duh!" Harrison said. "Look the handicapper can use her brain," he put his index finger on her head and pushed her head to the side.

"Stop that."

"Who's going to make me? It's not like you can."

"I can do a lot of things."

"Can you use that little pelvis of yours?"

"That's none of your business."

"Can you feel it or do you just lay there like a fish while the guy does all of the work?"

"You are a mean, cruel drunk."

"And you a homeless whore. Let's call a spade a spade now."

Max went to get away from him. Harrison in his drunken stupor grabbed her. "Come on you sexy ass, show me what you can do?"

The flood lights came on. The front door flung open. "HARRISON!" Joanna yelled. He tried to straighten up, but he lost his balance and his footing. Joanna now saw Max huddled into herself. "Max. Max, are you ok? Come let's go in the house. Can you sit up?" Joanna came over and put her hands on Max's back and sat her up. She saw her blouse was ripped. "Max, what happened?"

Grant came out on the porch. Within a few seconds he saw the whole picture. He grabbed his son by the back of shirt and pulled him around the back of the house. Then he doused him with the hose. "What the fuck are you doing?" Grant yelled at him. "What were you planning on doing? You drove here drunk and then you were going to do what? Have your way with Max? What the fuck is wrong with you?"

"She's nothing more than a homeless slut," Harrison said.

Instead on hitting his son, Grant blasted him with the hose again.

"COME ON! STOP WITH THE FUCKING HOSE ALREADY!"

"You need to sleep this off and then we will talk in the morning."

"Can I come sleep in my bed?"

"Not a chance in hell," Grant said.

"But this my house."

"No, son, this is your mother's and my house."

"I think I hit something with my car."

"What? HARRISON!" Grant went running to look at the car. There was no damage to it at all. He went back to his son and brought him to the pool house. "You can sleep it off in here. And I'm telling you not to go anywhere near Max."

Joanna had brought Max in the house. Max seemed like she was galaxies away. Grant came back in the house. He looked at Max. "Did he hurt you?" She had a glazed over stare. Grant now lifted her carrying her into the bathroom, where he put her in the shower and turned the water on. When the water hit Max, a scream quaked out from her. "It's ok," Grant assured her.

Max got dressed. She stayed in the bedroom for the rest of the night. She wrote a letter to her dad and Gwen.

> Dear Dad and Mommy,
>
> Mom, I just wanted to thank you for always believing in me and helping me through this and out of this as well. I could never prove to you how grateful I am.

What will happen now. Joanna mentioned a transition period, but to where? When I was imprisoned at Desiree's all I wanted was to live on my own and be by myself, but now I just don't know. I am not sure. I mean I can take care of myself. I've been doing that for the better part of eighteen years, but the thing is, I afraid to be alone. I'm afraid to be myself again.

I don't know if you'd want your 30-year-old kid living with you. But maybe just for a little while we can try it? I don't have too many bad habits. I will follow whatever rules you have for your house. I try not to take up too much room.

Mom, why is it that because I was a dancer that people insinuate that I am a whore. I have had two partners. Though I do love the affection and feeling of being in someone's arms, I don't need to be. I really like Trent, but since…well, you know…he is different now. He barely talks to me. The COP in him has taken over. Oh, well, I will get over that as well.

I have been let down and have known what it is to be let down and I don't want to do that to the boys. I love them and I want them to know that I always will be here or there for them. I want to be here or there for them.

Dad, I want us to really get to know each other. I want to be able to trust in you. I have missed you the most over the years. And not knowing how to reach out and get in touch with you has really burrowed a hole in my heart. I thought for sure when Desiree told you that I was gone that you would have come looking for me. I dreamed of you finding me. Of you taking me warm and snug in your arms and you bringing me home, but then I would wake up and blink away the tears that I cried because it wasn't real. A week went by, nobody. A week turned into a month, a month turned into another and then another.

I had gotten into a spill a school and as I sat in the office bleeding from the spat with Scott, one of my fellow dancers, they told me to call my parents. I refused. I mean who could I call? I had tried calling Desiree, but they changed the number. By then she was with Jordan I think or maybe she just changed the number. I don't really know when her life or your life went on. I don't really know how my life did too, but then it did. A person from child services came in and told me that I was going to go to a foster home. I told her that I would never stay in someone else's home without my parents' permission. They said I could stay where I was staying as long as I came to school every day and I followed the rules.

Hannah Grace learned about the fight and she punished both of us for a week from dance. For a punishment, she had us take off our shoes and socks and stand on the balls our feet for the whole practice. Scott would whine and cry, but I never did. After the first twenty minutes or so, your calves just start burning. By the end of class, my legs shook so bad that it hurt to walk. I don't know why I am remembering this now. I don't know why it is important to let you know, but I want you to know. And Mommy too.

After that, I followed the rules. I walked the straight line. While my teammates were getting high, I never did. I studied in a coffee shop. I slept in an alley between two large trash bins. I made myself invisible, for I was invisible to you and Desiree. You two were gone from each other's lives and so was I. Where you both found someone else, I was alone. I didn't want to disappoint you or be a disappointment, so I worked hard graduating top of my class, but that accomplishment only came down to a piece of paper, a ribbon and a pin. Nothing to tell me that my parents were proud of me. No one to say, "hey, you did it. You did a great job." I still had no one, so I chose to enlist because at least then, for 365 days a year, I would be surrounded by others. They may not like or love me, but I would have a place to call home. The United States

Air Force became the first home that I had known in six years. It wasn't one place. But at least I had someone to report to and someone who knew where I was at all times.

When it was over or I chose to leave, I went to an apartment that I had bought when I was twenty-two. My real first home now twelve years in the making. And Dad and Mom, shit my life was good. But I was a fool. I didn't see the shit that my teammates had started and were doing. I let Lucy, Scott and Elliot move in with me. To find out after the accident that they had stashed stolen shit in my house. I took the ultimate fall and then I took the fall for them because I didn't have any one there to vouche that I would never do that.

I know that I can't go back to Desiree's house. I would never go there. If I never see her again, I am truly fine and ok with that, so the predicament that stands now is where I will reside. My apartment. My home went up in flames. It burned to the ground. If I weren't paralyzed, I would consider returning to the streets as hard as that really was, but I can't do that. So, I am asking you if you would consider letting me live with you for the year and half that the judge says I have to live in one place for? Will you let me say that your home is my home too.

I love you both and the boys too.

Love,
Max

Max hugged the elephant from Gwen. She got on the bed and buried herself deep under the comforter. Joanna looked in on her. She saw Max covered to her left ear. The stuffed elephant's face peered over Max's shoulder. Joanna saw the neatly written letter sitting on the side table by the bed. She picked it up and read it. Joanna put the letter back on the table before leaving the room. Joanna called Gwen and Matt. "What would it take for you to allow Max to come live with you for the terms that the judge said that she has to have placement?"

"We need about a month or so," Matt said. "We are having renovations done. Ramps installed to the house, a lift for the pool, the bathrooms doors are being widened, one bathroom is being made larger so that she will be able to maneuver in there. In the room that has been her room since she was twelve, the furniture is being changed out so that she can access everything."

"Matt, you need to tell her that you have always had a bedroom for her in your house," Joanna said.

"I will let her know tomorrow. Will she able to have someone bring her here tomorrow?"

"Yes."

Hank had gone to the captain. "Sir, I have met someone, who had been in trouble with the law, that it turns out that she was not or never was involved in. I would like to know if it would be ok to have a relationship with her?"

"Yes," he said.

"Will my job be on the line?"

"No."

"Sir, I have to let you know that we were intimate on more than one occasion. It was consensual. I was off duty when it occurred."

"Trent, what you do in your off time is completely and totally your business. Good luck with the relationship."

"Thank you, sir."

"I hope that she makes you happy."

Hank left the station after taking the next two weeks off. He called Joanna asking her if he could come there. With Joanna's permission, Hank went to the house.

Grant had rented a car with hand controls in it. He had taken Max to an empty parking lot and after demonstrating how it worked, he put Max in the driver's seat.

"I can't do this."

"Yes, you can. Let's just try."

Max pressed the break in as she shifted the car to drive and then she hit the gas and screamed when it jumped forward. She slammed hard on the breaks. "Ok. Not exactly like that, but you will learn. It's like the first time you do anything, you don't get it right right off the bat. Ease on the gas. Let's try it again."

Within ten minutes they had worked out the kinks and then Grant told her to pull out on the street. "Do what now?"

"Come on. Drive us home."

"You want me to drive us home?"

"Yes. I want you to drive us home. Max, you can do this."

Max pulled out on the street. With Grant telling her how to go, she drove them back to the house. Hank sat on the front porch waiting for them. "Hey, look who is driving," Hank said.

"Who's ready to go take her driver's test?" Joanna asked.

"When I am done, will someone take me to see my dad, Gwen, and the kids?"

"Yes."

The three of them took her to the DMV, where Max was given an eye exam, a hearing test, and then the written test. She would have to get a doctor's note saying that she was permanently deaf in her left ear before she could get her license, but she had aced the driver's written test.

"I don't have a doctor."

"That's ok," Gwen said.

"Mom! You are here."

"Yes, I am here."

Matt came around the other side of her with a beautiful bouquet of flowers. This was the first time that Max was ever receiving flowers. Max looked at them. "Max, these are you for you."

"Thank you. They are beautiful."

"You are acting like you've never had flowers before," Matt said.

"I haven't," she said. "I've seen others get flowers before, but I never have. I had never had family members there waiting for me." Max started to sneeze.

"Are you allergic?" Gwen asked.

Max sneezed three more times. "I don't know." She laughed and then sneezed again and again. "They are really pretty. I like them."

"Here. Let's take them away from you."

Max smiled at Gwen. She looked at Matt. "Thank you, dad."

After a visit to Gwen and Matt's doctor, where Max's deafness was documented for the first time since the accident, a note was written on Max's behalf saying that although she is completely deaf with zero percent hearing in her left ear, her other sensory body parts work just fine and he was granting her permission to get her driver's license.

"We will deal with this at the beginning of next week," Gwen said.

"Sure. Thank you."

After keeping her promise and seeing the boys and spending time with them at Matt and Gwen's house, Max noticed the construction being done. Construction that was already at least a week into work.

"Max, can I talk to you a minute please," Matt said.

"Here," she said putting Jackson on the couch. "I'll be right back. Let me go talk to your daddy."

"He's your daddy too," both boys said.

"Yes," Max said looking at Matt. "He is my daddy too. I'll be right back and then we will finish this awesome puzzle. Don't go on without me ok. I don't want to miss anything."

"We won't," the boys said.

Max went over to Matt. "I want to show you something." He took her by the hand. He brought her into a room that Max had not seen.

"What's this?"

"This is your room."

"But this looks like a young girl's room."

"Max, I always had a room for you and your brother in my house."

"But I don't understand. You were so mad. I remember. You asked if we wanted to live with you or her. I let Logan answer first. He said that he wanted to live with her. I never got the chance to answer. You made us go to school and carry on with our day like nothing was happening. I went to dance and danced an amazing dance and then when I got home, you weren't there. All of your stuff was gone. Your address was on the paper. I came here. You were hugging and kissing Gwen. I heard you say that you were free."

"I didn't mean of you and your brother, Max." Matt sat on the bed. "Parents make mistakes. I never knew that your mother threw you out."

"Did you ask about me?"

"Yes. Every time I called, she would say that you were out, you were at dance, you were reading a book. She had Logan tell me that you didn't want to come. That went on for years, Maxine. It's not like I just moved out and forgot about you."

"But you did, dad. I haven't seen you in eighteen years. You were like the genie from Aladdin. One second you were there and POOF – nothing."

"Why did your mom throw you out?"

"Because I told her that I would rather have you yell at me every day then live with someone who cheats on her husband and destroys the family. At least with you, I knew what I was going to get. Her choices scared me. I caught her kissing Dean's dad one day at practice. She told me if I ever told you that she would get rid of me. I lied to her. I screamed at her that I had told you."

"But you did tell me, Max. In your own innocent kid's way, you did tell me."

"So it was like you and her said."

"What was?"

"Your marriage ended because of me."

"No, Maxine, and I am so sorry that I ever said that to you. I should have never blamed you and neither should have your mother. We had fallen out of love. We had fallen apart. And the lies that your mother told me, changed the way I looked at you. I truly wish it hadn't. I know that I missed out on your whole life because of thoughts that your mother put in my head and led me to believe. I was made to believe that you were not my child. I should have..."

"That's in the past now. Here. I have something for you," Max said handing him the letter that she wrote. "Read it later though. After I leave ok. This room would have been nice to grow up in, dad. It's pretty."

"It can still be your room," Matt said. "We can change it to however you like. The renovations shouldn't take too much longer."

"Renovations for what?"

"For you to come here and live with Gwen, the boys and I until you are ready to move on."

"Just read the letter ok. Show it to Gwen too." Max rushed out of the room. She went back and finished the puzzle with the boys and then she had Grant take her back to their house.

Matt and Gwen sat that night after the boys were tucked into bed and they read Max's letter together. "Well, then I guess it's settled," Gwen said. "She wants to live here, and we want her to live here, so when can we move her in?"

"Well, I want it so that she can come and go as freely as the boys do," Matt said. "The ramps won't be done for at least another week."

"Matt, you look hesitant. I remember seeing that look before and it wasn't about you and I buying this house or moving in together."

"I don't know what it will be like living with my daughter."

"So we will learn together. She's not a child anymore. Twenty years separates the age gap between your oldest and our oldest, Matthew."

"I don't want her to feel obligated."

"Trent, I don't want them to feel obligated."

"Max, they won't."

"He…They had a bedroom for me since I was twelve. I was so hasty. I was bull headed. I mean I knew for sure that I couldn't live with the shit, who is my mother, but I didn't stick around and wait to see what happened next. He left and so did I. Though it was always hard and I was constantly getting yelled at, at least he spoke to me. She barely uttered a word to me. Maybe if I had stuck around this wouldn't have happened."

"Max, don't do that."

"Don't do what?"

"Think about the what ifs," Trent said. "It's because of what happened that I got to meet you," he kissed her. "I'm off for the next two weeks. I want to take you away. I want us to be intimate like we were where no one else will know."

"I would really like that."

Trent took Max to his cabin on a lake. It wasn't in the middle of nowhere, but it was private. Trent had come up here a few weeks ago hoping that he could bring Max here. He himself had installed a ramp to the porch. He had someone come in land install rails in the shower and a shower bench.

"So is this where you bring all your girl friends?"

Trent laughed. "Maxine, you are the first woman that I have ever brought here." He took her in his arms. He kissed her. He brought her over to the bed and gently placed her down. Max sat up and took a pillow in her hands. "What are you doing?" Trent asked as Max hit him with a pillow and then laughed and laughed. "Do you really want to do this?" She playfully hit him again with the pillow. He now grabbed the other pillow. Max scooted herself to the edge of the bed. She swung it again and hit him. "Maxie, this is the start of a war," he said. Max stopped. Trent stopped mid swing. He let the pillow fall to the floor.

"What is in the bucket?"

"What? Where are you looking?"

"Are those snowballs?"

Trent turned and looked. "Yeah. It's for when I bring my nephews and nieces here."

"Can we play with them?"

"Sure."

Trent put her wheelchair by the bed. Max got herself in her chair. She went over to the bucket and took a plush made snowball in her hand and then she turned around with a bright smile and threw it at Trent. "Ok, missy. This is it."

They had an indoor snowball fight which led them back to the bed. Trent put Max on the bed. She sat up and put her hands on his chest. He gently pulled her closer to him bringing her legs over his thighs, but she was still sitting on the bed. She leaned her head back to look at him. He closed the gab between them and kissed her. Soon they were undressing each other and then they lay naked together, Trent started to glide a hand over her nipples one at a time. Where his hand touched, his mouth soon followed and then his hand was between her legs. Max laid herself back and then soon after, Trent was on top of her. And once again, Max's body was answering to the calls of Trent's member. It wasn't rushed. It was passionate and intense all at the same time. They went another two rounds before they just lay together on the bed.

"Do you feel any of it?" Trent asked.

"Yes," Max said. "It's the only time that I seem to have feeling other than when I have to go to the bathroom."

Trent kissed her on the lips. As they kissed, Trent brought his hand down between her legs, he eased his finger inside of her and he brought her into a full exploding orgasm. An orgasm that had her legs, pelvis, and torso fluttering like a dancing butterfly. When it was over, she lay there completely drained but urning and desiring more.

He took her and they went for a swim in the lake. In the water, she moved freely. It was she who initiated yet another go at it. They had mind blowing sex in the lake together.

Joanna had called Trent's phone to make sure that they had gotten there safely because she hadn't heard from him. After they had showered, Trent saw his phone. They were both dressed now. Trent had made all of the preparations, yet he had forgotten to get food.

He called Joanna. "Hi, mom!" he teased. "Yes, we got here safely. Hey, we are going to run out to get a bite to eat. Would you and Grant like to join us?"

Max and Trent spent the whole two weeks away, but not in the cabin the whole time. They would go back there and stay there at night, but during the waking hours, they went to museums and to places that Max had never been to. Trent took Max to buy a car and hand controls were ordered the next day. Trent even had hand controls installed in his Hummer, so that Max could drive that too.

On one of their ventures out, Max saw her mother. Desiree saw her. She watched her daughter as if watching a stranger. She watched her move with elegance and grace. Desiree was reminded of seeing Max dance when she was a child and seeing her flow through the space. Max did that now. Max and Trent had started up the street the other way. The man that Desiree was with watched as well. He didn't make any shitty comments. "She's beautiful," he said.

"What?" Desiree asked. For the first time drawing her gaze away from Max.

"I said she's beautiful. It's almost as if she were a dancer the way she carries herself and moves with ease and grace down the street. Even the way she playfully pushes the guy that she is with, it is done with grace and fun. Do you know her?"

"Yes," Desiree said absently.

"How do you know her?"

"She's my daughter."

"What?" the guy said. "She's like twenty years old. How come this is the first time that I am ever hearing that you have this daughter."

"She is thirty," Desiree said going up on her toes trying not to lose sight of Max, but they had gone into a store and were now out of sight.

"Desiree, you have a thirty-year-old daughter? Where has she been?"

"We have been estranged since she was twelve. But then three years ago she had to come live with me."

"But I have been in your house for the past three years. I mean not every day, but still I have been there. Where was she? Why is she in a wheelchair?"

"She was a dancer and she was in an accident," Desiree said. "She is paralyzed from the waist down. She was or is a thief. She stole a lot of things. She has been on house arrest. She just recently was released from it I think."

"What? No. I know your children. They are Logan, who is twenty-five, Caitlin, who is eighteen, Leah, is fourteen and Harrison, he is five."

"Robert, Maxine is my oldest child."

"No one and I mean no one has ever talked about her."

"Logan is the only one who knows about her. He was seven when the divorce to his father Matt was over. The day that he moved out, I was mad and hurt and I threw Max out of the house. I never thought that she would have stayed gone. If it weren't for her accident and going on house arrest, I would never have seen her."

"Desiree, I was in that house. I never saw or heard her. Where was she?"

"When you were coming over, I would lock her in the bedroom."

"Oh my god. And when we went to New York for a month. Your neighbor called telling us that your power was out. Did you turn the power off? You mistreated her? Have you ever been remotely close to this child?"

"When she was young. Before I collaborated a lie to her father that she wasn't his child. As he grew to hate her and despise her and me, I hated her and despised her as well."

"What happened to her? Where did she go when you wouldn't let her return?"

"I don't know."

"She lived in your house for three years. Didn't you ever talk to her?"

"No, not really."

"Where does she live now?"

"I don't know. She was taken from my house four months ago. I believe she was taken to county lockup, but I don't know. She is no longer on house arrest."

"Who is she with?"

"I don't know."

"Is she in a relationship?"

"I don't know, Robert."

"Was she before the accident?"

"I don't know. I hadn't seen her in fifteen years," Desiree said.

"Desiree! What do you know?"

"That she was dancing and there was an accident, and she was severely injured."

"Did you see her when she was in the hospital or after that?"

"No. I saw her when I had to go pick her up from the courthouse. Her mouth was wired shut."

"Why?"

"I don't know. She's deaf in her left ear."

"Why?"

"I don't know."

"Can I meet her?"

"She won't speak to me."

"Have you tried?"

"Robert, who's side are you on?"

"There aren't sides, Desiree. Kids aren't sides."

Max and Trent went to eat and then they went shopping. It was while shopping that again their paths crossed. Max had been speaking and now dropped her head. "Can we go?"

"What's wrong?"

"Please. Can we just go?"

"Max, who is it?"

"That's Desiree. My mother. Trent, I want to go."

"Do you trust me?"

"What?"

"Look at me." Max brought her head up. She turned her head to the right to look at him. "Do you trust me?"

"Yes."

"Then trust me when I say that everything is going to be ok. Did you hear me?"

"Yes."

He took hold of Max's hand.

"Hello, Max," Desiree said.

"Hi," Max said. Her voice was small.

"How are you doing?"

"Why do you care? You didn't give a fucking shit how I have been for the past eighteen years of my life. What's the concern now?" Max looked at Robert. "Right. I see. You want your man friend here to think that you love all of your children and that you speak to them."

"I want the chance to get to know you."

"I lived in your house for three fucking years and you never tried once. I was mad that I had to come there just as you were mad that I did too. It wasn't a goddamn choice."

"What have you done with your life?" Robert asked. Max heard him speaking but couldn't make out what he said.

"I'm sorry, sir, I didn't quite get that. Can you please move closer to my right side? I have one hundred percent hearing loss in my left ear."

Robert stepped to his left. "I've asked what you have done with your life?"

"I was a dancer, sir."

"Did you go to college?" Desiree asked.

"I was going when the accident happened."

"What were you studying?"

"Psychology, sir. My scholarship was terminated when I couldn't return and my grades tanked because I couldn't return and I couldn't call anyone because for more than the first month after it happened, I was in an induced coma. You can't ask my mother or even my father to confirm that because neither of them was there. My jaw had been wired shut for just shy of a year."

"Max, maybe we shouldn't do this in the middle of this nice store," Trent said.

"Oh, shit! I'm sorry. You're right. I'm so sorry." Max took off as fast as she could go. Max ran as fast as she could. Trent ran after her.

"Desiree, we have to go with them," Robert said. "DESIREE! We have to go find your daughter."

Trent was running after her. Max went down a hill and picked up speed and was flying. Trent stopped running at the top of the hill. "SHIT!" He pulled his phone out and called Joanna. "Max took off. We were…in a… store."

"Slow down, Hank. What is going on?"

"Max saw Desiree with I guess her boyfriend. We were in a store and there they were in front of us. They started to question Max."

"NOW?" Joanna said.

"Yes. I simply said that maybe we shouldn't do this in the middle of the store and Max got embarrassed and took off. I almost had her, but then she went down a hill and got away from me. I don't know where she would go."

Joanna and Grant came to where Hank was. Desiree was standing there. "Next time you want to have a sit down and talk to your daughter, it will have to be in police presence," a man's voice said from behind them. They all turned to see the captain.

"Where is Max? Did you find her?"

"No, Hank. And I don't know. We have units out looking for her right now. Where would she go?"

"She doesn't have anywhere to go, Captain."

Max went to Joanna's house. The house was all locked up, but the garage door wasn't, so Max went into the garage and she blared music as she just moved through the space. She filled the cavity of the room.

Ashley had gone to the house. Hearing music coming from the garage, she called her mother. "Max is here," she said.

"How is she?"

"I'm not going to disturb her."

"Is she sleeping?"

"No. The house is locked up tight. She's in the garage dancing. Mom, did something happen?"

"Yeah, Ash, something happened."

"Is she in trouble?"

"No. Nothing like that. We will come home. Thank you, sweetheart."

Ashley climbed up in the loft of the garage. She muted her phone and she sat there watching the power, the emotion, the anger, the frustration, the passion, the elegance, and the grace come flowing out of Max. And when the CD finally stopped, Max went to one of the bars along the side of the room, she gripped it as tight as she could and tried to pull herself up. Her wheelchair went sliding out behind her; Max clung to that bar holding on as long as she could and she screamed the whole entire time. Ashley flew out of the loft hoping to get down there before she hit the ground, but she didn't make it. When she got there, Max was in a heap just completely and utterly distraught.

Trent, Grant, Joanna, Robert, and Desiree came into the garage. The first thing they saw was the abandoned wheelchair and then they saw Ashley standing there looking down and crying. Max lay on the floor, face down unresponsive.

"JESUS CHRST!" Trent yelled. "MAX!" He went racing to her.

"No. Don't move her," Robert said. "I'm a doctor." Robert got down next to her on the floor. Grant came running over. "We need to stabilize her and then move her gently."

"What happened to her?" Desiree asked. "What caused her to be in a wheelchair?" Desiree knew the answer to that question, but she verbalized it now.

"She lived with you for almost three years, didn't it ever come up?" Hank asked.

"She lived with you for almost three years, and I never knew that." Robert said. "What did you do? Lock her in a room or something?"

"I was mad that she had to come live with me."

"Desiree!" Robert said.

"You want to know and see what caused your beautiful daughter to become disabled?" Joanna asked.

Desiree looked at her. "Yes," she said.

Joanna grabbed Desiree's arm and brought her into the house. "SIT!" Joanna sternly said. Joanna put the disc in. Desiree sat up straighter as she watched the first performance. Then Joanna changed the discs and put on the accident. Desiree sat intently watching and then seeing her daughter hit the way she was and then laying there pinned under the light and rail, Desiree screamed out and then cried.

"Oh my god. I didn't know it was like that."

"What did you know?"

"They said that she had an accident. I assumed it was a car accident."

"Your daughter doesn't drive."

Hank carried her in the house. Robert stopped and looked at the TV. "My god. Oh, the poor girl. Desiree, did you know about this?"

"No."

"Didn't you ever talk to her?" Joanna, Ashley, Grant, and Robert asked her at the same time.

"Not about the accident. I told her that I hated that she had to come back and live with me."

"Trust me, lady, it was mutual feelings from Max," Ashley said.

"She was on house arrest, so I lost custody of my children because of her. I didn't have a choice."

"And you think that she did?"

"Ashley!"

"No, mom. She mistreated Max her whole life. Well for the first twelve years. Tell me, Robert, did you know that Desiree even had this daughter?"

"No."

"Wow, she got stuck with two horrible parents."

"You never told me about this daughter," Robert said. "What is she like twenty or so?" He found himself repeating what he had asked her earlier in town that day.

"I'm thirty," Max said from behind them.

"Are you ok?" Desiree asked.

"What the fuck do you care?"

"Don't you dare talk to me that way in front of these people," Desiree said.

"She can talk to you anyway she fucking pleases in this house," Ashley defended.

"Max, are you ok?"

"Yes, Jo, thank you. I knocked the wind out of myself when I fell, but I'm ok. Thank you, sir, for your help."

"Did you go to college?"

"Yeah, but I was put out when the accident happened."

"Did the hospital call you?" Grant asked Desiree.

"Yes."

"What did they tell you?"

"That my daughter had been in an accident."

"Did you go see her?"

"Maybe Max shouldn't hear this," Ashley said.

"Awe, your so sweet, Ashley, but it's ok. I already know the answer."

"No," Desiree said. "She had made her choice when she was twelve. She went to live with her father."

"Did she really?" Joanna asked.

"Yes. Matt told them to choose. Logan chose me. Max chose him."

"When she came back to your house what did you do?"

"I smacked her across the face for choosing him over me. I was so mad at her because she drove her father away."

"How does a child do that?" Robert asked.

"Matthew and I had been married for about three years before we became pregnant. We had already grown apart. When she was born, Matt never put her down. He took her with him everywhere he went. It was adorable, but I couldn't stand it. When she was three, I told Matt that she wasn't his."

"Why?" Joanna and Robert asked.

"I wanted him to hate her so maybe he would love me again. Instead, he hated us both. Then when Logan was born, he was happy again. Max was five when Logan was born. We put her in dance to keep her out of the house most of the day. Whenever, Matt had to get her, he would get pissed just to be asked. He would say, "Why don't you go ask her father to do it?" I felt bad at first, but then it didn't seem to matter anymore.

"I always knew that she was thief. She started stealing at five. Things from her dance team members started to disappear. She would get so mad and say that she never took anything, but we knew different. And then when I was called to come pick her up from the courthouse because she was on house arrest, I knew that it had finally caught up with her.

"I told them to keep her locked up. The judge told me that they couldn't because the women's prison is on the second floor with no elevator. People came into my house and made renovations to my house."

"Modifications," Max said.

"What?"

"They made modifications."

"Oh, whatever," Desiree said. "She now had to come live with me. I had to send my babies to go live with their fathers. My beautiful girls and my little Harrison. He was just a little baby when they had to go. When Max first came to the house, I locked her in the bedroom."

"Which bedroom?" Robert asked.

"The one when you come in the house and go to the left. That very first room." Max said.

"The room without any windows," he stated.

"That's right. She was on house arrest. It wasn't a damn luxurious vacation."

"Your place will never be a fucking vacation," Max said. "Why did you follow me today?"

"It's the first time I saw you out in the community. I wanted to see how you did. I wanted to see where you would go."

"Did you ever come looking for me?"

"No. Why would you I?"

"Oh, maybe because I was your daughter, and I was homeless."

"You were homeless?"

"Well, where the fuck do you think I went?"

"To your father's house."

"No, you asshole. He didn't want me and then you threw me out. Leave! Please leave! You threw me out twice without a fucking thought or care in the world."

"Max, did you go to school every day? You obviously continued to dance. Did you graduate high school?"

"I'm done talking to you." Max turned so her left side was now facing Desiree.

"Max. Max, I'm talking to you!"

"She's one hundred percent deaf in her left ear," Hank said.

"It's a joke. She's faking it."

"No," Robert said. "She's not faking it."

"Why are you taking her side?" Desiree whined and looked at him with sad puppy dog like eyes.

"Desiree!"

Max had gone into the bedroom. Ashley went into the room. "Are you ok?"

"Yeah. Why wouldn't I be?"

"After hearing that."

"Ashley, that's that cunt as a light weight."

"Why do you call her that?"

"Because she is worse than a piece of shit. I want Gwen," Max said almost like a child.

Ashley left the room and called Gwen. "Can you come here."

"Yes. I'm not too far. I'll be there soon."

Gwen went to the house. When she walked in, she saw Desiree. "You should be locked up for what you have done to my daughter."

"You want her then she is yours," Desiree said. "She's always been…"

"Don't you dare finish that statement. You lied to Matt for years making him think that she wasn't his daughter. By the time he learned the truth, the damage was already done, and you did that. You kept her locked up in a room as if she were in solitary confinement. What the fuck gave you that right," Gwen asked and then smacked Desiree as hard as she could across the face. "You both punished an innocent child and for what? For a fucking lie that you concocted." Gwen smacked her across the face again. Joanna came and put her arms around Gwen. She pulled her away from Desiree. "I want to press charges against this bitch."

"For what?" Desiree asked.

"For abusing a disabled person." Gwen had gotten away from Joanna. She was now face to face to Desiree. "You left her for a month with no fucking electricity and barely any food. Were you planning on coming home and maybe finding my daughter dead?"

"If she is your daughter like you claim, then how come you didn't take her when she was on house arrest?"

"ENOUGH!" Joanna yelled. "Back up. Both of you back up right now."

"Tell us, Des, were you planning on killing her?"

"No, I just wanted her to suffer for making Matt hate me."

"That happened long before that child came into this world."

"So then how come Matt didn't take her all of those years ago?"

"Because he heard your son say that he wanted to live with you. He thought for sure that Logan, who you let him baby and spoil, would want to live with him, but Logan chose you. Max chose her father, but you had already turned him against her, so he didn't want to hear it. Did you ever think of the date that your divorce went through on?"

"Of course," she said. "Her birthday. I wanted to ruin her life as she ruined ours."

"STOP IT!" Joanna said. "Desiree, you are under arrest for child abuse, child neglect, child abandonment, abusing a disabled woman, and abusing your power of detainer."

"But that was eighteen years ago. Isn't there a statute of limitation?"

The police came to Joanna's and took Desiree away. Max had stayed in the room listening to music, so she hadn't known what was going on. Gwen came into the room. Max looked up and saw her. Gwen went to her and took her in her arms.

"I wanted you to come."

Gwen took the earphone's off of Max's head. "Well, of course I would come."

"She came here. Desiree. She is or was here. Before that she was out with a guy. He seems nice. But we had gone into the little town to do a little shopping and there she was. We went the other way to avoid them and then she was there in one of the stores and she was in front of me. I took off. I came back here. She followed me. Why? Why now?"

"I don't know, angel."

"What does she want?"

"I don't know."

"Mom, she made my heart pound in my chest." Max picked up the elephant that Gwen had given to her and she brought it to her body and then she hugged it as tight as she could. She reached and took hold of Gwen's opened hand and she placed it over her heart. Gwen felt Max's heart pounding. "I don't want to see her. Please, mom, I don't want…"

"She's gone now Max."

"She will take…"

"No, angel, you aren't going to be taken anywhere."

"I'm so tired, but I'm so afraid right now."

"Max, I won't let anyone hurt you. Come. Come lay on the bed. I'll stay with you."

Gwen texted Matt. *Desiree came to see Max. I don't know why. Ashley called and told me that Max wanted me, so I came here to see her. I'm going to stay with her, Matt. Love you and the boys. See you all tomorrow.*

Gwen got on the bed with Max and she took her in her arms. Gwen rocked her. She rubbed her hand over her head and her hair and then she put her arms around her again and she continued to rock with her. They both slept.

Gwen had of course slept with her sons over the years. As she now held Matt's and her adult daughter, she could imagine Maxine as a child — running around, dancing around. Talking about this or that. Playing and having fun.

She had been in Matt's life back then. They had met by chance at the bank. Gwen was new in town. She didn't know anyone. She had gone to the bank to take out a loan to rent an apartment, but she didn't have credit, so the bank wouldn't give her a loan. She sat outside the bank crying. Matt had walked up and had come down on one knee asking what he could to do to help. She explained her situation to a total stranger. He had wiped away her tears and they had gone into the bank together. Matt didn't help her take out a loan. Instead, he had opened up an account for her. He had put ten thousand dollars in the bank for her. He then took her to a grand apartment building, and he had showed her a wonderfully furnished apartment and then he bought it for her.

"But you don't know me," Gwen had said to him.

"I know, but I want to get to you know. You should know that I am in a marriage that I hate. I have two children. A beautiful little girl and my son is a baby. My marriage, I hope will be over soon. But I would surely love to get to know you better."

Gwen opened her eyes. "He told me about you," she said. "I had never met you, but your father did tell me about you." She kissed Max lightly on the cheek. Max slept soundly in her arms. "I'm sorry that I never met you when you were little. I wish things would have been different."

CHAPTER FOURTEEN

The renovations and accommodations had been fully made to Matt and Gwen's house. They had brought Max to the house on a Friday morning after taking the boys to school. The boys were going to get a surprise of their very own. They would each have their own rooms. Max after trying everything new that was put into the house, she then helped paint walls in another bedroom and then helped take apart a bed in one room and then helped put it together again in the other room. They had left Jackson in the old room because it was closest to their bedroom and they had moved Gunnar to a vacant room. A room that he had played in and went in to read when he wanted to be alone. This was now his very own bedroom.

By the time the boys got home from school, the changes had been done.

"When do you get your car?" Matt asked. He realized his mistake of being on Max's left and simply moved to her right side. "When do you get your car?"

"Ah, I think…" Max was putting something together. She looked up at her father and smiled. "I'm sorry. What did you ask?"

"What are you doing?"

"Making gifts for the boys. But you asked me…oh the car. The hand controls come from Michigan, so they said about three weeks, so in retrospect, I should get the car back next Wednesday."

They hadn't shown her her room yet. "So when are going to move in permanently?"

"Whenever you are ready to have me."

"She is completely moved in," Gwen said. "All of your stuff is here."

"I haven't seen the room."

"Max. Angel, you can say your or my room."

Max smiled and lowered her head. "I haven't had a real room to call my room for a long time."

"Come on. Let's show her," Gwen said. She took Max's hand, while Matt went behind her and pushed the wheelchair. They brought her to a wing of the house that she had never seen before. A private wing. As they went in, there was a room on the left with bars and mirrors lining the walls. "We will see that room in a minute," Gwen said. "First, we wanted to show you this."

They brought her into a suite. Her medals from the service hung on a wall. There were pictures of her in her plane and climbing the ladder to her plane. Those too hung on the wall. On another wall, there were shelves for her dance trophies. Trophies that had never been displayed before. There was a king size bed in the room, a table with four chairs, and a huge flat screen TV.

"This is for me?"

"Yes, but this is for when you completely want privacy and want to be alone with a special man friend," Gwen said.

Max laughed. "How hard was that for you to hear?" Max asked Matt.

"Harder than you know."

Max laughed again.

"Max, look. This door closes and it closes off this section of the house to the other. Now come with us."

"There is more to see?"

"Yes, angel," Gwen said.

Max went with them into a bathroom that was made especially for her use. "Is this doable?" Matt asked.

"Oh, my god yes. Thank you, daddy. Thank you, mommy," Max said.

They then took her to see the dance room. "Oh, my god!" She immediately saw the track in the ceiling. "What is that?"

"To help you fly when you dance," Matt said. "Your new dance instructor will be here on Tuesday."

"What?"

"It's your dream to be a dancer," he said. "You wrote it one thousand times in your journal."

"I did," Max said.

"Well, then you are going to still be able to live your dream."

"Oh, dad!" Max said.

"You can come in here whenever you like. It is never off limits."

"Thank you so so much."

"Angel, there is more to see."

"More?"

"Yes."

"Wait! Are those ariel ribbons?"

"Have you used those before?"

"Yes. I did a whole dance with them when I was eighteen. I was accepted into this dance academy."

"Why didn't you go?" Gwen asked.

"It was in France. I was scared. I didn't know anyone there."

"So you went into the service?"

"Yeah. I wouldn't change that for the world. In France, I wouldn't have had a place to live. You had to earn your room and board there, so I chose the Air Force."

"Why?"

"Because I saw there was more of a possibility that I could fly in the Air Force."

"Were you ever injured?"

"No."

"Did you get beat up?"

"Beat up?"

"Yeah," Matt said. "You know. Like they show."

"No. I was never beaten up. Yelled at. Yes, but never physically hit. The service gave me a sense of stability. A taste of home. I was given three meals to eat every day. I could lay my head down on the pillow at night and not have to worry if someone called the police to say that someone was sleeping on a park bench or they heard strange noises in an alley way. It was home for six years.

"I had my apartment too."

"Did your friends always live there?"

"No. Not until I came back from the service. I was twenty-four. I was out on my own again and I didn't want to be, so I went against myself and let Lucy move in first. Then it was Scott. Dean suddenly started coming around at mealtimes. He'd show up and come and cook for us. We would have these wicked competitions and then he started staying over. Elliot and I were an off again on-again thing, so he lived with me as well. The others would come occasionally. And one thing led to another, I now had roommates."

"Did they pay for anything?"

"No. Not really. Food and laundry every once in a blue moon."

"Did you ever see any of the stolen things?" Gwen asked.

"No. I was rarely there."

"Where were you?"

"I'd spend my days at the studio. I had to catch up on dance moves that I missed while I was away for six years, so I spent as much time as I could at the studio dancing."

They brought her and showed her the other bedroom that was for her as well. More of her things were hung on the walls.

The boys came in from school. "Daddy!" Gunnar called. "Daddy!"

"Yeah. I'm in here, Gunny."

Both boys came and found him. They saw that Gwen was home. "Mommy!" they said together. They both ran and hugged her. Gunnar ran and hugged Matt.

"How was your day?" Gwen asked.

"I got put on the timeout bench today," Gunnar said proudly.

"What did you do?"

"I leaped over Amanda's head, but my shoelace hit her in the eyebrow. She fell to the floor crying. The teacher asked me why I did it and I told her that Amanda dared me."

"Did she?" Matt asked.

"Yes. She said I dare you to jump over my head, so I did."

"Gunnar, did you land it?" Max asked.

"MAX! YOU ARE HERE! ARE YOU GOING TO STAY?"

Max brought her hands up. "Not so loud," she said. "But to answer your question. Yes."

"Have you seen our room?"

"Funny you should say that," Gwen said.

"What do you mean?"

"Well, come see."

They went down the hall and went into the vacant room. "This is my room?"

"Yes."

"Wow! I get my own room! I get my own room! Look Max!"

"I see."

"Thank you, mommy and daddy. Thank you. I always wanted my own room."

"Where is my room?"

"Your room is still your room, Jackson," Matt said.

"Does Max have a room here now?"

"Yes, Jackson," Matt said.

"So you are going to live with us?"

"Yes."

They went to go see Jackson's room. He went in and hugged one of his stuffed animals.

"So can we tell people that we have a sister?"

"Yes, of course," Matt and Gwen said together.

"Can we have a party for her?" Gunnar asked.

"You want to have a party for me?"

"YES!" Gunnar said. He was so excited that she was there.

"Hey, come with me," she said to both of them, but Jackson wanted to stay in his room and check it out. Max took Gunnar into the dance studio. He was the first person that she danced with in there. He was still so excited. Max danced with him for a little while. When they were done, he threw his arms around her and then he took off to go play. Max stayed in the dance room. She pulled herself up on the ariel ribbons. She got herself secure into them and then she started to swing back and forth. She pulled herself up higher into them. "DAD! DAD!"

Matt went running. He saw the empty wheelchair. He looked up and saw Max air bound. Gwen came into the room now too. "Now how are you going to get yourself down?" Gwen asked.

"Oh, god no!" Matt said.

Max laughed as she let go and her body spiraled down. Laughter filled the room. "Ta da!" she said.

"Ta da?" Matt asked. "Ta da?"

"Yeah. Ta…" she threw her arms up high. "Da."

Matt grabbed her and tickled her. The scream that filled the room and the house played on complete fun. It was the first time that he was tickling her in twenty-seven years. He took her in his arms, and he hugged her. A warm hearty hug. "I love you, Maxine," he said.

Her first night in her own bedroom for the first time in four years, Max's bed was so comforting and inviting. She put her head down on new clean sheets and she was sleeping within minutes. She slept soundly. Both Matt and Gwen went to check on her.

When Max up woke up the next morning, she woke to someone sitting on her. "Are you getting up now?" Gunnar asked.

"What time is it?"

"Seven thirty."

"Yes. I'm getting up."

"Are you going to come to our ball games today?"

"Sure. I would love that."

"I play short stop and I sometimes pitch."

"Well, that's amazing."

"Can you play baseball?"

"I think I can."

"So when you were on house punishment, what would you do all day long?"

"I read books."

"Did you dance? Like you did here last night?"

"No."

"What's your mom like?"

"Nothing like yours," Max said. "But your mom is now my mom."

"But she wasn't before?"

"No, Gunnar. It's different. Here. Let me get up." The boy climbed off of her. Max got out of bed. "Sometimes a stranger comes into someone's life and they are really nice to that person and it makes a lasting impression. That is what your mom has done for me. She has showed me kindness like

I have never known a mother to be kind. She has showed me love and the support the way a mother should show her child."

"Did daddy do that with you?"

"In his own way he did."

They had breakfast together as a family. "Dad, does Logan come here and stay here?"

"Not anymore," Jackson said. "He comes, but he doesn't stay over."

"Do you like Logan?" Gunnar asked.

"Yeah. I like him. He's my brother."

"Do you like us?"

"I more than like you two. I love you two."

Smiles and giggles filled the breakfast table. Matt was watching Max.

They all went to the ball field. Jackson was playing first. A five-inning tee ball game.

"Matt, who is this with you and Gwen this morning?" a woman asked.

"She's our daughter."

"Where have you been hiding her?"

"I was away for long time," Max said. "I'm Max."

"It seems like Gunny really enjoys her."

"Hey, why don't we go play catch," Max said in Gunnar's ear. "Dad, do you have a glove with you?"

"Yes. It's in the car."

After Max went away with Gunnar to the car to get the glove, the women turned and looked at them. "Why is she in the chair?"

"She got injured dancing," both Matt and Gwen said together.

"So was she away at rehab learning how to function again?"

Gwen put her hand on Matt's chest. "Let's go," she said to him. "Let's move away from here."

"Aren't you going to stay and watch Jackson?"

"Yes, of course we are going to stay and watch our son. Maybe you should think of what you say to people. That was hurtful," Gwen said.

"Well, she's your adult child and yet she's never been here before now."

Max came back with Gunnar, who was eating potato chips on her lap. Max had heard every word. "Dad, why not just tell them the truth?" Matt looked at her. "They won't believe you anyway."

"Come on dear. Just come out with it."

"I lived in Brooks Town. I was on house arrest…" Max said. They went away from the area.

They moved to a different location. Gunnar was content sitting perched on Max's lap. "What's the big guy's name?"

"His name is Trent."

"Is Trent going to come see you?"

"Yes, but not this weekend. He's working."

Gunnar went and played. Ten-year old's play a full game of baseball. He got up to bat and he hit a homerun. Matt and Gwen were cheering. Max now had Jackson on her lap, and they were cheering too.

"That's my first homerun!" Gunnar said. "It's because my sister is here. She is a good luck charm."

Gunnar played one hell of a game. He was in at short stop. A ball was hit high up in the air, and he jumped up snagging the ball right out of the air.

"ALRIGHT GUNNY!" Gwen cheered.

His team beat a team that they had lost to every other time that they had played them.

"What's the secret weapon," the coach on the other team asked.

"There isn't one," Gunnar's coach said.

"No, Coach. That isn't true. It's because Max is here."

"Who is Max?" Gunnar's coach asked.

"My sister. She's right over there holding Jackson."

The other coach bent down close to Gunnar. "You know what then?" Gunnar looked at him. "You go over to her and thank her for being here for you today. But before you go, Gunnar Brandon…" The coach stood up. "THE V.I.P. AWARD FOR THIS GAME IN THE TOURNAMENT GOES TO GUNNAR BRANDON FOR MOST IMPROVED PLAYER THIS SEASON." They all watched Gunnar take his award and saw him thank him and then he walked over to the family. They all hugged him.

"I want Max to have it," he said.

"What? No, Gunnar, I can't take your award. It really sounds like you deserve this award."

"IS THERE A MAX BRANDON HERE? MAX BRANDON?"

"SHE'S RIGHT HERE," both boys started to jump up and down and point to her.

"MAX BRANDON, PLEASE COME OUT HERE."

Max went out on the field with both boys on each side of her. "LADIES AND GENTLEMEN, IF YOU CAN PLEASE STAND AS WE PRESENT THIS AWARD TO MAXINE "MAX" BRANDON."

"I don't understand."

"YOU SEE EVERYONE, MAX USED TO FLY FOR THE UNITED STATES AIR FORCE AND ALTHOUGH SHE HAS BEEN OUT OF THE SERVICE FOR SOME YEARS NOW, THIS AWARD WAS NEVER AWARDED TO HER."

"What award?"

Just then two big men from the Air Force came over and came on either side of Max. Together they lifted her to a standing position.

"THIS AWARD IS APPOINTED TO BEST FEMALE PILOT," The guy announced. "WE WOULD LOVE FOR HER FAMILY TO GATHER AROUND HER AND TAKE A PICTURE WITH HER AT THIS TIME."

A picture was taken with her standing at first and then with her sitting. When she was back in her wheelchair, Gunnar sat on her shoulder. Matt stood on her left side with Gwen on her right, and Jackson sat on her lap. Max looked at the medal that was presented to her.

One of the guys that had helped to hold her up, waited till they were all done and then he squatted down next to her. "I have a question for you." Max looked at him. "Have you thought about flying again?"

"I think about it every day. That and dancing. And walking," she said.

"I would like to arrange to take you up in an aircraft."

"Yeah. Ok. I would love that."

"With your family there to see you fly."

"Like I said, sir, I would love that."

"I have your number. I'll be in touch."

"Thank you, sir."

Trent came over on Sunday night for dinner. The boys were running around chasing each other. Max was in her studio dancing. Gwen and

Matt were preparing dinner. Trent brought brownies. When he got to the house, he was first greeted by the boys.

"Hi," Gunnar said.

"Hey, little buds."

"Max is in the house."

"Ok. Thank you."

"Would you want to play video games with us?"

"Yes. I would love that. Have you asked Max?"

"Not yet," Gunnar said. "I just thought about it."

Trent laughed. He went to the door and knocked on it. Gwen came and opened the door. "Oh. Hello."

"Hi. I came to see Max. Is that ok?"

"Yes, that is more than fine," Gwen said.

"I thought I'd let her settle in. I thought maybe it might be overwhelming for her moving into a new place. I was there when she was brought to Jo's house."

"So you were there when Desiree kicked her out?"

"Yes," he said to Matt.

"Can you tell us how it happened?"

Trent sat down at the counter. "We got dispatched out for a domestic dispute. When we got there, there was smoke coming from the back of the house. We followed the fire fighters back there. The neighbor was yelling at Max to put the fucking thing out. Joanna went over to Max and told her to put it out or the fire department would. They did. Joanna told Max to go into the house. She went to the back door and it was locked. Desiree opened the back window and told her that she was done. That Max couldn't live there anymore."

"Did you take her in handcuffs?"

"No. She didn't resist. She came with us calmy. She was yelling at the neighbor, but when Joanna told her stop, she did. Then the next day, Jo went and got Max's stuff. Desiree told her to take everything otherwise she was going to discard it. She signed surrender papers saying that Max couldn't finish her house arrest in her household."

"She surrendered her?" Gwen asked.

"Yes. She said that she had done the same after the divorce."

"What?" both Gwen and Matt asked.

"It's in the documents that she gave Jo."

"I never saw that," Gwen said. "So she terminated her rights to her when she was twelve?"

"Yes."

"Please don't mention that to Max."

"No, ma'am," Trent said. "I don't want to hurt her. I just want to be in her life and be here for her."

Max came in from the studio. She was drenched in sweat and dripping. "Dad. Mom. The only thing that needs to be changed on that side is where the towels are placed."

"Shit!" Matt said. "I forgot."

"No. It's ok," Max said. "Also, I need a broom in there please."

"I'll get it for you tomorrow," Gwen said.

Max turned around and saw Trent sitting there. "Oh, hi," she said. "I didn't know you were here. Give me a few minutes. I'm a little gross right now."

"I'll be right here."

"Is there a video game system?"

"Yes," Gwen answered Max.

"Can I maybe play it?"

"Of course, angel."

"I'll be right back." Max went and took a shower. She got dressed and then came back.

"Why were you so sweaty?" Trent asked.

"Oh, you don't know. Come with me." Max took his hand. He went with her. She showed him her personal wing. "So if you sleep over, we have this section all to ourselves."

"They did this for you?"

"Yes. No one has ever done anything like this for me. I have a bedroom on the family side of the house too."

"Wow."

"I know. Can you stay for dinner?"

"Yes."

They went and joined Gwen and Matt in the kitchen. The boys came running in the house. "It's starting to rain."

"Really?" Max said.

"Yes," Jackson said.

"Excuse me please." Max went outside. The five of them went to go see what she was doing. Max went in the middle of the driveway. It was now pouring. Max closed her eyes, leaned her head up to the sky, put her arms up stretched high over her head. Gwen saw that she was crying.

"Take the boys inside," she said. She came off the front porch and went to Max. She grabbed her in a hug. Max wrapped her arms around her. She sobbed in Gwen's arms.

"She had me locked in a room!"

"I'm so sorry."

"I couldn't call anyone. I didn't have anyone to tell. I don't want to protect her anymore."

"What? What are you protecting her from?"

"She only feed me every two days," Max cried. "I couldn't leave that room. I never saw sunlight when I was in her house. She came to see me."

"She did what?" Gwen made like she didn't know about this.

"She did. We saw her in town. She watched me with Trent. She followed us. I ran from her, mom. I ran away from her.

"The first time I was free from being hurt was when I was twelve, mom," Max cried. "Free from dad yelling at me and free from her telling me how much I ruined their lives. When I went back to live there because I had to, it start..." Max choked on the words. "It started all over again. I left rehab getting a wrap and hold on my new life and I went to jail and then I went to her house."

"Max, we need to get inside."

"I want to sue her."

"Yes. You can do that. Come. Let's go inside."

After they both changed, they had dinner together. "Is everything ok?" Matt asked Gwen in private.

"I think it will be."

"She confides in you."

"And I love every minute of it, Matthew. She should have been able to come eighteen years ago, but I understand. I saw how angry you were, and I know how long it took to get you to calm down, but that girl in there made something out of nothing. Her little broken self was able to find a way to move on and make something of her life and then Desiree tried to destroy her all over again."

The boys showed Max and Trent where the games were. "Oh, yeah!" Max said. "Dad! Dad!" Matt came into the room. "We are keeping the boys home from school until we have played each one of these games."

"YES!" the boys said together.

"Max, they get out of school…"

"Please, dad?"

"Yes. That's fine, but just this once."

The boys both laughed. "Did he ever tell you that?"

"Um. Yeah. He probably did, Gun, but I don't remember. It was a long, long time ago since I was a child."

"Did daddy ever read to you?"

"Yes," Max said. "He read me a princess book until I told him that it was bullshit."

"What?" Gwen said.

"That wasn't my life. Those girls needed someone to pull them out of their shitty lives. They needed rescuing. I did that myself."

"What book was it?" Gunnar asked.

"What?"

"What book was it?'

"Sleeping Beauty," Matt said.

"There's a dragon in that book," Jackson said.

"There's a what?" Max asked.

"Yeah. There's a dragon in the book."

Max looked up at Matt. "I guess we didn't make it that far."

"No, angel, we definitely didn't."

"How far did you get?"

"The trolls had her."

"Trolls?" Gwen asked. "What the hell version were you reading to her."

"They aren't trolls," Jackson said.

"Then what the hell are they?"

"Fairies," Gwen said.

"Fairies?"

Jackson got up. "Be right back." Gunnar went to the bathroom.

"You read the boys princess books?"

"There are boys or men in the books, Max," Matt said.

Jackson came back. He handed her a heavy fat book. "It's all the fairy tales."

"So, all of these stories have fairies in them?"

"No," Gwen said.

They played video games for hours with the boys.

"I know you are staying home at least tomorrow so far, but you still have to go bed on time," Gwen said.

"Good night," Gunnar said.

"Good night. Come. I'll put you to bed."

Trent took Jackson, who was already asleep. Max brought Gunnar in his room. "Put on your pajamas." He went into the bathroom to change. Max pulled his bedding down for him. When he came back, Max was sitting on his bed waiting for him. "What do you have there? What book is that?"

"It's about a dragon."

"Here. Let me see it. What page are you on?"

"Like twenty I think."

"Can I start it from the beginning?"

"Yeah,"

"Come on. We can go lay in my bed ok."

"Yeah, ok."

Max brought him in her room. Trent went into the room with them. He sat on the bed with them. Gunnar snuggled in next to Max on the bed. Max started to read from chapter one. Gunnar was fighting sleep. "Close your eyes, little brother. We will read more tomorrow. I'm not going anywhere."

He put his arm across her shoulders. His head was on her left shoulder. He closed his eyes and fell asleep. Max put her hand on his back. She too closed her eyes and fell asleep. Trent went and found Matt. "Is there a place where I can sleep tonight?"

"Yes. We have a guest room. Come. Let me show you."

"Thank you."

As Gunnar slept with Max, he was woken to her crying, shivering, and shaking. Gunnar got up and ran into his parents' room. "Daddy! Daddy!" Matt opened his eyes. He glanced at the clock seeing that it was four in the morning. "It's Maxie," he said. Matt got out of bed quickly.

"Go in your room ok, Gunnar."

"Yes, daddy."

"And Gunnar, thank you."

Matt went to Max. She was crying in her sleep. Matt sat on her bed. He took her into his arms. Max took a deep breath. "It's cold," she said. Matt put a blanket on her and held her.

"Daddy has you," he said. He kissed her forehead. The chills rocked through her body. Her body temperature was cold. Matt had brought his phone with him. He called Gwen waking her up. "It's Max," he said. She came running into the room. Max shivered. Her teeth were chattering. Her skin was so cold.

"We need to get her warm," they said together.

Max's head rolled back off Matt's shoulder. "She was so little, Gwen. She was smaller than the boys ever were. She danced before she walked. She would get up on her little skinny legs and just bounce about and move her arms. And then when she started to walk, she would flutter all over the house. Gwen it was cutest thing in the world. And then when Des told me that she wasn't my child, it crushed me. I stayed away. My marriage was over and now I couldn't even look at my own child.

"The best thing was meeting you, Gwen. You changed me. You softened me. I did go to visit her. She would have been about fourteen. I stopped being angry. I went to the house. She wasn't there. I went to the studio. She wasn't there. I didn't know where else to look for her. Logan said that she was at a friend's house studying. I took his word. He was nine by then. He hadn't seen his sister in two years and the kid never said a fucking word."

"You have to tell her that, Matt."

"I went a few times looking for her. Des and I didn't speak, and I was always ok with that. But she had our son lying as well. And then for Maxine to have to go back there and be mistreated. Can we sue?"

"We? No. Can she? Yes."

With them having Max wrapped up in blankets, her body temperature started to climb. Her teeth stopped chattering. Max moved in Matt's arms. She reached down to move her legs. Though she was sleeping, she repositioned herself on him. She extended her arm placing it on Gwen's leg. They both stayed with her the rest of the night.

CHAPTER FIFTEEN

A guy name Jonathan from the Air Force called and made plans for Max to come to the airfield. She had finally gotten her car. On the day that they went, she drove them to the airfield. She got out of the car after Trent had given her her wheelchair. She got into it and started to go towards the planes.

"Hi, Max. I'm Jonathan."

"Hi, Jonathan."

"So how long has it been since you've been up?"

"Six years."

"Ok. So let's go over a few things."

"You bet."

"First. Who did you bring with you today?"

"This is my dad, Matthew Brandon. My mom, Gwen. My little brothers, Gunnar and Jackson, and this is my boyfriend, Trent."

"It's nice to meet you all. Why don't you go make yourselves comfortable in the hangar for awhile. We will let you know when she is ready to fly."

Max went with Jonathan. A half hour later, they were going back to the hangar. Matt and Trent had the boys high on their shoulders as they stood at the chain link fence facing the airfield. Gwen stood with her fingers looped in the chain fence. Jonathan piggy backed Max to the plane and then up the ladder. He put Max in and then he got in. The engine started.

"Oh, my god, Matt," Gwen said.

Someone came over to them. "Here. You might need these," she said handing them binoculars. "Don't use them until the plane is up. And you will need these too for the little ones," she said handing them protective ear muffs. "I swear Jonathan loses his head when it comes to flying."

The engines now roared and glowed and then it tore off down the runway and seconds later was air bound. When they got up to a good height, Jonathan told her to take it over. And now Max brought the hornet straight up in the air and then she spiraled it as they came down. She did loop after loop before bringing it back up and then flew it upside down before bringing it down. It landed like a butterfly on a flower. They sat in the plane for a few minutes and then the cockpit opened up. Jonathan climbed out easing Max up first and then got her so he could climb down.

"Thank you for that wonderful experience," Max said.

Jonathan brought her back to her wheelchair. He lowered her. She hugged him. He hugged her. "You are amazing, Maxine."

"Thank you. As are you."

"I will see you again, Elegant Dancer."

"Thank you, Jonathan."

He smiled at her. She smiled back at him. He bent and kissed her on the head.

Max went back over to where the others were waiting for her. The smile plastered on her face brought Matt back to a memory when she was about six and she had danced a flawless routine. He remembered watching her and seeing her twirling and spinning and that adorable little laugh that she had.

"Dad! Are you ok? Dad!"

He pulled out of the memory. "Yes, Maxie, I'm fine. I got caught up watching you."

"Mommy filmed the whole thing."

"Oh, thank you, mom," Max said.

"What do you want to do now?"

"Eat!" Max, Gunnar, and Jackson said.

They went to get something to eat at Le Café Diner.

"Dad, I can't go in there."

"No, Max, it's ok," Gwen said.

"But, mom, they won't serve me in there."

"Yes, angel, they will."

They went in and the boys ran to their usual table. Gunnar pulled a chair aside for Max. They ate breakfast in the diner and the food was by far the best that Max had had in a diner before.

The boys went back to school on Wednesday morning. Trent had called out of work taking a few more vacations days. He went with Max as she drove to the airfield again. She and Jonathan went up again. Trent was taken back at how elegant and graceful it really was. He had seen jets fly, but never like this. When they landed and she was getting out of the plane; Jonathan lowered her into Trent's arms this time. As she was in his arms, they fox trotted back to her wheelchair. Max had thrown her head back laughing. They went back to the house now. Trent followed her into the studio. She moved in a passionate playful like kind of way. She hooked herself up to the track and then she went into the middle of the dance floor. Trent went to her. He took her hands in his and they started to move together across the dance floor. The next thing she knew, she was in his arms again. Her weight being completely supported be the track in the ceiling. He took her into a hold like a tango. Although, she couldn't move her legs to meet his, they danced a steamy hot tango together. After the dance was over, Trent stood there. Both of them breathless as they started to passionately kiss each other. Even their lips moved together like a dance.

Max sat with the others in the backyard. A firepit was burning: The fire started off small and slow. Like Max had once been as a child learning how to dance. As it gained more heat and oxygen, it started to grow; as Max had grown through the years. Yellow turned into an orange. There were tints of blue as that could be seen too. The smoke started off in puffs and now climbed higher and higher in the air. The crackling was intense and grew louder and louder. The light grew bigger and bigger. The fire jumped and danced like a dancer on center stage. Tonight, it was contained. As a cold wind blew, the flames waved along with the flowing air. Maxine "Max" Brandon sat close to the warmth of the fire. She watched it dance and flicker in the air. She closed her eyes and saw her disabled self on center stage.

Max's Dance

My sister was a dancer, who suffered an incredible accident. She now uses a wheelchair and can't use her legs anymore, but my brother, mom, dad, and I have witnessed her dance. She dances with my brother and I in her studio at the house. And we have seen her dance with an airplane. We watched as she was carried up into it and put down in the seat. We watched it take off fast and loud. Everything shook including me. And then we witnessed the most beautiful thing I have ever seen. A woman dancer in the arms of that massive plane as they climbed and then spun and twirled, it was like watching my sister dance. I watch her spinning from the confines of her wheelchair. She twirls on the apparatuses that my parents had put in the studio for her, and I have seen her not only fly a plane, but I have seen her flying while she dances. And that is Max's Dance: Elegant. Graceful. Powerful. Gentle. Explosive. Heart Racing and Completely Breathtaking. At times she is like exploding fireworks and at other times she is like a precious fluttering butterfly – That is Max's Dance – that is Maxine "Max" Brandon – my older sister. ELEGANT DANCER By: Gunnar Brandon

~ THE END ~

MAX'S DANCE

Maxine "Max" Brandon finds herself trapped in a world that she wants nothing to do with. A world that she thought she left behind when she was young. Max moves through her life always in a dance.

A contained, controlled fire seems to be her savior. It brings her out of the darkness of where she is in life and opens her up and brings her into a strange new kind of dance - this strong, beautiful - Elegant Dancer.

This story came to be as I was burning a fire in my backyard, and I watched as the fire went from a flicker to a flame. The fire danced – was soft and then intense. It tangoed, it seemed to hip hop about, it raged and broke; it inspired me to write; and POOF: Maxine "Max" Brandon was born. I wrote this in a total of twenty-five days. As Max is a dancer; she spun, twirled, and danced right out of me. It's Max's Dance
– GINA M. IACIOFANO

216